"Walk where the ground is hard, and step only in my footsteps..."

Nile Barrabas—decorated veteran and ex-prisoner—led his men into combat.

Barrabas looked down at the center hut. Half its roof was in flames and the fire was spreading.

Billy and Alex lobbed grenades toward it. Lee's and Nate's guns were already barrel-hot from firing at it.

A solid sheet of bullets covered the air inches above their heads.

Suddenly Billy howled, craning his eyes down the length of his body in the mud.

"You hit?"

"Yeah," he groaned. "Some bastard just shot off my little toe.... Slide that goddamn grenade launcher over here!"

SOBs

THE BARRABAS RUN

JACK HILD

A GOLD EAGLE BOOK FROM

W⊕RLDWIDE

TORONTO · NEW YORK · LONDON · PARIS
AMSTERDAM · STOCKHOLM · HAMBURG
ATHENS · MILAN · TOKYO · SYDNEY

First edition September 1983

ISBN 0-373-61601-5

Special thanks and acknowledgment to Jack Canon, Robin Hardy
and Alan Bomack for their contributions to this work.

Printed in Canada

NILE BARRABAS:
SERVICE RECORD

1958: age 18, enlists in Cheyenne, Wyoming
—basic training, Fort Knox KY
—advanced individual training—Army aviation
—paratrooper training, Fort Benning GA
—assigned to 11th Air Assault Division at Fort Benning
—promotions to corporal, sergeant
1960: Intelligence School, Fort Holabird, MA
1960: West Point Preparatory at Fort Belvoir VA
1961 to 1964: West Point—specialist in communications
  and intelligence, infantry tactics and strategic warfare.
1964: 3rd Lieutenant. Special Forces Training in Bad
  Tolz, Bavaria, Germany; learns German
1965: Lieut. to 1st Cavalry Division (Airmobile)
—Military Operations Specialty
  Special Warfare Training at Fort Bragg
  Jungle Warfare Training, Panama
1966: receives Special Infantry Badge
1967: transfer to 5th Special Forces Group (Airborne),
  Vietnam Company C, 1st Cavalry Div. (Airmobile) as
  Captain
1967: receives Silver Star for gallantry
1968: receives Silver Star for gallantry
1969: receives Distinguished Service Cross
1969: promotion to Major, transfer to Military Assistance Command (Intelligence) Saigon, Operation
  Achilles
1970: promotion to Lt. Colonel, transfer to Defense
  Intelligence Agency, the Pentagon, Washington DC
1972: Commander, Operation Conquistador, Guatemala,
  Honduras, El Salvador, Panama, Costa Rica.
1973: promotion to Colonel, transfer to Military Attaché
  Liaison Office, MAC Saigon
1975: receives Medal of Honor
1975: retires from US Army; returns to civilian life.

Local war hero fails to attend medal ceremony

(Special to the Weekly Tribune)

WASHINGTON, July 14—Col. Nile Barrabas, a much decorated war hero and native of Green River, Wyoming, disappointed White House officials last Friday when he did not attend a ceremony at which he was to receive the Medal of Honor, this country's highest award for bravery.

An Army spokesman told a Weekly Tribune correspondent that Col. Barrabas, a career soldier, had resigned from the service and was returning to civilian life.

Failure to make an appearance at the ceremony was an embarrassment to President Ford's staff and considered strange by Green River residents who have known Barrabas since he was a boy. He grew up on a ranch near that town.

Bystander kill

LAST MAN OUT

A tense silence settled over the murky waters of the old
canal. There were no birdcalls now from the bushes along
the bank. Even the chorus of insects seemed to have
stopped. It was an oppressive, menacing stillness that
reeked of rotting vegetation and marsh gas.

Lieutenant "Deke" Howard, of the 17th Waterborne
Assault Group, scanned the gently waving screen of elephant grass that marked the junction with the main river
channel. Ahead of the *Callisto* the waterway narrowed
where it joined the lazy, rippling current of the Kap Long,
the river that would take them clear down to the coast and
safety. If the VC planned an ambush it would have to be
here, where a submerged finger of accumulated silt,
marked only by a thin fringe of reeds, poked out from the
left-hand shore, forcing any traffic to hug uncomfortably
close to the dense undergrowth along the right bank.

"Trouble?" asked Jessup. He was a CIA field officer—
clandestine service, Howard assumed. He had arrived at
the very last minute, identification papers in order, to
accompany them to the rendezvous point. On the voyage
upriver Jessup had been reserved, politely patient, but now
that he had the war plans in his hands he was edgy, eager to
get back to base.

Well, so was "Deke" Howard. And the rest of the crew.

The *Callisto*'s commander pursed his lips and merely
shrugged in reply as he raised the glasses to his eyes once
more and began another careful sweep. The river level
would rise after the next rainy spell, but at the moment it
seemed they had little choice but to pass close on the right.
The young officer didn't like it.

The setting sun angled through the topmost branches and
lit the scene with an eerie golden-greenish glow. Howard let
the *Callisto* drift quietly under the tangled canopy of vine-
hung trees that lined the leeside of the canal. Gary Murr, the

engineman, was ready to bring its two 220-horsepower diesels roaring into life at a moment's notice. There was a faint, menacing click as Les Hannell, a veteran seaman, slid the safety catches off the twin .50-caliber machine guns, mounted forward, and hunched lower behind the sights.

"Deke" Howard chewed his lower lip; no, he didn't like it one bit.

The *Callisto* had been serviced in a hurry. A halfhearted daub of paint no more than partially obscured the combat graffiti "Sat Kong!"; if captured, this sign—"Kill the Vietcong!"—would mean immediate execution for all the men aboard.

Howard had been seconded by V-WAG HQ in Saigon to command the 31-foot patrol boat for this solo run to pick up any survivors of a Special Forces elite team returning from a classified mission deep in VC territory. There had been only one—he was behind Jessup, sitting with his back to the bridge coaming. A taciturn man, with red-rimmed eyes and dark stubble. When they picked him up he offered no greetings, no thanks, no rank. Just one word—his name, "Barrabas." And Barrabas inspected the CIA officer's identification very carefully before handing over the plans he had stolen from Chan Minh Chung's command center.

"Seems okay," grunted Howard, still biting on his lip. He addressed Jessup, but half turned so that Barrabas could hear his explanation: "We'll wait till it's a little darker. We're nearly home free. No point in taking unnecessary risks."

The youthful commando ran his fingers through his thick, chestnut hair, wearily signaling his resignation to the delay. Absentmindedly he scratched under the heavy nylon flak jacket that Howard insisted everyone aboard should wear.

Howard had taken an instinctive dislike to Barrabas. The lieutenant thought him too boyish-looking, his features too finely chiseled, to be one of Special Forces' most lethal killers. A few years ago he would have been one of those high-school heroes who won a place on every team without seeming to try, and who never had to work too hard to do well in their academic subjects either. Howard had had an elder brother like that. And he'd always resented having to live up to him. But Robert was killed while serving as a U.S. "advisor" in the defense of Ira Dihn. God, it seemed so long ago now.

Actually, "Deke" Howard was wrong about Nile Barrabas.

About as wrong as he could be.

Barrabas had had to work for everything in his life. Work hard. There were few silver spoons handed out in that high-country corner of Wyoming where Barrabas was born. No lucky breaks for him. Sure, sometimes he'd been a winner... but Barrabas had trained hard and played hard for that football scholarship to Purnell. And on top of his ranch work, he'd had to burn the midnight oil just to keep up with his classmates.

The fact that he had worked so hard and done so well made his family all the more surprised when, instead of preparing to go off to college, he told them he was enlisting in the Army.

But why the Army, asked Nile's mother again and again; after all, surely Uncle Edward pulled enough rank in the Navy to ensure that his nephew would not have to go overseas. But Nile did not try to explain it to her; he couldn't, he'd thought about it for a long time, but still found it difficult to express his reasons.

Luke Barrabas, his old man, kept his feelings to himself—as he always did—but he was secretly proud of his son's refusal to take the easy way out and never more so than the day he learned Nile had got into the Special Forces.

Nile Barrabas never regretted his decision.

There were times during his training, especially in the early days, when he didn't think he could go on... but he always managed to grit his teeth and hang in there.

In the swamps of Georgia and Louisiana he'd learned every trick in the book for a combat rifleman, and a few more that had never been written down. He'd practiced communications under all conceivable conditions. He'd passed the parachute course at Fort Benning; he'd been shown how to use every kind of weapon and how to improvise them if the need arose; and he'd absorbed the deadly skills of the guerrilla and the saboteur. His whole body—

his feet, his knees, his hands, even his fingertips—had been turned into a frighteningly efficient killing machine.

Nile Barrabas was a one-man army.

But none of it had come easy.

Howard could not even guess the significance of the bloody mission Barrabas had just completed in the fetid jungle swamps of the Kap Long's upper delta, and he sure wasn't about to ask. The papers he had seen Barrabas turn over were now in the thin case securely locked to Jessup's wrist. The lieutenant's sole responsibility was to get these two men back in one piece and—

There was a sound.

A surreptitious clink.

He heard it again.

Howard ducked his head for a moment, then peered cautiously over the bridge with his glasses. That was no jungle sound. Howard kept a mental tape of all the slithery splashes and soft sucking sounds one could hear along the riverways. This didn't fit.

It was too metallic.

It was Charlie.

"Dammit, let's get some help," Howard nodded to his number two, Boatswain's Mate Cassidy. "Call up some firepower!"

"This is *Callisto* . . . come in, Big Boy." Cassidy, crouching by the radio, had already anticipated him. "This is *Callisto*. We need support. . . ."

"Okay, *Callisto*, we read you," drawled a bored voice, "what are your coordinates?"

Howard checked the map, rattled off their position, and Cassidy passed it on to the operator at District HQ, who meshed the efforts of the artillery and Air Support Center.

Barrabas was just pulling on his helmet when the tallest stalks of elephant grass were shredded by the sweeping arcs of VC machine-gun fire. *Callisto*'s engines roared into reverse. As he ducked forward, the windshield above Barrabas's head disintegrated into flying splinters.

Whooosh! Whooosh! The first artillery shells exploded in the middle of the channel ahead.

"Range okay!" instructed Cassidy. "Correct three degrees right."

More shells landed in the churning water, exploding several of the mines that the VC had sown across the canal entrance. Foam-capped gouts of slimy yellowish water mushroomed upward.

"Right, you assholes, right!" shouted Cassidy, although there had not been time for his initial correction to be relayed.

The next barrage struck home.

"Bull's-eye!" exclaimed Howard.

A VC mortar coughed twice—the explosions straddled the bow of the *Callisto*, lifting it high from the water. In the glimmering dusk a veteran F-100 came out of the dying sun to grease the VC ambush.

The searing fireball of napalm splashed through the trees at an angle to the canal. It left the thick undergrowth right at the entrance untouched, although the vines overhead were already crackling with flame. A 57mm recoilless barked. It missed. More muzzle-flashes. . . .

"Now!" shouted Howard. "We're going through!"

The boat surged forward, the Jacuzzi-designed pumps forcing high-powered jets of water from her stern as the *Callisto* darted over the churning surface of the canal. Hannell, at the twin fifties, was spraying Charlie's last hiding place, glowing streaks of tracer stitching a deadly pattern through the burning trees.

Barrabas hand-held an M-60. The machine gun bucked and writhed against the strength of his grip as he fired burst after burst at the bank ahead.

The *Callisto* was closing on the junction. It was an inferno of roaring engines, screams of pain and rage, flickering shadows and the numbing concussion of heavy gunfire.

Howard veered left, praying there would be at least nine or ten inches of water over the hidden finger of silt that now partly blocked the canal. At a snarling twenty-seven knots, the *Callisto* smashed her fiberglass hull over the submerged obstruction and leaped out into the main channel of the Kap Long.

As the patrol boat pulled in a tight arc to starboard, the crew turned their blazing guns, pouring out a continuous leaden stream of destruction at the VC ambush point. They were almost broadside to the canal opening now. Charlie's position was an impossible furnace lighting the wide stretch of the open river. One last shot. . . .

The 57mm shell clipped the edge of the thin steel-sheet armor and the aft sweep of the bridge exploded in a fatal flurry of fiberglass fragments and metal splinters. A white-hot shard sliced into the groin of Jay Newman, the rear machine gunner. "Deke" Howard collapsed, his now sightless eyes still gazing up at the night sky. But Jessup was miraculously untouched. The dazed CIA operative grabbed for the wheel and regained control of the *Callisto*.

They left a foam-spewing wake behind them as they raced south down the river. Several moments passed before Jessup realized that Barrabas too had been hit.

He was sprawled to one side, his nylon flak jacket peppered by the blast. Jessup stared in morbid fascination at the hole in Barrabas's helmet—a jagged tongue of steel had been peeled back as if by a can opener that slipped. The dark wet stain covering his cheek was a sheet of blood leaking from under the helmet and dripping down to soak into his collar. His eyes were still open. Barrabas was watching Jessup.

He knew it was night, but Jessup's face looked down from faraway, peering at him through a halo of brilliant light. Cassidy had a medic pack. The light was so intense. Barrabas screwed his eyes shut.

It was pure pain. His head...

...just a glaring agony of white light.

He was walking through the fire.

And then, the darkness.

Impenetrable.

No night so black.

No river. No boat. No Jessup. No more gunfire. No more war.

Just darkness.

THEY WERE CAUGHT IN THE MAELSTROM.

It seemed like half the population of overcrowded Saigon was rushing the gates of the U.S. Embassy.

The final hours before dawn had been quiet, but it was the deceptive calm before the storm. It was only 7:15 in the morning, but the grim overcast made it seem much later in the day; indeed, for the desperate South Vietnamese it was the final failing twilight of freedom.

The iron-gray clouds clamped an oppressive lid over the

teeming city, just as it was being suffocated by the ten divisions of Vietcong troops that encircled it. They were holding six more divisions in reserve to quash any attempt at a counteroffensive. But there would be no such retaliation.

Brian Calvert, an old Asian hand for the Canadian newsmagazine *Now*, focused his Nikon on the tall Army officer who had just tossed a match into the gasoline-soaked pile of official papers on the lawn.

There was no mistaking Colonel Nile Barrabas.

Calvert had heard plenty of stories about the man, in Jimmy's Kitchen and in countless dark bars in Saigon's sidestreets...of how his hair had turned a steely silver gray overnight from the trauma of a head wound...some people claimed it had turned him crazy, others said he was just plain fighting mad...anyway, he was mad enough to have mounted an unauthorized rescue of U.S. airmen held prisoner deep in Indian country.

They had tried to court-martial him for the raid, even though it was a success. Instead, he'd walked away with another citation. Barrabas had more lives than a cat, and he always seemed to land on his feet.

But someone over at Pentagon East was still angry that the charges had not stuck, angry enough to ensure Barrabas was detailed to remain behind with a small detachment of Marines as a rear guard at the embassy during this final phase of evacuation. Barrabas didn't know who to thank for his orders, but he wouldn't have wanted it any other way.

"Why the hell aren't you out at the airport?" Barrabas asked the Canadian photographer. He had to shout to make himself heard above the noise. Screams and wailing pleas mounted in a panic-stricken chorus from the crowd outside; the frustrated snap of small-arms fire echoed through the streets, and in the distance could be heard the rapid explosions of a rocket barrage. "Go on...get the hell out of here!"

Calvert tried to reply but he was drowned out by the throbbing racket of a Jolly Green Giant heading for Tan Son Nhut. It was followed by a twin-tailed flying boxcar—probably full of some politician's loot, guessed Calvert, glancing up as it flew over them.

He tried to excuse himself: "We've both got our jobs to do, Colonel."

But Barrabas was already racing through the smoke across the lawn. A small boy had somehow clambered over the corner of the ten-foot-high wall.

The American recognized him; it was little Bay Tin. He was the kid who used to bring round the copies of the *Saigon Post*—but more important than the newspapers under his arm had been the hard-to-get information he carried by word of mouth. Barrabas hustled the kid across to the front porch.

"Look after the lad," he instructed Calvert. "Take him up to the roof. Now. The next chopper in is likely to be the last."

Civilian or not, the journalist knew this was an order to be obeyed.

The creases above his left temple were not a friendly wrinkle but the ridges of old scar tissue. And the eyes of Barrabas were ice-cold and authoritative.

As the colonel turned away, shouting to catch the attention of the Marines by the gate, signaling them to withdraw, Calvert hurried the youngster inside. He was surprised how cool it was. The air conditioner was still working.

BARRABAS DOUBLE-CHECKED that most of the papers were burning as the Marines backed off toward the embassy's main entrance.

Leaping up from a cyclo, one man clawed his way onto the top of the wall. He was holding a Molotov cocktail.

"Giai phong! Giai phong!" he chanted, as he lit the fuse of the homemade incendiary. He spotted Barrabas and spat out: *"Do-mai!"*

"Don't call me a motherfucker, you son-of-a-bitch," said Barrabas, drawing his side arm.

He gave the VC sympathizer the liberation he'd been yelling for—a .45 slug below the third rib. It knocked the would-be arsonist back into the street, where he landed in a fiery puddle of his own making.

THE BUILDING WAS A SHAMBLES INSIDE. Desk drawers had been dragged open and their contents spilled across the floor.

Filing cabinets had been emptied in the search for sensitive documents. Office furniture lay everywhere, overturned and often broken.

Calvert and Bay Tin took the steps two at a time, not willing to risk the elevators.

A telephone, half-buried under a mound of abandoned paperwork, began to ring. The Canadian put his arm round the boy's shoulder, helping to push him faster up the stairs. The camera case was banging uncomfortably into his hip. Below them they could hear the crashing echo of the Marines' boots following after them.

They had to stop on the fourth floor to catch their breath. Through an open door they caught sight of an official, whose well-cut bush jacket could not conceal his growing paunch, standing over the biggest pile of money either of them had ever seen.

Jessup was setting fire to the embassy's cash fund of $100 bills. The mountain of money had just started to smolder.

"Clear out!" he shouted at the two strangers, but then added, "And tell the chopper pilot to wait for me!"

HANDS CLUTCHING PAPERS promising safe passage were thrust through the railings. The sheer pressure of people had almost burst open the gates. It was time for Barrabas to hightail it too. He hated to go like this...on the run. It wasn't his way.

Damn it all! They had been sold short on strategy from the very beginning. And in the end they had been sold out at a conference table half a world away.

So it all came down to this—nothing! The living and the dead were being left behind. Barrabas turned his back on the tumultuous rush of refugees as they broke into the grounds. Even worse, he felt as if he were turning his back on those buddies who would never go home. Like the four men who had died in the stinking swamps of Kap Long. This final betrayal meant it was all for nothing.

Well, never again. Barrabas was never going to fight again for empty words and even emptier promises. From now on it would be for money. Cold, hard cash. In advance. And spare the rhetoric.

Barrabas felt the bile rising in his throat as he charged up the stairs. So many men had died. And their South Vietnamese friends were being cruelly abandoned. Only the politicians won. Wasn't that always the way? On one side they would claim a revolutionary victory, and on the other "peace with honor." Honor? They didn't know the meaning of the word.

"Watch out, Colonel!" Two floors above him one of the Marines dropped a tear gas canister down the stairwell.

A bunch of freshly cut flowers lay among the shattered fragments of a delicate vase. The edges of the carpet were beginning to burn around the smoking heap of currency Jessup had torched. As Barrabas passed the last office he saw a map of Vietnam lying on the desk. A half-drunk bottle of wine had been knocked over and its contents had seeped down across the south in a broad red stain. There was a second bottle too, an unopened fifth of Johnny Walker. Barrabas ran inside and grabbed it, as the Marines threw more tear gas to deter the milling crowd that now turned to looting.

By the time Barrabas reached the top landing, the Marines had withdrawn. The last chopper was loading. He ran out onto the roof. The wind of the rotor wash tore at his clothes.

The pilot, assuming everyone was aboard, began to lift off.

"Hey, there's one more!" shouted Calvert. But the pilot couldn't hear.

Jessup was in the open doorway. He got one foot balanced on the landing skid; then, with his hands wrapped around the grabrail, he stretched out his other arm.

In five long strides Barrabas closed the gap. And leaped for his life.

His fingers closed around the chopper's skid. Jessup grasped his wrist. Jesus, under that shock of almost white hair, it was Nile Barrabas! "You crazy bastard, gimme your other hand...."

"I can't! Just haul me in."

Jessup put his not inconsiderable weight behind the effort and pulled Barrabas up to the door.

Soldiers in the streets below, men from both sides, were firing up at the last evac chopper to fly off the embassy roof. But it was too late.

Jessup wrapped his beefy forearm around the colonel's shoulder to steady him. Calvert had taken his final picture of the war. Tomorrow it would flash around the wire services of the world. He could already see the caption: "Last man out!"

"Thanks," said Barrabas, then produced what he was holding in his other hand. "I thought we might need this."

Jessup saw the whisky and shook his head. "You really are a crazy bastard!"

PART ONE
THE TERMS

1

The cell was solid stone on three sides, with a rusting iron door making up the fourth. The only air came from sporadic breezes wafting through a high paneless window that was just too small for a man to crawl through.

Barrabas knew. He had already tried it. In fact he had made three escape attempts in the six weeks of his captivity. They had all ended in frustration. Right back where he started.

Now he was trying to squeeze his bulky six-foot-four frame into the five-foot-ten cot in a futile attempt to get comfortable. Sleep was out of the question.

He could hear the squeaking and scratching from the rats' nest high on the ledge in one corner of the cell. His furry neighbors had extended their family group since his arrival. He'd asked one of the guards to get rid of them; not out of fear, but because their noise kept him awake.

Chavez, his belly jiggling, had laughed at that.

"So, *señor*, you have only a few days...a couple of weeks at most. Spend them awake." Then Chavez had leered. "But be sure to clean any food from your lips and fingers. The agony from a rat's bite is often more painful than death itself."

Barrabas had kept himself as clean as possible, and made an equitable truce with his rodent companions—they stayed in the rock crevice, he stayed below it. What else could he do? Captured mercenaries could not expect lodgings at the local Hilton.

Nile Barrabas figured he had no one to blame but himself. There was always someone ready to sell you out. It was no different this time. But he should have expected it.

In Nam it had been greedy bastards like that Aussie journalist who blew the whistle on a covert operation just to sell a few more copies of his lousy newspaper. Or the guys who were the linchpins in the drug trade. Like Karl

Heiss. But at least Barrabas had lived to see *him* die. His only regret was that he hadn't been the one to pull the trigger. And you could always count on the politicians and diplomats to shaft you. They were the ones who precipitated these bloody conflicts—then when the going gets rough, they're quick to sell out the poor slobs on the sharp end.

This time it was the United Nations. General Ramon Perez, Barrabas's erstwhile employer, had gotten the Marxist Liberation Front on the run. But a ceasefire agreement hastily rammed through the Security Council had given the Cuban-backed MLF the time it so desperately needed to regroup. When they were good and ready, they staged enough violations of the truce to allow themselves to be "provoked" into retaliating, which they did in strength. Zamarga was turned into a sweltering tropical Stalingrad. Barrabas had been one of the last to be taken prisoner.

Why did he pick this lousy war? Barrabas smiled grimly at the ceiling: it was a bad career move for a mercenary. He should have stuck with Africa. That was a merc's playground compared with this banana republic. He hadn't got much faith left in Perez' expected counterattack.

The verdict of the kangaroo court that tried Barrabas had been a foregone conclusion.

Now it was only a matter of time before the sentence would be carried out.

And time, as the guard was fond of reminding him, was running out fast. . . .

THEY WERE a long mottled green column, forty men strong, moving through the bush.

The jungle in front of them was too thick to see through.

The dark trees were so close together, so intertwined with their own climbing vines and roots that the whole wall of foliage seemed to breathe. Grasping creepers twisted the life from weaker vegetation and reached up to snare the human intruders.

But these intruders knew the bush well. They knew the secret passages deep inside those unseen depths. Their black faces gleamed with mesmerized intent and glistening sweat as they seemed to will openings in the green curtain that closed abruptly once they had passed through. Now and then they would glide through a clearing between the giant trees above, and the blistering shafts of sunlight would turn the sheen of their faces a dappled gray.

They had been on the move since early morning. Soon they would be expected to fight, and then there would be a return march far into the night.

Marching and killing: the most common duties of a bush solider with a cause. And even more so for a mercenary.

Their work had already begun. In the last hour they had left eleven outlying perimeter guards dead with their throats cut. Now they were within a mile of their objective, and it was minutes until dusk. Just after the sun takes its last dip behind the green hills and the dark jungle folds in in upon itself is the perfect time for an attack in the bush.

A whisper from a low, guttural voice at the front of the column halted it. Lyinga's order rolled back in a rippling wave and they immediately melded into the heavy growth on both sides of the path. In seconds they were indistinguishable from their surroundings. Without orders now, working from instinct and experience, they fanned out in a jagged line and once again began moving forward.

The three bazooka teams took the points of the triple spearhead. They would begin the firing, hopefully to knock out half the resistance before any serious retaliation could be mounted.

Each man in the column had been carefully briefed days before, and General Lyinga's orders were very clear: "We want him alive. Knock out the machine guns and destroy the outbuildings first. Control your small-arms fire into the main hut and by no means use anything heavier than small arms in the vicinity of where Noboctu might be."

Behind the bazooka teams the main force checked its weapons and ammunition as light from palm-oil lanterns and campfires pierced the foliage ahead. Above the sound of scurrying bush rats and the light hum of locusts could be heard the steady clicks as safeties were shifted to the off position.

The weapons were as varied in background as the men who carried them. Several Makonde warriors, left over from the revolution in Mozambique, carried Russian AK-10s and French Marcid submachine guns. These Makondes had fought on the Portuguese side and now fought for whoever would pay them. They were the fiercest of the group and respected, as well as feared, by the others. Often their appearance alone served to frighten the enemy. At puberty in the Makonde tribe, both boys and girls went through the rite of making incisions in their faces and then rubbing charcoal into the open, deep wounds. This, plus the tradition of filing their teeth down to sharp fangs, gave them the appearance of something straight from hell. Very effective in combat.

The same was true of their Balante brothers, many of them lightly caressing new Crisobal .30-caliber carbines supplied by a rebel force from a country not their own.

There were Ugandan exiles, ex-rebels from Chad and the Congo, and Nubian mercenaries from the Sudan.

But the leaders, five in number, were all from the same land. They were tall, sturdily built men with a high degree of trained military bearing from the island of Kaluba.

It was *their* revolution.

Another order was passed along in Swahili and then discussed by smaller groups in French, Portuguese and many tribal languages including the clicking language of the Bantu.

Then they were halted. Light streamed through the undergrowth in wide patches now. Directly in front of them lay their objective, and each man carefully checked the area against the briefing instructions.

The clearing's perimeter was dotted with thatched huts. The native materials used in their construction merged so well into the tangled landscape that they were barely visible from a few yards away.

In the center was a decaying building of whitewashed mud brick. The yard around it was grassless but had gone to weed. Part of the corrugated tin roof had slipped away and now lay where it had fallen.

Around the whole was a barbed-wire fence with platform-mounted machine guns on each of four corners. These guns, and the men nodding in the oppressive heat behind them, were the only real indication that the pretending President of Kaluba, Joseph Noboctu, was running his self-proclaimed government-in-exile from inside the building.

This time the command was silent, nothing more than

the fluttering of a bush cap. The three bazookas fired almost simultaneously and the whirring scream of their shells seemed to precede the actual sound of their firing.

Three of the machine guns lifted from their mountings and turned over and over idly in the air with the effortless grace of steel gymnasts as they fell back to earth. The men behind them were disintegrated on impact, leaving only bits of charred clothing as evidence of their existence.

Reaction from the fourth gunner was instant. He started firing when the first shell exploded and before he could even turn the muzzle of his gun toward the invaders.

The .30-caliber slugs sprayed the ground knee high and crippled three men before an AK-10 in the hands of another rebel stitched an even line of dark, quick bloody holes across the gunner's chest.

The machine guns were hardly dispatched before the bazookas were reloaded and firing point-blank at the mess hut.

The result was implosion rather than explosion. The thin-sheeted metal roof disappeared into the jungle beyond, and the walls seemed to crumble inward as if suctioned by a huge vacuum in the hut's center.

Out of the smoke and powdered adobe came screaming bodies. Some were armed, but being blinded, fired wildly. Others were weaponless and half-naked as they ran for the jungle with only survival in mind.

All were cut down within six feet of the demolished building by automatic-rifle fire and the stuttering chatter of submachine guns.

On signal, rebel green filled the clearing, firing at any moving object. Grenades were lobbed, three at a time, into the smaller huts. The explosions followed each other in staccato bursts and were quickly followed in turn by more screams and groans of dying men.

A few defenders managed a gap-filled defense line between two of the huts. They were able to fire one futile burst, mostly in the air, before being overrun and dispatched by bayonet or panga—the long, curved knife so good for clearing the bush or decapitating the enemy.

Lyinga and his cohorts had already headed for the main hut. Two sentries, at the break in the barbed fence, dropped to their knees and raised their weapons. Both rifles misfired and the men died with frustration on their faces.

The Kaluban officers, backed by three Nubians, spread around one room of the hut, easily covering the two windows and single door. A burst of machine pistol brought answering fire from the room. It was of little consequence, the slugs going into the air or scattering in puffs of dried mud in the clearing beyond.

Lyinga, a surprisingly young, dour-faced black man with heavily hooded eyes, directed two of the Nubians to the door. Blindly they obeyed, charging the panel with their shoulders and bringing a fusillade of gunfire from inside the room. The door splintered, killing both of them at once.

With the defenders' attention on the door, the remaining Nubian was hoisted above the rear window ledge. A quick survey of the four surprised faces in the room told him they were all much younger than the face in the picture he had been shown before the mission; the face of the man that was to be taken alive.

This established, he sprayed the room until the bodies fell, and then sprayed the bodies until there was no more sound or movement from the floor.

The corpses of the fallen Nubians were unceremoniously kicked out of the way and the leader, followed by his two officers, entered the room. A single door now separated the men from the second room in the hut.

One of the officers fired a short burst through the door near the top lintel, much higher than a man's head, and shouted in Swahili, "Further resistance is useless. The compound is ours. Surrender now!"

There were muffled curses from the opposite side of the door and it soon opened. Four men stepped out, two in civilian clothes, more rags than garments, and two in tattered uniforms.

"Place your guns on the floor!"

The four gingerly bent and slid their guns forward before dropping them. When they were upright again they formed a ragged line and attempted some degree of military bearing.

With a slight wave of the hand and a wiggling of fingers for a command, all four were killed where they stood.

The ranking officer turned to his lieutenants. "Take care of the rest of them with the minimum ammunition necessary!"

They nodded in reply.

"And the hardware?"

He moved to the window and surveyed the compound. Most of their arms were still stacked neatly by the huts and around the center cookfire. As his experienced eyes took in the caliber, make and age of the Enfields, the stockless Berettas, and the ancient single-shot small-caliber rifles left over from sons of colonial hunters, his lip curled into a slight sneer.

"No, leave it. The machine guns were the only weapons usable and they are destroyed. The rest of this ordnance probably won't fire half the time."

Again they nodded and the room cleared. The leader stood at the window a moment longer, watching his orders being carried out as groaning men were silenced forever with short bursts from an automatic rifle or single, popping sounds from unholstered Mausers.

He nodded in satisfaction and looked at his watch. He had brought forty men on the raid. As near as he could tell he had three dead and three wounded. The base defenders had numbered one hundred. There would be no survivors.

It had been six minutes and twenty seconds since the first bazooka had opened fire.

Turning briskly, he walked into the second room where a tall, lean black man stood hunched in the center of the room feeding papers into a hastily constructed fire.

"Joseph Noboctu."

The gray head turned around. The dark, piercing eyes quickly surveyed the young intruder, dismissed him, and returned to the task at hand.

"Joseph Noboctu, I am General Joshua Lyinga, first officer in the Revolutionary Army of Field Marshal Haile Mogabe."

"A little young for a general, aren't you?"

"Revolution breeds early maturity, sir. We have come to liberate you."

The last of the papers fell from the graying man's hands into the sputtering fire. He turned, his mocking eyes now intently fixed on the younger man, as if he were trying to penetrate the brash look of arrogance he saw before him.

"Is that what you call it...this butchery? You call it liberation?"

"They were puppet troops of an imperialist government. Now you are free to fight that government alongside Field Marshal Mogabe!"

"I've been fighting the imperialist government *and* Mogabe for ten years. What if I refuse to go with you? Will you shoot me?"

Lyinga shook his head, but gave no spoken assurance.

The young general turned to the door and barked a brisk command. Three soldiers appeared and whisked the old man from the room to the carnage in the compound. He surveyed what he saw stoically and made no complaint as he was pushed into the column that now marched into the darkness of the jungle.

WALKER JESSUP gave a small grunt as he squeezed his large bulk into the chair that sat opposite the imposing massiveness of the senator's desk. The office was at a top-floor corner of one of the main administrative buildings. The furniture was really much too large for these cramped quarters.

Behind the desk, the diminutive figure of the senator stared distastefully at Jessup through the split lenses of his bifocals. The big man returned the look under sleepy eyes that suggested bored indifference.

"So we have a problem in Kaluba?" The senator's voice was as dry and hard as his handshake.

"It appears so," conceded Jessup. "They've grabbed Noboctu."

"I must confess the committee has been so busy with the growing danger to Costa Rica that I've not stayed on top of African affairs." The senator shrugged. He was a busy man. Jessup refrained from reminding him that it was largely his own backroom politicking that had scuttled the President's plan to extend aid to El Salvador. And that particular shortfall left the Central American trouble-makers free to work their mischief in Costa Rica. His eyes merely wandered above the senator's head, until the other man placed his hands on the desk top and instructed: "So brief me. . . and keep it brief."

With an air of exaggerated patience, Jessup painted the picture with bold brushstrokes. The senator was a careful listener, or at least he gave that impression as Jessup concluded his simplified lecture. "So now Kaluba has a South African puppet dictator in power. And he's bleeding the country dry. On the other hand we have another Idi Amin, in the person of Haile Mogabe, just waiting to take over."

"And it was this Mogabe's mob that grabbed Noboctu?"

"Yeah. They snatched him right out of that jungle base camp we set up for him."

"Stubborn fool." The senator shook his head. "He should have got out. . . he could have had our protection."

"Noboctu is stubborn," Jessup agreed, "but he's not a fool. He's an honest man. And he's the only one the people would pick to lead them if they had a free choice. We should have backed him in the first place."

"We couldn't! And you know that." The senator slapped his hand on the desk top harder than he'd intended. "How the hell could we when the man would give no clear indication of his intentions. Which way was he going to lean. . . right or left, West or East?"

Jessup said nothing. He had given his opinion and he was sticking by it.

The senator ran his finger under the rim of his heavily starched collar. "We're not here, Jessup, to discuss the reasons for the current situation, but to find a way to solve this mess. We've got to get Noboctu back. In time for the proposed elections."

"You think we should send in the Marines?" Jessup tested the senator, knowing full well that would be an invitation to disaster.

"No, not the Marines." The senator seized the initiative. He searched carefully for the right words. "But I am authorized to suggest you create a small, highly trained, and very mobile unit to take care of this problem. . . and any others like it that should arise in the future."

The senator had Jessup's undivided attention—he'd been arguing for something like this for years, but never thought it would meet with the committee's approval. Now he knew why this morning's meeting had been set up in this small office. And why the senator wanted to meet with him alone.

The senior man did not especially like Walker Jessup, or men like him. This overweight Texan had a mysterious, somewhat shady past, but his record as a soldier and, later on, as an operative for various intelligence agencies was enviable. If something needed to be done—a fast operation put together, clandestine or otherwise—Jessup had a one-hundred-percent record of accomplishment. Even the senator had heard of him referred to as "The Fixer." That's how he was known in the trade.

Well, this time the wily senator was going to fix Jessup. He'd teach him how the game was played, how to score the big points. The senator enjoyed the certain knowledge that he was about to set Walker Jessup an impossible task. And that should finish off any suggestion of setting up such an undercover squad ever again.

"Of course, such a unit . . . ."

"A 'dirty tricks' team."

He had heard some of his fellow senators call it that, but chose to ignore Jessup's remark: "The existence and operation of such a unit depends entirely on finding the right man to lead it."

The Texan nodded. He couldn't have agreed more.

"You will need to find a man who is fiercely independent, yet knows his patriotic duty. He'll have to have an exceptional record and at the same time be willing to take on the dirtiest jobs with no thought of personal glory." The senator was warming to his task. He was enjoying this. He reached for further contradictory qualities. "He must care for his men, cherish them even, but have the instincts of a ruthless killer . . . ."

The corners of Jessup's mouth began to twitch. He was trying to suppress a grin.

"This man, if it were possible to find him, would have to be bullheaded but never blind. He'd have to be just a little bit crazy but never stupid." Suddenly the senator didn't like the way Jessup was looking at him. "You know such a man?"

"I met him once," Jessup nodded. "Twice, to be exact."

"Who is he? Where is he?"

"I'm not sure," confessed Jessup. "But I'm on speaking terms with a couple of friendly computers. They'll give me a detailed profile and I'll soon find out out where he is...."

The senator's knuckles turned white. He had the sickening feeling he had just lost game, set and match.

2

The man's experience was broader than Jessup had even dared hope for—Nile Barrabas had been through it all, and then some.

The big Texan propped his heels on the edge of his desk and glanced through the file that lay open on his lap. Few men had a service record that could equal that of Colonel Barrabas. The numerous commendations for bravery more than outweighed the reports of brawling and breaches of strict military protocol.

The phone console buzzed softly.

"Yes?"

"Your call to the Defense Intelligence Agency is through, sir. Doctor Noll is on the line. He's the head of the Operative Selection, Monitoring and Assessment Board."

"Thanks, Jane." There was a click as the girl made the connection. "Hello, Doctor Noll. This is Walker Jessup."

"Hi, you asked for the documentation on Nile Barrabas, ex-Colonel Barrabas."

"That's right. I've already obtained the standard service material."

"Well, I've got you some notes from the CIA and other agency files. At this short notice, it's not as comprehensive as it might be."

"What's your assessment of this Heiss affair?" asked Jessup.

"I think the two men may have crossed paths even earlier than 1975—but there's nothing on paper to prove it. I'm not sure the rivalry was intentional on the part of Karl Heiss. It's just that Barrabas, who it seems was very good at his job, kept crossing paths with. . . well, a guy who was a bad apple."

"Uh-huh," Jessup grunted; he would have used stronger language to describe that rat, if half of what he'd read was true.

"As you know, the Operation Achilles pacification program gave Barrabas the chance to 'wage war with a human face'—"

"I'm beginning to think he often does," murmured Jessup.

"—and then along came Karl Heiss, who scuttled the Colonel's efforts."

"Why? Why did Heiss do that?"

"Drugs, basically. Heiss undermined Barrabas in order to cement his ties with various dope smugglers and other unsavory elements within the Vietnamese armed forces."

"I suspected as much."

"At the same time he also prevented Barrabas's excellent intelligence-gathering machine from uncovering any of his own illegal operations," added Noll. "You can read more about it in the material I'll send over. The documents collected for the Colonel's court-martial make interesting reading. I've also included clippings from various Saigon newspapers that will give you some idea of Barrabas's 'social standing' during the height of his career over there."

"The Colonel was a ladies' man?"

"He was certainly sought after by some of the capital's most attractive women. It appears that Barrabas was often the center of attention in very sophisticated, chic and high-powered circles." Noll sounded disapproving. "Of course, he left all that behind him when he quit the Army to become a mercenary."

"But is he the man I'm looking for? Give me your professional opinion, Doctor Noll."

"From the specifications in your notes, I'd say Barrabas more than measures up. He has an exemplary service record—much of it in action. And that unfortunate court-martial affair was quite unnecessary." It was clear that Noll regarded the black marks against Barrabas as pluses in judging his fitness for Jessup's operation. "I should warn you that he'll be an odd character to deal with...he may be a soldier for hire, but even his mercenary career has shown a strict sense of ethics. Above all, treat him as the professional he is, and I think he'll respond like one."

Jessup had no intention of treating him any other way.

He had come to the same conclusions about Barrabas's moral character himself.

He was beginning to think he had found his man. "Thank you, Doctor Noll. I look forward to reading that material."

He placed the phone back on its sloping cradle just as Jane walked into his office. She handed Jessup a torn-off sheet of computer printout. "This is the latest information regarding Nile Barrabas."

He read the newest findings quickly. Then read them again. "Are you sure this is right? This is where he is now?"

"The Digimax 6000 is certain that information is correct, sir," Jane tartly reminded him. "I just carried the paper in here."

Jessup shook his head and read the computer's answer for the third time. He couldn't help but grin.

Walker Jessup knew he had found his man.

JESSUP WAS SMILING when he entered that very private office for the second time.

The senator did not look quite so happy. "So, you've assembled all the information needed for this project?"

The Texan opened his case and pulled out a thick wad of files. "Twenty-five potential recruits have been selected by computer analysis. This number will be cut to ten, which is the perfect size group for the type of 'dirty tricks' strike force your committee has requested."

"Damn!" the senator swore under his breath. It betrayed the liberal promises with which he had bought himself votes in each of his winning elections. "They wouldn't be needed at all if every hawk on the Hill or every general over at the Pentagon didn't scream for us to take action every time some tinpot dictator takes a dump on another one!"

"Oh, I'm sure your objectives are completely honorable, Senator." Jessup couldn't resist the barb.

The smaller man overlooked the remark. It was to be done and he could come to terms with it. "You realize there's little over a month left now."

Jessup nodded. "Thirty-seven days, to be precise. The elections in Kaluba have been set for the twenty-sixth."

"It isn't good enough just to produce Noboctu in time for the polls. He's got to be able to show the people what's been going on. He's got to be furnished with proof." The senator's hands fluttered with despair. "If he isn't there on the twenty-sixth...." The politician let the rest of his statement trail off as if it left too sour a taste in his mouth.

Jessup finished the thought for him: "Then the Kaluban diamond mines and the gold fields could find their way into very dangerous hands."

"Can you reduce your selection to a short list, recruit them, and get them whipped into shape by then?"

"I can't," said Jessup. "But the man I've chosen to lead them can. He's a born commander, an experienced soldier and a killer. And, at present, he's in something of a predicament."

"I suppose he's as rebellious and crazy as the men we're going to ask him to lead?"

"He has the very qualities you asked for, Senator," smiled Jessup. "He's an ex-colonel. Ruthless when he has to be, highly seasoned in the fine points of war, and he has already had some dealings with the intelligence community."

The Texan riffled open the top file and flipped an eight-by-ten glossy across the desk. It showed a bare-chested man carrying a handgun and a submachine gun and a couple of grenades and a knife and pouches....

"My God!"

"Interesting-looking sight, isn't it? Barrabas became a mercenary after his regular military service, so he already has a close knowledge of the kind of areas this unit is likely to be dispatched to—particularly in this instance. He's done a good deal of fighting in that bush country."

"And are you sure he can be recruited?" the senator asked, handling the picture as if it might burn his fingers. "After all, he's just a soldier of fortune...."

"His fighting skills are for hire, Senator. That much is true. But he isn't the kind of man who can be easily bought." Jessup gave a knowing grin. "But I do, in fact, think he'll listen to what we have to offer."

He stood up, retrieved the photograph and slid the files back in his case. "At this moment, Nile Barrabas is waiting to die in a South American prison. In forty-eight hours, he's got a date with a firing squad."

RUMOR HAD IT that Perez would finally launch his long-awaited counteroffensive within the next few days. Chavez had promised Barrabas would be shot in his cell if the loyalist troops so much as got near the prison. And Barrabas had more reason to believe the guard's jeering threat than in gossip whispered from the next cell after dark.

He had chosen the life of a mercenary. He worked for the people who could afford his price. They put up the money and he took the chances. You couldn't bet to show, only to win. Simple. Only this time he had lost.

How could he have played it differently? Where would he have ended up? Pushing papers from one side of a desk to the other? Sending men he didn't know out on missions he could never be part of...then scrubbing their names from the duty list when they were terminated? Killing is real easy when all you have to do is push buttons, draw up lists, and sign orders. But that wasn't for Barrabas. No way. Never would be.

Yet he could not shift the responsibility.

Sure, he was a killer too.

He was a professional.

But it never came easy. He never wanted it to. Nile Barrabas was a mercenary with a heart. He was a living, breathing, fighting, killing contradiction-in-terms.

He was more complicated than the rules. They were simple: kill or be killed.

Simple, yeah, but never easy.

You know the other guy is going to fight like hell for his life, and you know that when you pull the trigger—when you looked into his eyes just before pulling the trigger—you would see yourself reflected in those terrified mirrors, silently screaming, struggling to survive, grasping for life. But the trigger gets pulled. Always will—as long as you're fighting for your life. And so you lived, and he died. You can only hope to be so lucky next time.

But if you're not, if it's time to buy the farm, then you know your eyes are going to look just like his did when someone pulls the trigger on you.

No, it wasn't easy.

But simple as hell.

Barrabas wanted it that way.

From now to the end.

He had had enough of politics. Nam had taught him that. He'd had a bellyful of people promising to do good, of trying to do *their* idea of what was good for others, when it was always at someone else's expense. He tried to go along with it. But he saw that the lust for power that compelled men to seek public office contained the seeds of their own corruption.

Barrabas had found a simpler way.

But now he'd played out the string....

"*Señor!*"

"*Sí.*"

The iron door creaked open. "You will come with me."

Barrabas, on his bunk, turned his lined and weathered face toward the pale square of light. He scowled at the guard. "Not until dawn, *amigo*."

"Oh, no, *señor*," said Chavez, "it is not that. Not yet. But you have a visitor."

"I told you, no priest," growled the prisoner. Barrabas ran his hand through the short brush of gray white hair and rolled back to face the wall.

"You would be advised to see this man, *señor*. He is an official...an *americano*."

That was different. Barrabas sat up. Perhaps the lawyer back home had finally gotten through to the State Department. He preceded the puffing guard up the stone steps to the fresh air and growing light.

His eyes adjusted slowly as a second guard joined in the procession, and he was led through a maze of dank corridors until he found himself in the familiar surroundings of the claustrophobic interrogation room.

They sat him at a table. The guards turned back and shut the door.

The naked bulbs stung his eyes. It was so bright he had to squint to see the glass of whisky that was shoved toward him and the nearly full bottle of Johnny Walker that followed.

"Now Barabbas was a robber..." drawled the stranger on the other side of the table. His voice still retained a hint of the open plains of Texas.

"That would be the least of my worries," grunted Barrabas. "Robbery isn't a capital offense down here."

"I was thinking of the time you stole those plans from

Chan Minh Chung's offensive. That saved a lot of lives."

Barrabas stared at the bulky shadow outlined by the lights. He lowered the glass from his lips: "Jessup?"

"Yep, it's me. Walker Jessup."

"Damn, I can't say I'm sorry to see you," admitted Barrabas, leaning back in his chair. "Funny how we two seem to meet...."

"The first time was merely the chance dictates of a duty roster," shrugged the big intelligence officer. "The second time—well, I guess it was just a coincidence that we both got stuck in Saigon till the very end."

"And now, the third time?"

"This time? Coincidence has nothing to do with it. This time I've come looking for you." Jessup poured out another slug of whisky. "If I give you a hand—if I pull you out of the shit—then this time you're going to owe me."

"Who are you working for these days, Jessup? State?"

"A little higher than that."

Barrabas smiled for the first time. He felt the whisky burn his throat and warm his stomach, then he belched. "Good. So that means you do have some clout. Enough to get me out of here?"

"It can be arranged, even with the MLF. Of course, as I said, there would be some, er, considerations."

The merc's lip curled tighter, giving a cynical edge to his smile. He downed the second shot and reached for another refill. "Yeah, well, considerations are what got me in here. I backed Perez. I didn't know it was rigged for him to lose."

"Go easy on that stuff! I've got some talking to do," Jessup said. "And you've got a decision to make. So sit back and listen."

The voice had a certain tone that arrested Barrabas's dismissive gesture. It was the tone used to command. Barrabas knew it well; it was in his own voice. He understood it and gave it his grudging respect, when it came from someone who knew how to use it. Like Walker Jessup.

"You were a mercenary officer employed by the losers and captured by the MLF."

"Yeah, I know that."

"And now they are going to stick you in front of a firing squad. All according to law."

"And I know that too."

"This time tomorrow you'll be dead. Unless...."

"Unless you get my butt out of here for...considerations."

"Right. When was the last time you saw Karl Heiss?"

"The night before he died."

"He was spotted two months ago in Amsterdam."

The glass was halfway to Barrabas's lips. He paused, digested the words, and then swallowed the burning liquid in one quick flip of his wrist.

"I saw his body...with a hundred holes in it."

"What you saw were remains. With too many holes to recognize him properly."

"I'm listening," Barrabas said, pushing the empty glass away from his hand. This time he didn't refill it.

"Because of certain differences of opinion, a minor revolution was encouraged in Kaluba a few months ago. It was fronted by Haile Mogabe—"

"A butcher."

"True, but the only alternative available at the time. To make it short, we eventually withdrew our support. But Mogabe didn't quit, even without our aid. About six months ago a shipment of raw diamonds, worth over two million dollars, was lifted from an African country. It was a gutsy heist, too gutsy for profit alone to have been the motive. It smelled of a cause, a fanatical cause. They had to be fanatics...six of them were killed.

"We think Heiss brokered the stones. About two months later the usual ads for 'farm workers' appeared in the Paris papers under Heiss's old code name. Then he was spotted in Amsterdam."

"Setting up a buy." Barrabas said it tonelessly without emotion. He knew the procedure so well he could recite it like a litany.

"You got it. Munitions, boat, uniforms, the works."

"Sounds like you already got a war started. What the hell do you need me for?"

"Sometimes it takes a small war to stop a big one. You should know that already. My employers—"

"Are?"

"Nameless, for the time being, but high...*very* high." He paused for emphasis. When Barrabas nodded, he continued. "My employers wish to organize a team that can handle any situation without making it appear that the Pentagon is interfering in foreign problems."

Barrabas spit. "Even when we *cause* the problems?"

"Alas, too true sometimes. As in the case of Heiss... crazy Heiss. All men in this business seem to have a kind of death wish, but Heiss is downright suicidal. No matter what a mercenary does, he does it for money...and he wants to believe that he'll live to spend it."

Barrabas's voice, when he spoke, was low, agreeing. "And Heiss does it for fun."

"Exactly. A man like that is very hard to control. Especially in the employ of a man very much like him, Mogabe."

Barrabas edged closer to the table. "I think I've got it. Some of your Sneaky Petes went off on their own to get a little revolt started. Maybe to jostle somebody—the present leaders of a country, probably—into thinking your way. After it got rolling, the revolutionaries decided that they didn't want to stop. Piss on your agreement. They want to go ahead and take over."

"That's basically it." Jessup's wheezing twang came back unruffled from the darkness.

"You cut off their funds. They hire Heiss and company, pull a heist for new capital, put together an army, and boom...full-scale war. Right?"

"Something like that. They have also captured our only alternative leader, Joseph Noboctu."

"And you want me to lead a team to get him out and stop a war before it starts."

"We've already compiled a list of men. You'll train out of the country and do your own buying. Funds are unlimited, but the source, of course, is top secret. Only a few people at the top will know of your existence and connections."

Barrabas went back to the whisky and leaned back in his chair. "What's in it for me?"

"Off the hook...not guilty. Safe passage out of the country."

Barrabas didn't bother to ask Jessup how he put the fix in with the MLF.

"What else?"

"You can keep your bank accounts in Zurich. And this will add to them. It pays fifty grand a job and all you can steal."

"A job? You sound like this is more than a one-shot deal."

"Knowing the state of the world and the propensity for 'disagreement' among ambitious men, I'm afraid there will always be a need for your talents, Barrabas," Jessup admitted wearily.

"One more thing...."

"Yes?"

"A clean passport."

"You know the rules. You've been fighting in the revolutionary army of another country. It's against policy."

"Screw policy!"

"It mattered to you once."

"That was a long time ago."

"It doesn't seem so long since you were a respected colonel in the Army of the United States. Now you're a general...a general without an army."

"I found out early, generals make more money."

"Only if they live to collect," Jessup reminded him, but then admitted: "I know, promotions are slow in our Army. But with you they came pretty fast...two Silver Stars, four Purple Hearts, DSC, Medal of Honor...."

"Don't wave the flag. Is it a deal?"

There was a wheezing grunt as the man's huge bulk was lifted from the chair, and then he emerged out of the darkness from behind the light with his hand extended.

"Okay. Pack!"

"I got all I need," Barrabas grinned, holding up the bottle.

PART TWO
THE TEAM

3

"I've got a terrible thirst. We'll have a couple of jars and then we'll go beddy-byes!"

Liam O'Toole barely managed not to choke on the smoke from his cigar as he spoke. He puffed up a thick haze and then studied her through it. She was pretty in a weathered sort of way through all the makeup. Her hair was sleek and long, even if the color was too deep a red to be believed. Her breasts spread over her arms and onto the table like overripe melons.

She was, as Liam had expected her to be, a rather stupid woman. Why else would she marry a wimp like Jacob Wheeler, Liam's ex-boss. Ex, because Wheeler had fired him that morning.

He had run into Thelma on the way out. She'd been trying hard for six months, ever since Liam had gone to work for her husband as a demolition expert. Now that he had lost his job, Liam decided to let the little lady succeed, and reap his revenge at the same time.

He'd almost backed out when they first sat down.

"Do you know how to make a Demon's Delight?" She had the habit of popping her gum after every third word.

"No," the bartender said, a pained expression on his face. "Could you kind of give me a hint?"

"Sure." The gum popped. "A shot of crème de menthe, two shots of rum, some orange bitters, float a few pineapple rings on it and cover it all with whipped cream."

"Whisky, neat with water back," ordered Liam. "Make it a double."

He sat, gazing in revulsion at the huge glass that was placed before her. The chunks of fruit and congealed peaks of cream floated listlessly on the surface as Thelma avidly brought the level down through a straw.

"Oh, that was so-o-o good!" she squealed, not-sodaintily wiping a glob of whipped cream from her upper lip. "I'd like another one!"

He ordered two more doubles.

Liam did not notice the two men sitting quietly in the corner booth—his attention was focused on Thelma. She was annoying him, but he became more good-natured and tolerant as he worked his way through the doubles and ordered another. The more booze he put away, the more he started liking the idea of sharing a bed with her later in the evening.

If she would only shut up.

"Would you like me to hold your gum while you drink that, darlin'?"

"Nah, it's okay. I just slip it out of the way with my tongue."

Her breasts did a wild St. Vitus dance under her sweater when she moved. It would be, he thought, like sinking into a huge, soft mattress made of baby pink flesh.

"Hey," she giggled, "I hope you're not drinkin' too much. You know. . . for later? A lotta guys have that problem."

"Sure, an' that's never a problem with me, darlin'. Why, even when I was a lad in Ireland, I'd do five pints better than my mates, and chase the lasses while they recovered!"

"Ireland? I thought you was American."

"I am, Thelma, darlin'. Me grandfather retired to Ireland from Chicago, an' I grew up there as a lad." He sipped his whisky, biting his lip. *And when I was seventeen, I was arrested and accused of being in the IRA, when I wasn't. So when I was released, I joined the IRA and learned soldierin' and makin' bombs. Yes, little Thelma, you're about to spread yer legs for a former IRA bomber!*

"Y'know, Jacob didn't fire ya just 'cause you got the men all stirred up."

"Oh? What then. . . makin' eyes at his pretty wife?"

She giggled, and slurped, and popped her gum. "Nah. Jacob's jealous 'cause you was a war hero and won all them medals."

Medals, Liam thought. *Yeah, I got eighteen medals, eighteen years of service, eight battle scars, two ex-wives, and forty dollars in the bank with no job.*

"How come you got out, Liam?"

"Huh?"

"I said, how come you got outta the service before you retired?"

" 'Cause there were no more wars to fight, darlin'. And the ones we was fightin', we was losin'.' "

"Did ya kill people? How many people did ya kill? I wanna hear. But first I gotta go to the potty!"

"Yeah, you do that, darlin'." Liam watched her buttocks work their way across the room in perfect time to a fast disco number, then he stepped up to the bar. "Do me again on this, and make another one of those messes for the lady."

"That's Jacob Wheeler's wife, ain't it?"

Liam nodded. "I worked for him until this mornin'. Land clearin'...did his explosives."

"Oh, you're the one they wrote about in the paper... told the army to go to hell, didn't ya?"

"Something like that, yeah."

The barman nodded toward the john door. "You plannin' on makin' her up in the motel?"

"Any objections?"

"Nah," the barman shrugged. "It's nothin' to me, but maybe you'd better get movin' soon. Her old man comes in here a lot with *his* dates."

"Jesus," Liam muttered, shaking his head and sipping his whisky. "Civilians."

"What's that?"

"Nothin'. Just thinkin' about what I got and what I gave up."

Besides a cursory glance at the white-haired stranger, Liam paid no heed to the guys who were studying him from their shadowy recess. His one thought now was to get Wheeler's old lady in the sack. As soon as possible.

Thelma staggered back to the booth and Liam joined her. They drank and played kneesies under the table while she grinned stupidly above it, and Liam tried to keep his hands from smacking things.

She was getting maudlin.

"I don't do this often, ya know. I mean, just go out with one of the workin' stiffs."

Liam swallowed and kept a smile on his face.

"I got a lot of problems. Bein' married to a money machine that treats you like an iceberg ain't no fun, ya know!"

"No, I wouldn't know."

"I used to be pretty, Liam, did you know that?"

"I'll bet you were."

"Well, I like that, you bastard!" Her words became very slurred now. "Anybody else, any of the gentlemen I know, would tell me I'm still pretty!"

"Oh, you're not hard to look at, darlin'...and you do have monumental breasts."

She was weaving backward and forward, her eyes smoldering, as she shifted her straw from the empty glass to the full one.

"Ya know somethin'...I don't think you was no officer."

"I was a captain."

"An officer is a gentleman. You ain't nothin' but a workin' slob. Hell, my old man could buy an' sell you ten times over. You ain't nothin', so shove off, 'cause I don't shack up with nothin's!"

Liam picked up the mess in the huge glass, extracted the straw, and carefully poured it over her head. He had to. It was the only choice left open to him.

He dropped a twenty on the bar as he passed. Thelma's language, a cross between a longshoreman and an irate New York cabdriver, followed him into the parking lot.

He was nearly to his car when the first figure stepped from the shadows.

"That's no way to treat a lady, Liam."

He stared with boozy uncertainty at the face under that steel-gray thatch. It couldn't be, no, not here...Jesus, it really was...Liam gasped and threw his arms around the man's shoulders. "A blessin' on me mother! Sure an' it's the Colonel, I thought the Simbas would have ye quartered and in a stew pot by now!"

"I'm too tough to eat, Liam. You know that. How is it?"

"Not good. You saw." Liam chuckled as he thought of the pineapple slices sliding down her face.

"Ever think of going back?" drawled the second man.

"I've thought of it," the big Irishman nodded, "but I doubt if they'd have me."

"Let's go get a drink."

"HE'S GOING TO HAVE TO quit drinking."

"You tell any of these men that, Jessup—hell, you tell me to do that!—and you're not going to get your little strike force," said Barrabas. "I promise you O'Toole will be sober on the job."

"It's your ass."

"Yeah, so let's not forget it."

Jessup shrugged his broad shoulders. O'Toole had been happy to accept their proposal. In fact, he insisted they all seal this new arrangement with another bottle of whisky. The man from Washington slipped the bill in his pocket— he did not look forward to explaining this month's expense account. They practically had to pour Liam O'Toole aboard the plane as they dispatched the Irishman to recruit Wiley Drew Boone.

"In a tight spot, I'd trust O'Toole with my life," said Barrabas, still wanting to underline his point. "You won't find a better man with explosives."

Jessup nodded as he scribbled a note in O'Toole's file. He scanned the data sheet. "French. Spanish. Some German. And a grasp of Russian. So he's a fair hand with languages."

"And he'll reel in our sailor."

Jessup touched the tip of his tongue and chalked an imaginary line in the air.

Barrabas checked his watch, shook his head, and held up two fingers.

"HONEY, my great-granddaddy was a Georgia sharecropper. He never had a pot to pee in or a window to throw it out of 'til the day he got run over by a train. My granddaddy turned that insurance money into five million. He was the crookedest politician in the South. Then my daddy turned that five into twenty-five. An' me? Why, honey, I've dedicated my life to spendin' that twenty-five mil!"

So went the philosophy of life as espoused by Wiley

Drew Boone to one of Madame Angela's girls in the last big-time bordello left east of the Mississippi.

"Yes, little darlin', it's true. I was nothin' but a wastrel, a beach bum, and a playboy. An' my daddy was angry. He says to me, 'Wiley Drew, boy, you git yore butt into the Army...make a man outta you!' So I joined the Navy. Won me a few medals an' came back a hero. Oh, I'm the same fun-lovin' boy I was, but now daddy says it's okay 'cause I'm a *hero* beach bum an' playboy!"

"Oh, Wiley Drew," cooed the girl, "y'all is so cute. Let's go upstairs."

"Later, honey, I'm not drunk enough to enjoy it yet. Let me tell ya about the evacuation of Mong Kong Bay. D'you know sweetheart, that I can sail anything that'll float?"

"Is that a fact? No, Ah didn't know that! Buy me another champagne cocktail, Wiley Drew. Is yore daddy really the richest man in Atlanta?"

"Hell, yes! Now, let me tell you...."

Few people in the room paid any attention as the boisterous, handsome young man related his war stories to the listless girl.

Except, that is, a wide-faced, broad-shouldered man with an unruly mop of red hair. He hunched over his whisky and compared Wiley Boone's embellished stories to the reality of the man's dossier he had just read back in his hotel room. Jessup had given it to him.

Wiley Drew Boone had two passions: women and the sea. In the Navy he had become a navigation and weather expert. He saw a lot of action, mostly in evacuation missions that brought him under fire more than once.

He had been wounded and decorated for singlehandedly taking charge of a dangerously overloaded boat full of refugees and guiding it to safe harbor. All of this against astounding odds and his senior officer's orders.

Wiley Boone did a lot of things against orders. The only reason he wasn't court-martialed for insubordination or cashiered out of the service completely was the fact that he was always right and his harebrained stunts came off.

"D'ya say the name was Boone?"

"That's right."

"O'Toole. Liam O'Toole. Do ya mind if I join ya? I think we served about the same time."

"Sit down! What are ya drinkin'?"

"Whisky."

"Hey, what about me? I gotta make a livin'—"

Liam rolled a fifty and slid it down the deep neckline of her dress. "Go pester someone else for a while, me darlin'. Mr. Boone and I want to swap some lies."

They swapped a lot of lies and a lot of truths, one of them being that Wiley Boone had grown jaded. Kicks were getting harder and harder to find, because there isn't a hell of a lot that money won't buy.

Then O'Toole began to relate another story. . .a story of a group of men and a mission. Halfway through the tale, he knew Boone was hooked.

"Believe me, son," promised O'Toole with a conspiratorial wink, "our little group will give you everything money can't buy!"

JESSUP PUT DOWN THE PHONE. "O'Toole has Boone signed on."

"Never doubted it," said Barrabas. "Who's next?"

"I've sent O'Toole on to Hong Kong. Perhaps we should speak to Lopez."

"Where do we find him?"

"Oh, you should feel right at home," chuckled the Texan. "He's in jail."

A SLIGHT, BARELY PERCEPTIBLE CHILL ran up Barrabas's spine as the gates of Yarmouth Federal Prison silently slid open and they drove through. Barrabas had no liking for prisons, and considered himself lucky to have been pulled out of that South American hellhole by Walker Jessup.

Emilio Lopez wasn't so lucky. He was doing hard time: fifteen years.

"If you'll just have a seat, the warden will be with you in a few minutes."

Jessup remained standing but Barrabas settled into a worn leather couch and opened the folder on Emilio Lopez.

Hispanic-American, born in El Paso, Texas. The child of immigrant farm workers, he traveled the southwestern

United States as a youth, where he was in constant trouble with the law. At sixteen he left his family and made his way to New York City.

The rugged demands of his early youth served him well on the streets of the city. He joined a gang and quickly became its leader. But seeing the futility of petty theft, Lopez studied hard to improve himself. He became an accomplished forger and cardsharper. He learned every con that had ever been pulled and then invented some new ones.

Business prospered and by the time he was nineteen Emilio was riding high.

But the draft threatened. To avoid it, Emilio joined the National Guard. He proved adept at tank and heavy artillery training. And, unknown to his superior officers, he proved even more adept at fleecing his fellow guardsmen during summer camps and after monthly meetings.

The regimen proved too strict for Lopez to contend with; it interfered with his work on the street. He allowed his attendance to lapse until it became nonexistent.

The Guard pursued, and he was finally caught and jailed.

But, to everyone's surprise, Emilio pleaded that he wanted the service, but the National Guard had allowed him to come home too often, where his "bad environment" and old cronies could lead him on the path to evil. He insisted that he be placed in the Coast Guard, where he could escape the social pressure. They bought it, and placed him in the Coast Guard.

For years, Lopez worked diligently and showed undeniable ability. He obtained an education and a commission, and soon was commanding his own ship. For a long time he functioned under the smiling praise of his senior officers, only to have the whole thing blow up when it was discovered that he was using his vessel to make dope pickups beyond the twelve-mile limit.

"I want to state emphatically, Mr., uh, Smith and Mr. Jones, that I don't approve of this sort of thing. Why should a criminal reform when some government agency will get him off?"

"Warden, may we see him now...alone?"

Emilio Lopez was short, with the wiry and firmly muscled body of an athlete. The almost traditional mustache covered all of his upper lip and his teeth gleamed like ivory in his dark face when he smiled. And he smiled often.

"Something funny, Lopez?"

"Maybe. What's comin' down here? Who the hell are you guys?"

"The prosecuting officer at your trial said you could con the gold out of Fort Knox. Is that true?"

Lopez shrugged.

"How much do you remember about your heavy weapons training?"

"Enough. What the...?

"Are you as good a thief and forger as your record says?" The two men were alternating questions.

Lopex smiled broadly. "Better. What do you want me to steal?"

"What's the first thing you'd do if you got out of here, Lopez?"

"Get laid."

"And then?"

"Make some bread so I could get laid again."

"Get your things together."

BARRABAS TOOK A DEEP BREATH as the gates of the federal pen closed behind them.

Colonel Nile Barrabas, Liam O'Toole, Wiley Drew Boone, and now Lopez. They were making progress. Jessup lifted his hand from the wheel, folded his thumb across his palm, and held up four fingers.

"Feel like a trip to Monte Carlo?" he asked. "You're going to need a driver. A good one."

4

"Out! Out, out, out, climb the hell out of there, Biondi!"

"I told ya...the fuel mixture was too lean!"

Coughing and clawing at the straps of his helmet, Vincent Biondi crawled from the cockpit of the smoking Formula One Ferrari.

"Mixture hell, lean hell! It was your damn foot, Biondi. It's heavier than your head!"

"Calm down, Angelo. I can put it back together by Sunday, don't worry about it."

The little Italian stopped jumping up and down and closed his eyes. He was obviously counting up to some predetermined number that would control his anger.

When he spoke again, his voice was even, nearly a monotone. "You amaze me, Vince. You've got the head and the hands to build the fastest cars in the world. But you ain't got the brains to drive them within their limits."

What Angelo was saying was true and Vince knew it. But he would never admit it, particularly to himself. Something happened to him when he settled down into that tiny slot, and the dark visor came down over his eyes. He was invincible. Nothing short of the very edge was any good. The danger of driving near death was more rewarding than life itself.

"I'll get the crew right to work on it, Angelo."

"You do that, Biondi, you do that. And Sunday maybe Botelli will make us a winner in Monaco."

Vince had started to move away toward the pits. Now he stopped and turned, his eyes two coals of quick, hard anger.

"No way, Angelo. I drive what I've worked on."

"Then, you maniac bastard, you work for somebody else. Get outta my sight!"

For a second, Vince thought of putting three fingers

through Angelo's windpipe, or using his knee to rupture the little owner's spleen.

But he changed his mind. What good would it do? It wouldn't get him another ride, and a driver couldn't be a driver without a ride.

No, let it go, and check with the Lotus team. Word was around that they needed a third backup who was also a mechanic.

But Lotus didn't need anyone. Neither did Deerling or the German team. The millionaire from Hong Kong who ran three cars on the Grand Prix circuit just to keep his hand in wouldn't even touch Vince. But at least he was honest about it.

"You're good, Biondi. In fact, you're probably the best. But you're too expensive, even for me. You take cars apart on the track faster than my boys could build them. And the way you drive? Crazy! No, thanks. I don't want you on my team when you buy it. And if you keep driving, Vince, you're going to buy it!"

Vince watched Botelli win Monaco for Ferrari in the car he would have driven. Then he sat in front of a big window in the hotel lounge and got quietly smashed staring at the lights dancing on the bay and the dark Mediterranean beyond.

He was deep in the decision-making struggle, trying to decide whether he should follow the tour across Europe or give up and return to the States, when the waiter arrived with a fresh bottle of wine.

"I didn't order...."

"I did. The name's Barrabas. I've seen you drive. Mind if I join you?"

"You're buyin' the bottle...hell, yes, sit down."

Barrabas slid into the opposite chair and filled their glasses. "This is the most expensive bottle in the house... eighty bucks."

"So you got dough," Vince shrugged.

"You didn't drive today."

"I wasn't feeling well."

"You were canned." Vince started to rise. "Sit down, Vince."

Vince sat down. "You an owner? I mean, you lookin' for a driver?"

"Perhaps." Barrabas took a map from his pocket and spread it on the table between them. He was glad Jessup had stayed behind in Washington. "It's eleven miles from here to the Italian border. Can you make it in twelve minutes?"

"That's right through the middle of Monte Carlo!"

"That's right. Can you do it, Vince...at high noon... for a thousand dollars?"

"Oh, no. You want a wheel man for a heist, get somebody else. I pulled that crap when I was a kid. That's what landed me in the Corps. It was either that or prison. No way!"

"You got it all wrong. I just want to make sure you can do it in traffic as well as in an open-road race."

Vince studied the other man's face. Something about the steady gleam in Barrabas's eyes told him that the man was straight.

"A thousand bucks?"

"That's right."

"You got a deal."

They met at eleven-thirty the following morning, two miles west of Monte Carlo on the Nice highway.

"Are you nuts? This is a pickup truck!"

"Can't you do it, Vince?"

Christ, the guy is crazy! I'll have to average seventy, with S-curves, mountains, and heavy traffic...in a truck?

"Two thousand, Vince. And maybe more, if you can do it."

"Get in!"

He made it in eleven minutes and thirty seconds with half the army of Monaco forming a posse behind him. Vince was hoping the gray-haired man would need a change of underwear, but he was totally unruffled as he counted out the money.

"You flew Marine H-34s and later Hueys in Nam, Vince."

"Yeah. So what? Hey, how do you know so much...?"

"Can you still fly, Vince?"

Their eyes met and Vince sensed that there was a lot more behind this than a crazy ride in a pickup through Monaco.

"My guess is you know I can fly or drive anything that's got a power plant."

"Your guess would be right," Barrabas smiled. "Now I suggest we get over to the Italian side before we're both thrown into a French jail."

BIONDI DROVE. Fast, as usual. And this time speed was of the essence.

Barrabas checked the newspaper story again. He shook his head: sometimes there was no understanding women... maybe that's what made them so interesting.

"NATE, I won't let you do it. It's wrong!"

"It's done, Beverly. There's nothing we can do about it now. I fed the last program through the computer this afternoon."

"Oh, Jesus."

Shit, why did she have to find the plane ticket. How the hell do you explain to your wife that you're just hopping over to Geneva for a few days to convert the million dollars you just stole into diamonds? You tell her the truth, that's how.

"Jeez, what's with you? You ain't no macho, big-time thief!"

"I am now."

But she wouldn't let up. "You collect guns, you jump out of airplanes on weekends, you live in some fantasy world you get out of all those crazy spy novels you read. Why don't you just be what you are?"

He was getting angry. "Maybe that's what I am."

"Nonsense!" she cried, and wept. "You're a nice Jewish boy from the Bronx with a hundred seventy I.Q. and you happen to be a genius with computers."

And I've got a Jewish princess for a wife who doesn't understand me, the real me. Under this scrawny chest beats the heart of Errol Flynn.

"You got responsibilities! You got a wife, a home....."

"A mortgage."

"We got two cars, a boat. Money...we got money, Nate, why do you have to steal a million dollars?"

"To see if I could do it."

" 'To see if I could do it' he says!" She pulled at her hair, did some pacing and rubbed her sweaty palms on her flanks.

Nate watched her. She had nice flanks. But a man needs more than flanks sometimes. He needs a helpmate, a woman who understands his needs. She just didn't understand his need to steal a million dollars.

Beverly was like his father, then the Air Force, and now Big Business and society in general. No one had understood Nathaniel Beck from the beginning.

Nate was a genius in high school. With computers he tripled the efficiency factor of his father's business. Then he advised his father to get out of plastics and into computers.

His father didn't do it and went bankrupt.

University was too slow for Nate. He knew more than his professors. And when he programmed a student revolt through the computers that came off like a military campaign that even the National Guard couldn't put down, he was expelled.

He joined the Air Force two days ahead of the draft.

He went into communications, where some of his code formulas were so admired that they were ripped off by the intelligence agencies. He was quickly taken from active duty and placed in military research, where many of his ideas found their way into new communications systems and various electronic improvements. Although never under actual fire, Nate did receive some exposure to combat conditions in various NATO war games where he was called in to supervise the mechanical end of things. He accounted well for himself.

Try as they may, the Air Force could not get him to sign on for more duty.

But civilian life had changed. Computers were no longer in their infancy. What, for Nate, had been a creative art had now become a humdrum, monotonous tool of corporate business.

Once again the world wasn't moving fast enough for Nate Beck. All his life, his active mind had skirted the edges of Mittyesque fantasies. Eventually, with a marriage going stale and a job mired in boredom, he began to fuse fantasy with reality.

That's when he decided to program his firm's computers to transfer a million dollars through six banks and eventually into a dummy account Nate had set up in Switzerland. He skimmed the loose change from thousands of accounts—nickel and diming his way to a million overnight.

"What would your mother say? What happens if you get caught, tell me that! What happens to me when they put you in jail?"

He had finished his figures and now moved to the bedroom to pack a light bag. "I won't get caught. It's a foolproof scheme. And even if I did, you'd be all right. You said yourself, we got money."

"Jeez." Beverly sat on the bed, trembling, with her head in her hands. "My mother said marry a doctor, marry a lawyer! Jeez."

"I'll call you from New York when I get back." He checked the "London Fog" trench coat in the mirror and decided he liked the collar better turned up.

"Nate, if you do this, I swear I'll tell somebody. I'll... I'll tell the FBI...I'll tell the CIA...I'll phone Rabbi Rabinowitz!" She paused for breath, before adding the final threat: "I'll tell your mother."

"I'll call you."

Just getting on an international flight opened the floodgates of Nate's imagination. Halfway over the Atlantic, he started entertaining thoughts of not going back at all.

The solemnity of the Swiss bankers made him nervous, but he managed to make the switch from cash to diamonds without a hitch. He kept ten thousand in cash and put the stones in a safe-deposit box.

Back in his hotel room, Nate started doing some heavy thinking. Life with Beverly was a drag. Life as Nate Beck had become a drag. With a million dollars he might be able to become someone else.

He grabbed his trench coat. Somewhere there was a seedy bar, with a seedy character, who would take him to another seedy character, who, with a stroke of a pen, would give Nate Beck a new identity.

It was a new Nate Beck who yanked open his hotel room door and said, "Oh, shit."

There were two of them, both big, both in trench coats, worn more easily than his own, and both very meanlooking. The white-haired one spoke English like an American. The dark, Italian-looking one said nothing.

The Italian drove. Like a wild man he drove, while the other one sat with Nate in the back of the Mercedes.

"Interpol?" Nate asked, surprised at how even and calm his voice was.

"No."

"FBI?"

"No."

He didn't have the inclination for more questions. He was hanging on for dear life as the big sedan hurtled around curve after curve, until Nate was sure they would fly out into the dark void and become a fiery ball two thousand feet down the side of an Alp.

Then they were there. But where? It wasn't a police station. It was a well-appointed chalet, and Nate found himself sitting in front of a roaring fire with a brandy in his hand.

"You're not the police?"

"No. Quite the contrary. This is Vincent Biondi, and my name is Nile Barrabas."

They shook hands all around, and then a copy of the *International Herald Tribune* was shoved into his hand.

"Page two, Nate."

He turned to page two, read the whole article, and then drank the brandy in one long swallow.

"The bitch. She did turn me in."

"Too bad, Nate. Actually, you did pull it off...almost. We barely got you out of that hotel in time. I imagine the Swiss authorities are going through your room right now."

"But why? Who are you?"

The question was ignored. "What will you do now?"

Nate shrugged. "Turn myself in, I guess. The article says 'come home.' I'll only get three to five if I make restitution."

The white-haired man pulled his chair closer. The Italian refilled his glass.

"There are alternatives, Nate. Let me tell you about one."

BARRABAS FLEW ON TO NIGERIA. He called Jessup from Lagos.

"Yeah...yeah, I got him. Biondi's onside. Nate Beck too."

"O'Toole's having no luck in Hong Kong." The line was bad. Barrabas could barely hear Jessup. "Have you...Hayes...underwater demo...."

"I'll call you later," shouted Barrabas. "I'm going fishing."

CLAUDE HAYES was born at the age of twenty-four.

The boy that preceded the man came from Detroit, from a fairly affluent, middle-class black family. He was sent to the best schools, and early in his college career he became involved in the black movement. Highly intelligent, he became an expert in African languages and dialects, Swahili among them. In the sixties, he enrolled in a Southern college where he was instrumental in forming a black cultural curriculum.

But as his involvement in black affairs continued, his frustration and bitterness grew. He became sickened by white government manipulation and stalling, urban poverty and ghetto life, and even the politics and infighting of the blacks within the movement. His frustration reached the breaking point with Martin Luther King's death in 1968. He went on a one-man rampage of remorse that got him thrown into a Southern jail and put on one of the few remaining chain gangs in existence.

But for some odd reason, he suddenly seemed content. He became known to the other inmates as "The Mute," and some were even frightened by the silent withdrawal, not to mention the bursts of violent temper. But Hayes seemed to spend his time on the chain gang finding himself as a person, not a race, and he seemed to love the mindless simplicity of the work and the quiet serenity of the backwoods roads they worked.

But, while he was becoming a model prisoner, he was also planning his escape.

It took two years, and when the attempt was made it went off with the precision of a Swiss clock. His cross-country trek, with the aid of an old college professor, was like a modern version of the underground railroad. False papers were forged, and the real Claude Hayes was born.

He immediately joined the Navy, qualified for school in scuba and underwater demolition, and disappeared into the service like a fugitive into the Foreign Legion.

Beneath the waves he seemed to find the kind of peace, solitude, and escape from the world above that he had discovered to be the cornerstone of his nature. He volunteered for more missions, dangerous or not, than any other diver in his squad.

Though he was decorated several times, the regimentation of the military chafed. He slowly realized that he was truly a man who couldn't live with societies and systems, governments or causes. Discontented himself, Hayes sought freedom and solitude away from civilization and *its* discontents.

He roamed, becoming a citizen of the world, living by his wits. It was almost natural that he would eventually gravitate to Africa. Some of his early idealism surfaced when he witnessed the plight of his black brothers in Mozambique under the Portuguese.

He joined FRELIMO, the liberation army of Mozambique fighting for independence from Portuguese rule. With his knowledge of African tongues and his military background, Claude Hayes had no trouble fitting into the mainstream of African guerrilla warfare.

Indeed, it was quite the opposite. He found revolution, and being a rebel, a way of life that suited him. He had no home and no belongings except what he carried on his back. The compensation for this rootlessness was the unique bonds of friendship he formed within the guerrilla unit. They shared bush living, fighting, near starvation and other endless hardships, and found a comradeship that years of living across the street from one another in normal, suburban circumstances would never bring.

But eventually the fight was over and the politicians stepped forward. There was a place for Claude Hayes because they looked upon him as a citizen. But it was the revolution that interested him, not its aftermath.

He retired to Lagos, the capital of Nigeria, and opened a diving school and charter fishing service. But that was just something to do, something to kill time, until he found another revolution.

Then the tall man with the stark hair chartered his boat for a week. They talked and drank and fished and talked some more.

By the end of the week, Claude Hayes had found his next revolution.

LIAM COMPARED THE ADDRESS on the slip of paper against the crumbling numerals above the door. They checked and he knocked.

He was tired, dead tired. For a week he'd checked out leads in Hong Kong. All dead ends.

Then he had called Barrabas.

"Keep after him. We need him. Try Macao."

So here he was in Macao. But this time he might have struck gold. It had cost nearly three hundred in bribes, but he'd finally tracked down one of Al Chen's old brokers, a Eurasian who called himself "The Noodle Man." He ran a noodle factory as a front for the ton and a half of heroin that went through his hands every few months.

The Noodle Man had put Liam onto Royal Eastern Airways, who in turn—with the aid of another fat bribe—gave him the address of Lee Fong, an old flying mate of Al Chen's.

"Yes?"

The door was open a crack. Liam couldn't see the face, but the voice was female.

"Gotta see Lee Fong. I called. O'Toole."

"You wait."

The door closed and he waited. Five minutes, ten minutes, fingering the Beretta in his coat pocket. An unlit back alley in Macao's "butcher" district wasn't a comfortable place to be at three o'clock in the morning.

Again a shaft of light from the door. This time he could see an olive cheek, a shock of glistening black hair, and one dark eye.

"You come...hurry!"

The door opened just enough to allow the big Irishman to squeeze through and then slammed shut behind him.

"This way!"

Watching her compact little behind lead him down the dimly lit hallway was the best thing that had happened to Liam in the past two days. The cheongsam embraced her thighs, hips and buttocks like a silk skin, and every step made her youthful body under it vibrate in such a way that

Liam wished that for just two hours he could concentrate on something beside Al Chen.

"In here. . . sit. Lee Fong come."

The room was more Japanese than Chinese, with tatami-like mats on the floor and bamboo and rice paper sliding doors for walls. Cushiony pillows were arranged neatly around a low, black-lacquered table.

Lee Fong didn't "come," he appeared, as the sliding doors of one wall opened, revealing a room identical to the one in which O'Toole sat.

Lee Fong was a tiny man with a wizened face and of indeterminate age. He sat, Buddha-style, behind his tea table sucking on a pipe and filling both rooms with the acrid, sweet odor of hashish.

"You got gun?"

Liam nodded.

"Put on table. . . far side. Don't want you get pissed off, somebody get shot. Maybe me."

Liam put the Beretta on the table and slid it out of his own reach. "I want to contact Al Chen."

"You got money?" The man sucked a huge lungful of smoke and held it until Liam nodded. "Five hundred Hong Kong?"

"That's a lot. . . ."

"You got? Put it on table, too." Liam counted out the money and set it beside the Beretta. "Al Chen best fucking pilot in Far East. . . stoned or straight."

"That's what I want to see him about. I have a business proposition. . . ."

"Al Chen don't fly dope no more."

"That's not what. . . ."

"Al Chen don't fly refugees no more either. Too many damn fool die. . . Al Chen don't get paid."

Liam was starting to boil. "Look, you little. . . ."

"Al Chen dead. Hit mountain, go boom, nobody never find pieces." An Army issue .45 came out from under the table. In the tiny Oriental's hands it looked like a howitzer. "Leave money. Girl give you gun outside. Goodbye."

Two Chinese thugs opened the side door and beckoned to O'Toole. He had no choice.

The Beretta was returned by the girl who also pressed a

folded note into Liam's palm. He waited until he was well out of sight before examining it.

"Charter House. Wharf four. Hong Kong. Tomorrow, three."

The Charter House was one of over a hundred ramshackle sheds thrown up along Kowloon Harbor that served as the Hong Kong version of McDonald's.

Liam hoped "three" meant three o'clock. It did. She was right on time, sliding onto a barrel beside him that served as a stool.

For the sake of appearances, they both ordered fish, noodles and a bottle of wine before Liam got to the point.

"Do you know where Al Chen is?"

"I know. Al Chen very unhappy. You American like Al Chen. I think maybe you help him, make him happy."

"Are you in love with him?"

Her round little face under its dark halo of raven hair got very sad, and tears squeezed from the corners of her huge almond eyes.

"I Al Chen's wife, but he say no good marry to American gangster. He give me to Lee Fong."

O'Toole didn't pretend to understand the Oriental mind, even if it was born and raised in the United States. All he wanted to do was find Al Chen and get a yes or no.

Her name was Su Ling and her instructions were very clear.

Two days later, O'Toole found himself on a junk going upriver into the People's Republic of China. Every few hours they passed a Red gunboat, and Liam would sweat off another pound.

Then, on the third day, they swerved away from the main stream and chugged up a narrow tributary. Two hours later the single diesel shuddered into silence, and O'Toole heard the sound of grappling hooks and old rubber tires grinding against old rubber tires.

Liam was taken topside and discovered that they were tied to another junk. Over the rails he went and followed a pajama-clad sailor's motioning arm belowdeck.

The main cabin was like something out of *Playboy*. Muted teak walls flowed up from ankle-deep carpet, and the huge oval bed sat like a giant playpen under ten thousand dollars' worth of mirrors.

"Hey, man, I'm in here. Grab us a couple of beers and come on in! Fridge is behind the bar!"

It was a modern, double-door G.E. direct from the States. The freezer was full of USDA choice steaks and the refrigerator side sported both German and American beers.

Al Chen was obviously not hiding in poverty.

"Hey, somethin' wrong?"

"No, no," Liam called back. "Just admiring your layout."

"Ain't it a gas?"

O'Toole popped two beers and followed the voice down a passageway and into a large cabin that was as well-equipped a miniature gymnasium as the salon was a bachelor's paradise.

Al Chen's perfectly toned, sweat-gleaming body was just completing a tortuous set of exercises on the parallel bars. He ended with a perfectly executed two-and-a-half-twist that brought him to an equally perfect landing directly in front of O'Toole.

He took the beer from Liam's hand and then shook it in a viselike grip. "Al Chen."

"Liam O'Toole."

"I like to keep in shape. Between this and humping the help it's about all the exercise I get. Sit down."

They moved to an American-style sofa crowded between a wall exerciser and a set of barbells.

"I can see why you made the Olympics in '64," Liam offered.

"Yeah," Al Chen shrugged. "If athletes had made the kind of dough then that they make now I might never have started flyin'." He drained half his beer and turned to face O'Toole head-on. "So now I'm so loaded I don't even know how much I got, and I can't spend it. Su Ling says you got a proposition that might get me outta here."

Liam was a little bewildered and he showed it. "Just how do you manage to anchor five hundred miles inside Red China?"

Al Chen threw back his head and laughed. "Juice," he said. "Juice is the same the world over. Cross the right palms, they don't bother me, I don't bother them, and I don't take up much space." Then his young-old face creased into hard lines, and he leaned forward to stare deeply into O'Toole's eyes. ''But I start movin' this junk downriver and I'll have an army on my ass... and I don't mean a government army.''

''You didn't make a few deliveries.''

''You guessed it,'' Al Chen said, smiling again. ''You don't get this rich working for somebody else. I pissed off some very hard people.''

''You still got the touch, Al? And the nerve?''

''Mister, you get me outta here and I'll put wings on an orange crate and fly it to the fuckin' moon for ya!''

5

William Starfoot II sat in the lounge of the Miami Hilton, staring at a glass of the white man's redeye and wishing he was back in Oklahoma, or back on the reservation, or, hell, even back in his old man's oil-bought mansion.

He also wished he had never met the crazy Greek, Alex Nanos.

"Billy, where the hell have you been?" Alex slid onto the stool beside him.

"Sitting here, getting pissed."

"Billy, she's in there right now, waitin' for you! Her nervous little hand is clutching her checkbook and her panties are already damp!"

"I can't do it, Alex. It ruins my image. How does it look...a noble savage selling his body to a white squaw for Manhattan wampum."

"Listen, why she didn't go for the old Greek god like the rest of 'em, I don't know. But she didn't. She went for you. Now get in there and do your duty for Charter's Unlimited. We need a new boat!"

"We'd still have a boat if you hadn't insisted on following that school of tuna all the way to Cuba."

"How did I know that damn gunboat would open fire without warning? Billy Two, old friend, old comrade, she's only forty-eight and not bad to look at."

"I can't do it."

"Then call your old man and tell him we need twenty grand!"

"I can't do that, either. Alex, let's go to Alaska and hunt bear."

"No! I'm a sailor, and a fisherman, and a smuggler, and a gun- and dope-runner, but I ain't no bear hunter! And, besides, I won the flip, remember?"

Billy Two nodded and gagged down the rest of his drink, wondering if it had been a fair flip, wondering if there hadn't been collusion between the big-boobed little blonde and Alex that night.

The night referred to was two months after they had been mustered out of the Marine Corps and the Coast Guard.

William Starfoot II, the son of an oil-rich Oklahoma Indian family, and Alex Nanos, the son of a poor Greek fisherman from south Florida, met each other the day of their discharge, on the Oakland ferry.

Faced with the reality of impending civilian life and flush with a wad of mustering-out pay, they joined forces. Their friendship grew as they worked their way south from San Francisco to Acapulco.

When the money ran out, Billy Two—as Alex had started calling him—suddenly discovered his Greek comrade's considerable abilities as a gigolo. Women of all ages, sizes, nationalities and states of affluence fell at the darkly handsome Greek's feet with just a smile or a look from his sexy, sleepy eyes.

Alex was able to support them for another month, and then Billy got an attack of conscience.

They had picked up two schoolteachers from Dubuque at the hotel bar for a night of fun instead of profit. They were both blond, both sweet, both young and both very drunk by the time Billy and Alex got them to their respective rooms.

Billy was just about to consummate the evening, when she looked up at him with her big, blue eyes and asked what he and his friend did for a living.

Billy, being nearly as drunk as the young lady, saw no reason not to tell her. "My friend is a gigolo. We live off women."

"That's disgusting!"

Billy Two wilted immediately. He also started thinking. "You're right. It is disgusting."

At that moment he made up his mind to do something with his life. He'd joined the Marines because he wanted to follow in the path of his warrior ancestors, and here he was in Mexico with a crazy Greek, sucking up margaritas and humping schoolteachers from Dubuque.

Without bothering to dress, Billy Two pulled open the door and walked into Alex's room.

"Oh, baby...ohhhh, faster, honey...ohhhh, my God!"

"Yeah, baby, yeah."

Alex was doing what he did best.

"Alex, I've decided to re-up."

"Wha...what the fuck! Bil...Billy...are you nuts?"

"Oh, my God, don't stop, honey!"

Billy Two stood beside the bed, paying no attention to the writhing, gyrating bodies in his newfound, individualistic idealism.

"Bil...Billy...!"

"I've decided I've got to make something out of my life. I'm going back in the Corps."

"Jesus Christ, Billy, do we gotta talk about it *now*?"

Billy sat on the bed and craned his head low so he could look directly into Alex's eyes. "I wanted you to be the first to know."

"Swell," Alex said, rolling off of the girl, his urge totally depleted. "That's just goddamn swell."

Billy's girl appeared in the doorway. "Hey, what's with you two guys? You perverts or something?"

Then the argument started, with Alex finally convincing Billy not to reenlist. They would restructure their lives. They would go into business together.

What kind of business?

Billy Two grew up the scion of an oil-rich Oklahoma Indian family. The modernization of today's Indian repulsed him. He was also turned off by the vast difference between the rich and the poor among his people. He hated cities. He yearned to return to the wilder, freer life of his ancestors. Billy Two would like nothing better than to have been a Plains Indian, a warrior fighting for survival and glory. Because of that, he had become an expert in old style Indian "guerrilla" fighting, on survival lore and tracking. And that's why he had joined the Marine Corps.

Billy Two wanted to go to Alaska, live off the wild, and hunt bear.

Alex Nanos, on the other hand, loved the sea. He couldn't imagine being landlocked, following a trail of bear crap across frozen tundra.

Alex could sail anything that would float, and he was a fantastic navigator. He could sail around the world in an inner tube and, as a youth, practically did just that in the south Florida Keys running marijuana into the country. Two near arrests had driven him into refuge. He joined the Coast Guard and ended up chasing all his old smuggling buddies.

And now Billy wanted him to freeze his butt in Alaska? No way.

They couldn't agree.

They decided to flip for it.

They didn't have a coin. They were both naked.

They decided to flip the naked blond schoolteacher from Dubuque who was now screaming at them from the bed.

Bottoms up, they go to Florida. Boobs up, they go to Alaska.

They flipped the screaming girl and shook hands as her cute little butt bounced up at them from the bed.

No, Billy thought, as he swayed from the lounge into the lobby, it couldn't have been collusion. How could the blonde have known?

He spotted her imperial presence sitting by a huge palm, leafing through *The Wall Street Journal*. Her tall, angular body was draped in Dior silk and overflowed with a mass of jewelry.

My God, he thought, moving toward her, she looks like a vintage Buick.

"Hello, you savage!"

"How, Wampum Lady."

She slid her arm through his and skillfully guided him toward the elevators. "You know, my lawyer tells me that you two are the biggest losers on the Gold Coast. He calls you both clowns, says you've screwed up everything you've touched."

"Haven't screwed you up yet."

"Just an elevator ride away, Chief, just a high flying ride away."

She pressed Billy's arms against the side of a surprisingly firm breast and Billy thought this might not be so bad, after all.

Alex sighed in relief as he watched them get into the elevator. The woman was all over Billy Two before the doors closed.

Good old Billy. He'd come through, and this time he

wouldn't be sorry. This time they had a foolproof scam. Alex had discovered it when he found out the astronomical fees the local taxidermist got for mounting "the big ones" for one-shot fishermen down from the North.

It was simple.

They buy two boats, one in which Nanos takes the tourists out to catch the "big ones," the other which Billy Two takes out with the "big ones," already caught and dead. Billy Two hooks the baited line with a dead fish, the "mark" hauls it in, and Billy and Nanos split the very fat mounting fee with the local taxidermist. That, plus the charter fees and catch bonuses, would put them both in the bucks in no time.

And all they needed was twenty grand seed money for equipment. Alex hoped Sylvia Powers could be convinced. He also hoped Billy Two had twenty grand worth of staying power.

Damn, why didn't she go for Greeks. Alex knew he had twenty grand worth of staying power. He signaled the bartender for a drink and started sweating.

"Excuse me, lad. Is this stool vacant?"

"Sure."

The big redhead sat down, and an even bigger guy with gray white hair sat on his other side.

What the hell is this, Alex thought. The whole bar is empty and they gotta sit right here?

Then he really started sweating as he tried to remember whom he and Billy hadn't paid. These guys looked like they knew how to collect what they came for.

THE STRAPS of Sylvia Powers's dress were hanging around her shoulders in shreds when they came out of the elevator.

"Damn, I guess I pushed the right button," she gasped, fumbling for her key.

"Yeah, white squaw, I guess you did."

And she did. Even Billy Two couldn't explain it. He'd even put the twenty grand into the back of his head in favor of covering this woman's bones.

Maybe he had a latent mother complex.

Mustering an awesome amount of dignity, considering her state of disarray, Sylvia strode regally into the suite and addressed her maid.

"Louella, I would like you to...."

"Yes, Mrs. Powers, I know. I'm going." She'd seen it all before.

"Cute little maid," Billy Two said, letting his juices flow in every direction now.

"Forget her! I was the one who pushed your button, remember?"

"Oh yeah, woman, I remember."

"Jesus, you ignoble savage, take it easy!"

But the blood of his ancestors was boiling in Billy Two now. She became a captured squaw on the Mohawk Trail, part of the booty of war to a renegade Sioux.

He tore at her clothes.

"Billy, calm down a little...Billy...!"

Then he tore at his clothes.

"Billy...oh, my God!"

Then he tore at her, digging into her somewhat faded flesh with furious, driving lunges. He shot her like an arrow, sending her mind soaring somewhere in space to look back in awe as her body was ravaged. Faster and faster he lanced into her while she clutched at him, urging him on. Holding her throbbing body against him, he impaled her to the verge of complete surrender. He slackened his pace slightly and then drove forward again, full force, pounding his way into her aroused body.

She uttered a wailing cry. Her hair danced on the pillow, and then her head tilted back and away as her body arched into a taut bow. She yielded to him, and then they both slowly let their muscles slacken.

"Good Lord, how the hell did we ever manage to take the country away from you?" she managed to gasp.

"Too much fightin'...not enough fuckin'," Billy panted.

"How much you say these boats will cost?"

"How much you got?"

"Oh, no. We don't play it that way with my cash. You name it."

"Twenty grand ought to do it."

"You got it. C'mere!"

"Wait a minute, I gotta make a phone call."

Billy extracted himself from the clawing tentacles of her arms and legs and padded back into the living room.

Odd, he thought, *I don't even remember taking her into the bedroom. Must have been the redeye.*

He called the bar and had Alex paged.

"Yeah?"

"Alex, it's me. We're in"

"In what?"

"In business, you asshole. You should have seen me; I was magnificent. We got the twenty grand."

"Oh, yeah. Well, forget it."

The walls turned red. The phone turned red. The inside of Billy's eyeballs turned red.

"Forget it. *Forget it!* You greasy Greek bastard, you—"

"Easy, Billy, easy. We got a better deal...something with more security. Something worthwhile. You said you wanted to do something worthwhile."

Billy calmed down. Sylvia had entered the room. She was rubbing against him. He pushed her away.

"You remember a guy in Nam...Barrabas, Colonel Nile Barrabas?"

Billy thought. "Yeah, I think he's the crazy colonel that led that raid into the north and freed all the airmen."

"That's him. He's down here in the bar with me now."

"So what?"

"Billy, he made us an offer."

"What kind of an offer?"

"One we can't refuse."

BARRABAS WATCHED the amber liquid of the brandy fill his glass from the minibottle in the stewardess's hands. It was 9:30 P.M., and the lights of Long Island were quickly disappearing beneath the big 747. In twelve hours with, he hoped, a night's sleep, the plane would set down in Madrid.

Then, as per Jessup's order, it was on to Majorca and the training period.

"The operation has been set up," Jessup had informed him by phone from Washington. "Can you get them ready by then?"

"This crew I can."

"Good. I'll meet you in Palma, we'll go over everything then."

Barrabas ran his hand over the folder and smiled. Yes,

this crew could do anything. Vibrations of excitement slithered through his body and exploded in tiny bursts of anticipation in his brain. What was it Patton had said? "It's good we don't have perpetual war. We'd grow to love it."

"Will that be all, sir?"

"What? Oh, yes, fine. Thank you."

In his mind Barrabas went over the rest of the telephone conversation with Jessup and the stipulations they had both agreed to.

In the interests of security Barrabas would never know what agency or individuals in the government supported the team. He would work only through Jessup as liaison.

The men were hired like any other mercenary unit, with their allegiance totally to Barrabas. It would be Barrabas himself who would supply the pro-American sentiments, and that way, should any of them be captured, they could reveal nothing more than the fact that they belonged to an American mercenary unit, whose leader was "soft" on his native country...and fanatic in his desire to wage a one-man campaign to further its interests abroad. In this way, the government would never be implicated.

To further aid in secrecy, Barrabas suggested that the group function like any other mercenary army. They were hired *on contract*. The price? Determined by Barrabas and non-negotiable for each particular mission. They were to handle all aspects of the mission themselves, through normal black-market channels, and with normal illicit arms, only availing themselves of United States assistance through Jessup, and only when that assistance was determined to be absolutely untraceable.

Otherwise they were, in effect, an independent army... working on their own...with only Barrabas knowing the true nature and function of their existence.

As a last security measure, both he and Jessup had agreed that only they would know the true identities of the men involved. To society and family alike they had dropped off the face of the earth.

From that time on, Jessup's superiors would know them only by code names.

The big man opened the folder and sipped his brandy as he scanned down the page.

There was himself, of course, and...

(1) SHAMROCK (Liam O'Toole): age 37, Irish-American.

Languages:	French, Spanish, some German and Russian
Function:	weapons and explosives expert
Talents:	poetry, songs and booze
Experience:	Army

(2) FERRARI (Vincent Biondi): age 32, Italian-American

Languages:	Italian
Function:	vehicle expert (land, air and sea)
Talents:	mechanic, machinist, welder, driving and flying capabilities.
Experience:	Marines

(3) BEAVER BOY (Wiley Drew Boone): age 39, Southern American

Languages:	English only
Function:	nautical expert (motor and sail craft)
Talents:	women, girls and ladies
Experience:	Navy

(4) AQUAMAN (Claude Hayes): age 38, Black-American

Languages:	French, Swahili (fluent), adequate in several other African dialects
Function:	underwater expert, scuba, demolition and weaponry
Talents:	sailing, intimate knowledge of Africa
Experience:	Navy

(5) MR. WIZARD (Nathaniel "Nate" Beck): age 33, Jewish-American

Languages:	Hebrew, Yiddish, some Arabic
Function:	electronics and communications expert, codes and computers
Talents:	Very high I.Q.
Experience:	Air Force

(6) KAMIKAZI (Al Chen): age 32, Oriental-American

Languages:	Chinese (fluent Cantonese and Mandarin), adequate in Japanese and Korean

Function:	aircraft expert
Talents:	ballooning, skydiving, hang-gliding, stunt work, gymnastics, driving capabilities.
Experience:	Air Force

(7) CON MAN (Emilio Lopez): age 27, Hispanic-American

Languages:	Spanish
Function:	tanks and heavy artillery
Talents:	forger, con man, cardsharper, and underworld familiar
Experience:	National Guard, Coast Guard

(8) SPOOK (Alex Nanos): age 40, Greek/Slavic-American

Languages:	Greek, Russian, some German
Function:	Can sail anything, and loves a good fight
Experience:	Coast Guard

(9) BILLY TWO (William Starfoot II): age 33, American Indian

Function:	Wilderness and survival training, parachute training, personal defense and martial arts, charts and maps.
Talents:	Guerrilla warfare, tactician
Experience:	Marine Commandos

The plane's interior lights went out for night flying. Barrabas closed the folder and slid it into his briefcase, than locked it. With a tight grin on his lips he settled down into the seat and was asleep in seconds.

Ten men made up The Eagle Squad, as they would be known to a few people in Washington. But to the gray-haired Colonel, they were his boys—the Sons of Barrabas. Nine new guys, all right. Good men all. The SOBs were born again. They were back in business. The only business the SOBs cared for: waging war.

There was no way for Barrabas to know they were still one member short. Jessup was keeping Lee Hatton up his sleeve.

PART THREE
THE TRAINING

6

Heads of tourists and natives alike turned to follow his progress as Barrabas walked along the steamer's port side toward the gates. The men glared, shook their heads, and quickly returned their vacant stares to their nervous hands. The women's eyes followed him. Smiles fluttered around their lips as they gauged the tremendous well of power in the flowing muscles beneath the bush jacket. Their eyes widened as they mentally compared the rough, chiseled features of the weathered face with their husbands' overly fleshy counterparts.

"God, he's big."

"The man's hair is almost white."

"But at least he has it all...and then some."

The voices, like the women's eyes, followed him across the deck. He paid little attention. His mind was on the shoreline, on Palma.

It had been a long time since he had been to Majorca, and he had missed it. The island had been a wonderful place to hide and unwind after a war. Ironic that Jessup had chosen Majorca for the two-week training period.

The people parted like a sea before him, and he found himself at the rail, with the shoreline sparkling in the sunlight. He felt a twisting knot deep in the pit of his stomach.

"Changed," he whispered, "so changed, so different."

What had once been low, quaint buildings and row after row of charming shops was now towering monoliths of concrete and steel. Where there had been charm there was now progress, in the form of hotels and high-rise condominiums. They stretched as far as the eye could see, from the Cala Mayor to the Cathedral and beyond. What had once been a panoramic vista of mountains and green valleys beyond the old town was now nearly obscured from the bay.

And then two seamen were at the rail in front of him. The gates parted and, from behind, there was gentle pressure to move. With a bag under each arm, Barrabas navigated the gangway to the terminal.

He spotted Jessup by a station wagon with a bull's head emblem on the door. He moved toward him.

Jessup opened the rear door and tossed the keys to Barrabas after the big man had dumped his bags in the back.

"You drive," were Jessup's only words.

They rode through the city in silence. New construction, mostly hotels, was under way all around them. Motorized humanity clogged the tiny side streets as well as the main thoroughfares.

"A lot more traffic since the last time I was here."

"Don't worry," Jessup replied. "The Rancho is center island, isolated. You won't be bothered there."

"Anybody live there?"

"The owner's daughter, and a few servants. Place belongs to a friend of mine from the old days, Bryce Hatton."

"General Bryce Hatton?"

"Yeah," Jessup said, throwing a sidelong glance at Barrabas. "You know him?"

"I know of him. Worked under Donovan in the o.s.s., didn't he?"

Jessup nodded. "He was one of the best."

"Was?"

"Died two years ago, heart attack. Shame, bought this ranch to retire to and never got to enjoy it."

"The girl know why we're here?"

"She knows," Jessup said. "Take the left fork."

Barrabas was going to inquire further about the girl and the ranch but the road narrowed dangerously and started climbing away from Palma, forcing his concentration.

They left the city far behind and entered the island's southern plain, with its endless groves of orange and lemon trees. Before them lay a panoramic vista of greenery all the way to La Serra, the ridge of mountains along the north shore of the island.

"Beautiful country."

"If you like country," Jessup said.

Suddenly Barrabas knew why he didn't like Jessup too

much, he knew why he was uncomfortable around him. He guessed that most people were.

"What do you like, Jessup?"

"My work."

Barrabas digested that while he evaded a busload of gawking tourists and a trio of darting Vespas driven by dark, laughing boys and even darker, exotic-looking young girls.

"You ever kill anybody, Jessup...I mean, yourself?"

"Why do you ask?"

"Professional curiosity," Barrabas replied. "Just thinking that nobody I ever worked for ever got with it themselves. You know, down in the trenches where it gets dirty."

"It was plenty dirty that day on the Kap Long," Jessup reminded him.

Barrabas was forced to nod—Jessup was the one who had piloted the *Callisto* downriver. He got Barrabas into the medevac. That much couldn't be argued with. But Barrabas also knew that it had happened by chance, and certainly not by choice. Not on Jessup's part.

"Now I just push the buttons, Barrabas." The thin smile was far from endearing. "You're here to take care of the fighting."

"I'd like to get you back in the trenches someday."

Jessup changed the subject. "You satisfied with the nine?"

"Yeah. Aren't you?"

The fat man shrugged and wriggled his wide butt into a more comfortable part of the seat. "I think you might regret Lopez, and I don't know how you can hold down the clowns, Starfoot and Nanos. They don't take anything seriously, even dying."

"My problem," Barrabas said, lighting a cigar.

"That's right, your problem." Jessup paused and then jumped the line of thought again. "I've set up contacts with the firms you mentioned in Amsterdam, and set up the credit at Banco International."

"How much?"

Jessup smiled. "As much as you'll need."

"Who's the contact?"

"Brookler...remember him?"

"Simon Brookler." Barrabas nodded and chomped down hard on his cigar. He rolled his eyes away from the fat man so Jessup couldn't read what they were thinking. In the far distance, La Serra loomed larger. The jagged, angry peaks looked foreboding. Very much like Simon Brookler.

Brookler had worked a phony import-export outfit out of Marseille, peppered with a lot of smuggling. On the side he ran a profitable little business putting people together. If someone wanted to start a war or revolution, Brookler would put them in touch with the people who could do it. All, of course, for a fee. When and if the fee was high enough. And in his specialty, Brookler would often take on a job himself. His specialty was assassination. He was vermin, but Barrabas had gotten a couple of jobs through him in the past.

"As soon as you get the group rolling, let O'Toole take over and you fly to Amsterdam. He can handle it, can't he?"

"As well as I can."

"Good." It was very unlike Jessup to reach for thoughts or words. Now he seemed to, as he fiddled with an imperfection in the vinyl covering on the dash before continuing. "We think it was Brookler who set up all the buys for Heiss. He may have helped, too, with the brokering of the diamonds."

"Could be. Simon has the background for it."

"Yes." Again the long pause. "It would be no loss to the world, and probably a good security measure, if, after the transaction was completed and the goods shipped, you'd terminate Brookler's activities."

A white line appeared along Barrabas's jaw. It nearly matched his hair and did match his knuckles gripping the wheel.

"Go to hell, Jessup."

"It's a nasty business, Nile. Survival means taking precautions. If Brookler were to get word to Heiss that you were back in the game. . . ."

"Forget it! I'm a soldier, not an assassin."

"We'll see." Jessup stared blankly toward the windshield.

The rest of the drive was completed in silent anger,

soothed only slightly for Barrabas when they topped a final crest and began the descent toward their destination.

Even though Barrabas's body was trembling and anger burned like sheeted flame before his eyes, part of it was washed away by the sheer beauty of the valley laid before them. Groves of fig and almond trees swept through the valley, nearly reaching the wide expanse of lawn leading to the ranch itself. Open spaces between the groves were filled with wild flowers, and here and there the gnarled trunk of a thousand-year-old olive tree thrust its majestic green head toward the cloudless sky. From this natural beauty the rambling main house rose up, wreathed in bougainvillea and splashed with orange, purple and crimson creepers.

Jessup spoke as they passed under an ornate baroque arch and glided on up the wide, curving drive to the turn-around in front of the house. "Pull under the canopy. Leave your bags, a servant will take them."

"Servants?"

A gaunt, weathered old man hobbled toward Jessup from the pillared veranda. They exchanged a few words, then the fat man turned to Barrabas.

"This way. We've got a lot to settle. My plane leaves in three hours."

"You're not staying?"

"I've got to get back to my desk, remember?" Jessup needled him.

Barrabas followed him through the first-floor rooms, drinking in the old-world charm of the antique furnishings and the wood-paneled walls. As their heels echoed along the gray tiled floors, from room to room, a pattern began to emerge. Although each room was spotlessly clean, tell-tale signs of deterioration were everywhere. Slowly, Barrabas began to realize that the deterioration wasn't from neglect. It was from age. Ceilings and window casements weren't repaired and threadbare rugs weren't replaced.

And then a second pattern struck him. Most of the rooms were barely furnished.

Casa Hatton was going to pot.

They moved into what must have been the main salon. It, like the rest of the rooms, was spotlessly clean but showed decay.

The oak-paneled floor around a handwoven Catalan rug

was polished to a mirrorlike shine. The rug itself was threadbare and the floor showed through in many places.

Jessup waved Barrabas into one of the high-backed chairs and moved to a sideboard. He returned with a decanter and two glasses.

"You pour."

While Barrabas poured, Jessup spread a map on the table.

"They've moved Noboctu here...just above Albertville."

"That's Congo...Mobutu country."

"Right," Jessup nodded. "Can it be done?"

"I think so," Barrabas replied, checking the map and gauging the distance from the jungle camp, through the bush to the ocean, and across to the large island of Kaluba. "It'll be rough."

"You have ten days from tomorrow to mount the operation, and a week to pull it off."

"I'll need a copter," Barrabas mused. "We'll stick to the original plan in two stages...get him out and then get him home."

"Up to you." Jessup folded the map and passed it to him. He lifted his glass. "To success." They touched glasses and drank. "By the way, I've arranged for a doctor to be here during your training. It would be dangerous for you to use any of the locals in an emergency."

Before Barrabas could question this wisdom, a heel scraped on the threshold behind him and he whirled.

She was very tall for a woman, and beautiful, with an angular yet full-figured, firm body that was accented by the tight riding breeches and tailored blouse she wore.

The face was aristocratic, almost haughty, with pale skin and burning black eyes under equally dark, short hair.

"Nile Barrabas, let me present Lee Hatton...*Doctor* Leona Hatton."

Barrabas's head swiveled, his eyes boring into Jessup with alarm. *My God, man,* his look said, *not a woman!*

Jessup's eyes were blank again, saying nothing.

THE MEN ARRIVED and settled in quickly. Everyone was on time, except Lopez. He was six hours late because of "the most fascinating pair of tits in Palma!"

O'Toole straightened him out quickly. "Lopez, lad was it good? Was it really good?"

The little man smiled and rolled his dark eyes up into his head. "Good? It was fantastic!"

"That's good," O'Toole said, "because in this here army we don't have no court-martial or captain's mast or brig time for guys that screw up. All we got, Lopez, is your paycheck. I'm glad that piece of ass was good, because it cost you two thousand bucks."

Everyone got the picture.

They were rousted an hour before dawn the next morning for an initial briefing speech from Barrabas.

He was just about to start when Leona Hatton, dressed in shapeless fatigues and jump boots, stepped coolly through the door and took a seat with the men.

It was awkward. Puzzled frowns dotted foreheads around the room, along with low whispers and a growl or two.

"Good morning, Colonel. I think that if I'm to be of any help I should train along with the men."

"As you wish, Dr. Hatton," Barrabas said, unable to break the steady gaze she returned.

Don't worry, Jessup had said, *she's fully briefed. There's no security risk. She knows her job. Give her her head and let her do it.*

"Gentlemen, Dr. Leona Hatton. She is our hostess while we're here, and she will also serve as our medical officer."

"All right!" Nanos applauded.

Barrabas took note. "All sleeping and recreation will take place in these two bunkhouses until our gear arrives. At that time we will live in the field. The main house is off limits *at all times*."

He paused for emphasis. There were a few moans but mostly nods of agreement.

"You men were selected to cover the widest range of talents and capabilities. Areas where you are weak will be learned and mastered with the help of those who are the 'experts'...there will be no room for personal hangups and slacking. Lives depend on your cooperation, and you will not risk the lives of any of this group because of personal bull—uh...problems."

Leona smiled.

"You will all leave here 'soldiers'...definitely better prepared than the real GI when he takes the field. You are all of equal rank, with me as the general. At various times one or another of you will take command, depending on which field of expertise is required by circumstances. The rest will follow, and be followed in turn."

"Does anybody know where the hell we're goin'?" Wiley Boone asked.

"You'll be told specifics later. I will say this. We're going into the bush. Besides myself that makes Hayes our resident expert. He's not only been there, he's been in bush warfare." All eyes turned with a new show of respect toward the tall, brooding black. "Listen when he tells you something. It could save your ass—sorry, Dr. Hatton—when the time comes. Any questions?"

"Yeah, Colonel," Billy Two offered. "What's the hardware?"

"Basically light, no cannon or mortars. We'll be moving fast. Firepower will be AR-15s, Armalites. They're mostly aluminum and fiberglass, very light. As you know, they fire a .223, with a muzzle velocity so high a wound anywhere is usually fatal. Also, the Armalite can be switched over to fire like a submachine gun. It's perfect for our needs.

"Side arms will be Mausers, and a few of you will pack M-79 grenade guns. The bigger stuff, you'll find out about later.

"I'll be leaving you for a couple of days. I've got to go shopping for our ordnance. O'Toole is in command until I return. Till then it's tactics and physical shape-up. Any more questions?"

Silence.

"Liam, they're all yours."

"All right, everyone outside!" O'Toole barked. The scramble was instantaneous. O'Toole turned to Barrabas. "I don't know about this female business, Colonel."

"I agree. We'll just...."

"Excuse me."

They turned. Leona Hatton hadn't exited with the men.

"I think I ought to inform both of you gentlemen that being a woman doesn't mean I'm made of porcelain. I don't break easily, if at all. Both mentally and physically I think you will find that I can more than keep up with the men.

"As far as inhibiting their camaraderie and life-style, just give me a little time and I assure you they will not only respect me, but they will forget that I'm a woman.

"As far as them creating an uncomfortable situation for me, have no fear. I'm thirty-one years old. I've been married. I've had my share of love affairs, both one-nighters and those of a longer duration, and I'm quite accustomed to the language of men in the field and am at home with it.

"I know that by placing the bottom lip against the upper row of teeth, breathing out and hitting the roof of the mouth with the back of the tongue, one can perfectly sound the word fuck."

With a slight smile, she turned and walked from the room.

"Well, well, well," O'Toole grinned.

"Yeah," Barrabas agreed, "but lean on her anyway. Lean on her hard!"

Barrabas didn't explain why, because O'Toole didn't know about Jessup. But the big man guessed there was more to Leona Hatton than he'd been told.

7

Barrabas's plane hopped to Shannon, Ireland, and from there he took a KLM direct to Schipol Airport. The six-mile bus ride into Amsterdam put him at the Amstel Hotel just after six o'clock.

He registered for two rooms: one for himself, under the name of Carstairs, and an adjoining room for "Mr. Harrison," who would be arriving later.

It was past normal office hours but, as he guessed, that posed no problem. Arms dealers operate twenty-four hours a day.

He placed the call and patiently waited for the message to go through and the return call. Looking down at the wide Amstel River across the canopies of the stately old hotel, he wondered how right Jessup had been.

Simon Brookler had no loyalties. Was he selling information as well as arms to Karl Heiss? Indeed, was Heiss really still alive?

The phone jangled at his elbow. He waited three rings and picked it up.

"Yes."

"I understand you're on a buying trip, interested in fine china." The high, lisping voice was all too familiar.

"Delftware, to be exact. Vases, very fat, of a particular design. I believe my firm, Carstairs Limited, has already contacted you."

"Oh, yes. And where will you be staying while in Amsterdam, Mr. Carstairs?"

"Here at the Amstel...room 400."

"I'll be tied up until midnight."

"That will be fine."

The phone died. Barrabas clicked a few times and gave the switchboard another number.

"Hello?" Just one word from that low, honey-mellow

voice brought back a flood of memories. "Hello...who is it?"

"There is nothing more satisfying than an evening of Chopin from the Concertgebouw in the company of a beautiful woman and a bottle of fine wine later."

There was a gasp and then a barely audible, "Nile?"

"I'll wager you've grown younger and more beautiful, Erika."

"My God, I thought you were dead. Where are you?"

"At the Amstel."

"I'll be there in half an hour."

"No. I'll come there."

"My God, I thought you were dead."

"A half hour."

He hung up and grabbed a quick shower. Dressed in older, more nondescript clothes, he slipped from the room and left the hotel through the rear kitchen. He was sure that Brookler already had a man in the lobby, just in case a familiar face showed up.

Erika Dykstra lived sedately in a renovated eighteenth-century house in Begijne Hof, just off the bustling tourist and shopping areas of Kalverstraat. Most of Erika's neighbors were elderly little old lady pensioners.

Their hair would undoubtedly turn much grayer if they knew that the beautiful, youngish by their standards, woman who now seemed retired among them was, at one time, the head of one of the largest smuggling operations in northern Europe.

Barrabas trollied to the Begijnensteeg and walked on to the end of the street. There he stepped through a tiny gate almost hidden by greenery and found himself in a quadrangle of homes that seemed to have escaped time.

He had no need to look for the number. He knew the house well. And Erika too well to knock for admittance. Shunning the front door, he slipped around to the delivery entrance and let himself through the iron gate and into a rear courtyard.

As it had been so many times in years past, the inner door was unlocked. Silently he took the high, narrow stairwell two steps at a time and emerged in the upper hall.

He made no sound, but she must have sensed his presence. He had barely moved into the hall when she stepped, smiling, from one of the bedrooms and walked toward him.

She was wearing pants and a wispy blouse tied carelessly under her breasts. It was obvious that was all she was wearing. The pants were tight enough to have shown an outline had she been wearing panties. The blouse was sheer enough to show she wore no bra . . . nor did she need one.

She walked with the balanced grace of a dancer and the lithe strength of a jungle cat. Even her green eyes were slightly catlike as she glided wordlessly into his arms and tilted her full lips to be kissed.

The kiss was warm, sensuous and full of promise. Her generous breasts against his chest, coupled with her grinding pelvis, awakened a sense of lust in Barrabas that had lain dormant for too long.

Her eyes were closed when he pulled his lips away from hers, still keeping his lips close to her face. She opened them, and their eyes tried to find what was in their minds.

"I didn't think I'd ever see you again."

"Did you want to?"

She held him at arm's length and shrugged slightly, making her breasts do a dance under the thin material of the blouse. "You know me . . . one day, one night at a time."

He nodded. "It's business, too. Does your brother still take a job now and then?"

"I'm sure he would, for you and the right price. How much time do you have . . . now?"

Barrabas smiled and tugged her back toward him by the hips. "More than enough."

They kissed again, and his hand found the tie in her blouse. She trembled when his hand cupped her bare flesh, and held him tighter. His fingers stroked and squeezed gently.

She arched her back, thrusting her breast into his kneading hand, and whispered in his ear. "The bedroom."

For all of her size she was like a feather in his arms as he carried her and then deposited her gently on the big bed. His fingers deftly worked at the slacks as she shucked the rest of the way out of the blouse herself.

Then he chuckled.

"What?"

"You," he said. "I'd forgotten what a natural blonde you were."

LEONA HATTON was holding up, but not as well as she thought she would. She hadn't counted on O'Toole's over-zealousness. The first morning, they completed a ten-mile walk-march over the roughest terrain the big Irishman could find. Then after a brief break for a field lunch, they did an hour through a natural obstacle course before quick marching the ten miles back to the main area of the ranch.

All of this with improvised thirty-pound packs on their backs.

Halfway through the afternoon, Lee began to fade. Around her the men seemed as fresh as the moment they had started. They had obviously kept themselves in excellent physical condition all their lives. She thought she had, but now she was discovering muscles in her own body that she'd only known previously through an anatomy course.

She was numb from the knees down, and the straps of her pack had already chewed skin from her back and threatened to decrease her bra by two cup sizes.

It was on a particularly steep hill that she began falling behind. When she closed her eyes, everything turned red.

She did her best to keep her eyes open.

"Need a little hand, ma'am?"

"Let's see," she panted, concentrating on putting one foot in front of the other, "you're...."

"Wiley Drew Boone, ma'am. A true gentleman from the Old South who hates to see a pretty lady in pain."

He reached for her pack as Liam's voice barked from the front of the column. "What's the problem, Boone?"

"Just givin' the lady a hand."

"Forget it!"

"Sorry, ma'am."

"It's all right. I'll make it...even if my feet fall off, I'll show that bastard."

Wiley smiled and nodded. "I just believe you will, ma'am." His long legs quickly carried him away from her to catch up with the column.

Leona decided that even the chauvinistic O'Toole had some heart when, a half hour later, with her trudging along fifty yards behind them, he called a rest break.

She collapsed against a tree and drained the last of her canteen.

"You really a doctor?"

She nodded, out of habit, and then realized that the black man, Claude Hayes, was squatting beside her. "Yes, I am."

He seemed intent on studying the other men, the valley below them, or the hills in the distance. "Then you ought to know about plain water. It'll churn your guts up on a march like this. Tomorrow—"

"Good God, you mean we're going to do this again tomorrow?"

She wasn't sure, perhaps because of the haze over her eyes, but she thought she saw him smile. "Probably do fifteen tomorrow. Put tea in your canteen, with a lot of sugar in it. In the meantime, use these!"

She looked down at the small cellophane package. "What are they?"

"Glucose tablets. Chew 'em. They'll get you through the rest of the day." Without another word and without ever looking directly at her, he stood and ambled off toward the other men.

"Okay!" Liam yelled. "On your feet! Quick time the last five!"

Claude Hayes's small overture seemed to break the ice. In the next hour they approached her, one by one, and introduced themselves. And a few of them gave her little hints.

"Starfoot. William Starfoot the Second, but everybody just calls me Billy Two."

"You're a Navajo, aren't you?"

"Yeah. How'd you...?"

"I worked with VISTA in Arizona when the bureaucracy couldn't get medical aid to the reservations."

His stoic, high-cheekboned face broke into a wide grin. He slowed his jogging pace to match hers and lowered his voice. "If you'd reverse those straps, send 'em around your waist and crisscross 'em between, uh...between, uh...."

"My breasts? We both know they're there, Billy."

His grin spread. "Yeah, I guess we do."

It worked and the relief was monumental.

Lopez spoke to her in Spanish and was elated when she answered him in kind.

"Tell ya somethin', Doc, all that leather you're totin'

might be a great cushion from five thousand feet, but they're nothin' but lead overland."

She scanned the footwear up and down the column. They were all wearing lightweight sneakers or tennis shoes.

"Thanks."

"Sure, Doc. Maye I'll be lucky enough to contract a social disease before we leave and give you some work."

When they arrived back in the ranch compound, Lee had only three things on her mind; a long, hot bath, a tall, cold drink and twelve hours in her big soft bed.

"All right, short straw cooks tonight. Beans and stew meat out of one pot. A half hour for indigestion and then Hayes on survival."

Lee managed to get the drink and the bath before returning to the open fire. Al Chen had drawn the cook's duty. He saved her a plate.

"It doesn't look too good, but it will keep your navel away from your spine."

Nothing had ever tasted so good.

"You don't have to sit in on this, Doctor," O'Toole informed her.

"Oh, but I want to," she replied. "Suddenly survival of any kind seems important."

At ELEVEN-THIRTY SHARP, Barrabas slipped back into his room the same way he had left. Using a matchbook cover, he left the door to room 400 unlatched and entered 402—Mr. Harrison's room—through the connecting door.

Placing a chair by the hall door, he poured a glass of Jenever, lit a cigar and settled in to wait. The door was open a crack and Barrabas watched the elevator. The sweet, oily gin went down easily, and he was just finishing a second glass when the tall, gaunt figure with the dark, deathbed eyes stepped from the elevator.

Brookler moved directly to room 400 and the pressure of his knock opened the door. He reacted instinctively, reaching under his coat to the left side as he stepped into the room.

The floor indicator above the elevator rolled back to the lobby designation and stayed there. There was no sound from the stairwell, and the hall, both ways, was empty.

Satisfied, Barrabas opened the door to 402 wide and called Brookler's name.

The skull-like face appeared in the crack of the door. Recognition spread the thin lips into a wide grin. The lips didn't part far enough to reveal any teeth, and when he spoke they hardly moved.

"Barrabas. I'd heard you'd fired your last shot in South America," he said, walking into the hall toward Barrabas.

"Just a nasty rumor, Simon. In here."

Brookler closed the door to 400 behind him and slid past Barrabas into 402. "No need for all this, Nile. We're both respectable businessmen."

"Then why are you carrying?"

"Lawlessness," came the reply. "The city is full of it. I think your American youth imported it along with their guitars and visions of peace."

"Drink?" Barrabas produced the bottle of Jenever.

Brookler declined, patting his nearly nonexistent stomach with a bony hand. "I've given it up. Age and the pressures of our business."

"I've heard business was booming."

"Oh, it is, it is. But mostly in the heavy stuff. A little operation like me? Well...." He left it hanging and slid into a chair. "What can I do for you?"

"I've got a small war." Barrabas sat across from him and slid a neatly typed set of three stapled sheets into his hands.

Brookler mumbled aloud down the list, and Barrabas knew he was memorizing it as he read.

"Forty AR-15s, forty jungle-greens with full pack, six M-79s, forty side arms...Mausers?" Barrabas nodded. "Colts are easier to come by."

"I don't need the firepower."

Brookler grunted and finished out the list. "Would you settle for .30s instead of .60s for the machine guns? Hard to locate right now."

"S'okay, as long as they have mounts."

"Can do," Brookler mused and looked up. "Sounds like a bush operation. West Africa is turning up quite a few Belgian FNs right now. Get you a decent price."

Barrabas shook his head. "Armalites."

The thin shoulders shrugged as he handed back the sheets. "It's your money. A week?"

"Day after tomorrow."

"Not much notice, Nile. My suppliers. . . ."

"Can you do it?"

"I think so. Do I transport?"

"No, I have my own contacts. I want it split in two; half here and the other half through Hadege in Tangier. . . is he still in business?"

Again the thin smile. "At the same old stand. But. . . since you're going into the bush, I can deliver directly to the West side. . . or to Zanzibar, Dar es Salaam, anywhere in Mozambique."

Barrabas held back a smile of his own. Brookler was as subtle as a Sherman tank trying to draw him out. "I haven't said my war's in West Africa. There's bush in Angola and Guinea, too."

"Ah, but it's very quiet there now. Chad, Uganda, Kaluba. . . that's where the action is."

Barrabas sidestepped it all by getting down to money. "I'll move half the funds into your account tomorrow. The second half will be on delivery here and a cabled okay from Hadege. In diamonds, all right?"

Brookler stood. "Fine. Ring the same number in the morning. I'll give you the figure." He moved to the door and paused. "I take it you won't need an end-use certificate?"

There is was. An end-use certificate from a friendly country, stating that the purchased arms would not be reexported, would do away with any customs problems in their transportation. By declining such a certificate, Barrabas was practically telling Brookler that he had no government connections of any kind, and illicit smuggling would be his means of transportation.

Very risky knowledge in the hands of a man like Brookler.

"I might with the Tangier shipment. If I do, I'll set it up myself."

He slipped out the door and Barrabas quickly moved back into room 400. He overdressed, with both suits, and stuffed his pockets with toilet articles and the remaining contents of his bag. He then dumped more than enough guilders into the empty bag to cover both rooms for one night.

He would be leaving for good, but not checking out. If a chambermaid got the money instead of the desk? Well, too bad. But he doubted it. The Dutch are very honest people.

The phone jangled just as he was shoving the bag under the bed.

"Yes."

"Do you know the Lido, just off the Leidseplein?"

It was Erika. "I think so. . . just across the square from the opera."

"That's right. Gunther will meet you there in an hour."

"Do you mind a houseguest for a couple of nights?"

"I was afraid you wouldn't ask," she said, the smile in her voice shining through like a beacon.

LEONA WAS MIND WEARY and bone-wrenching tired. She was sure there was no possible way in the world that she could stay awake in the middle of a bombing, let alone a lecture.

She was wrong. The longer Claude spoke, the more attentive she became. And she sensed the same response from the others.

He prefaced his survival lecture with a short speech on the theme of "kill quick or be killed fast" when fighting in the jungles of black Africa. Around her, there were murmurs of agreement and emphatic nods when Claude would make a certain point. Leona found herself being fascinated by their calm acceptance of death. . . others or their own.

"If we find ourselves traveling in the bush for any length of time, it will probably mean that we're on the run. That means we sleep anywhere we drop at sunset. We won't find huts, and even if we did we'd have to steer clear of them. They're indefensible."

He held up a green sheet of cloth that resembled a large hunk of Saran Wrap.

"This is a bush sleeping bag. It might keep you dry and if you pull it over your head you can breathe through these holes. That way bush rats, snakes, lizards and seventeen hundred species of ants won't make you their evening meal."

The comments were plentiful.

"Is there room for two in that thing?"

"It would be see-through."

"Is there a piss tube?"

"Pipe down!" from Liam.

"If we run out of food, we eat whatever we find. . . roots, bananas, maybe a little fruit if we're near a river. Or we eat what we meet, like the bush rats and lizards I mentioned.

"Liam tells me that tomorrow we work on small arms. Part of that will be bows and arrows. Your department, Starfoot. There are gazelle, and a gunshot might attract the attention of who the hell we're running from."

Carefully he unfolded a pack.

"Jungle greens. We'll each have three pairs. Change and discard. Don't repack wet fatigues. They'd mildew in hours and ruin the rest of your pack. Wear tennis shoes, they adapt better."

Here he smiled at Lee who raised her arms, shrugged, and bowed to Emilio.

"That won't be a problem, will it, Doctor?" Liam said. "Since you're just with us for training."

The comment was pointed, and it brought on total silence. All eyes were on her. Lee kept not only a straight face, but a vacuous one. She focused her attention on Claude and smiled. "I see a red cross on one of those packages. I'm agog to know the medical end of all this."

For the second time that day she brought a smile to Claude Hayes's immobile black face. He took a deep breath and started in again.

"Leprosy, typhoid, yellow fever, cholera, tuberculosis, amoebic dysentery, tick-borne fever, malaria, bilharzia, ancylostomiasis, and elephantiasis just scratch the surface of the diseases that can be contracted in the bush. I assume we'll all be inoculated. . . ."

Here he nodded at Lee, which brought another smile to her face. "Yes," she said. "Several times."

"But let me tell you," Hayes continued, "they don't always take." Here he broke the red-crossed kit open and began holding up its contents, box by box. "Halazone tablets counteract all the bugs in the water—most of the time. Daraprim, antimalarial tablets. Use 'em! It's the quickest thing we'll get. The rest of this is antibiotics, anti-tetanus toxoid, injections against snakebite—quite common—or gangrene."

He paused and scanned the upturned faces.

"The one thing that ain't in here is an antibullet toxin. You get shot in the bush and start bleeding, ain't no way for a blood transfusion—so you just die."

This should have sobered them.

It didn't.

"Hell with this shit. Take me back to Nam!"

"It's these damn guns. The caliber's gettin' too big. Ya get hit in the arm, you lose a leg, too!"

"Just so they don't hit your bird, Nanos, you can always make a livin'!"

Liam stopped them. "Morning chow at five. On the hills by six-thirty. Small arms and hand-to-hand tomorrow afternoon. That's it."

Leona's thoughts were jumbled, but she found herself more alert than she had been in months as she walked across the compound.

Liam already guessed the truth. Barrabas probably did, too. Should she go ahead and tell them?

No. That was up to Jessup. Since she had agreed to work for him, she must follow his orders—to the letter.

Her mind went back to the men as she peeled out of her clothes and groped her way in the darkness to bed.

Everything battered at the back of her mind until it all exploded into one solid realization: no matter how much she had been trying to match them mentally and physically, there remained a huge psychological gap that she would have to overcome before she could consider herself a part of them.

She was a doctor, dedicated to preserving human life. They were soldiers and—one step further—mercenary soldiers. They were hired to kill and accepted it as a way of life.

Well, tomorrow she would start closing that gap. She'd wear tennis shoes, she'd drink tea, she'd eat glucose, and when they got to small arms and hand-to-hand she would show them that she'd had her share of the wars too.

BARRABAS PUSHED HIS WAY through the milling youth toward the Lido bar. His look, his height, and his age combined to get him instant service. Stein in hand, he moved on, booth by booth, until he saw him.

Gunther was as blond and imposingly handsome a figure as his sister was beautiful. He sat with a smaller, darker man, seemingly paying no attention to anything outside the environs of the booth.

But Barrabas knew he'd been spotted. When they slid from the booth and wound their way toward a rear door, Barrabas waited a short interval, then followed.

Narrow, dimly lit stairs led to a second door which Barrabas entered without knocking. Two steps into the room two huge, viselike arms enveloped him in a loving bear hug that threatened to break his spine.

"Ah, my friend, my friend! Gottdamn-to-hell, thought you was dead!"

After two resounding kisses, Barrabas's feet again touched the floor and he was released. "Like a cat, Gunther, I've got at least half my lives left."

"Sit down! Here, get rid of that swill. I have real Russian vodka!" He replaced the stein with a small but full glass of the clear oily spirits.

"To life!" Gunther raised his glass. Barrabas did the same, glancing at the third man. "Pepe, my bodyguard," Gunther offered. "He don't say much. Don't worry, you can talk. Pepe's very trustworthy. He's a shady character."

They drank, and the glass was refilled.

"How you like my joint?"

"You bought this place?"

"Sure! Hell, yes!" Gunther laughed. "Had to have a place for my ill-gotten gains." He coiled into a high-backed chair behind a desk and got serious. "Erika says you goin' back to the wars."

"It's my trade."

"That's bullshit. You got a death wish. How you like my English? Better, huh? I'm screwin' a lotta young American hippies...built-in dictionaries!"

"I'd swear I was in Berkeley," Barrabas smiled.

Gunther roared. "I know that...*Rolling Stone Magazine*! Why you want'a go back to the wars, Nile? Come work with me. We get rich and drink a lot. My sister loves your body. You got it made!"

Barrabas was used to the big blond man's constant jumps in thought. The best way to talk to Gunther was in the same vein. "I've got to return a favor. Your friend still got his bird?"

"Zelzig? Hell, yes. Got two now. He gutted one. Got a bedroom, living room and lounge in it. Flies big shots all over hell. You wanna do some screwin' at ten thousand feet?"

"No, but I need some pickups and drops made. And the use of the bird when the war's over."

"Full-time rent is a lotta bucks. How long?"

"Two weeks, give or take."

"Thousand a day for the bird, five hundred for Zelzig."

"Does that include your twenty-five precent?" Barrabas said, grinning.

"Hell, yes!" Gunther replied. "I don't rip off old friends!"

"It's a deal."

Gunther leaned across the desk, his eyes full of fire. "Sounds like you got a good war."

"But tricky," Barrabas replied, pulling a pouch from his inside pocket. From the couch he extracted two maps and spread them on the desk. "We truck the tools down to the canal. They'll be well mixed in with a legal shipment of Delftware. It's up to you to boat them out and down to Ostend. Is your Belgian contact still solid?"

Gunther shrugged. "Sure. Some things never change. We fly out of Brugge?"

"Right. Here's the drop, date and time." Barrabas pointed to penciled notations just off the island of Ibiza. "Zelzig goes on to Casablanca. The second shipment will come down from Tangier." He moved to the second map. "Here's the second drop."

"West Africa."

"Right. The bird goes on to Kaluba and stays. You and Zelzig take a commercial flight out."

"Sounds like a piece of cake, my friend. When do we move?"

"Day after tomorrow."

Gunther stood. "You want a young hippie for the night? I'll get one who takes baths."

"I'm staying with Erika."

"Good man. Pepe will drive you."

True to Gunther's word, Pepe never spoke all the way to Begijne Hof.

Erika was waiting for him with a prepared dinner and wearing a fetching nightgown. Halfway through the knockwurst, the day began to take its toll. His eyelids were lead and his head was getting too heavy for his shoulders.

"I don't think you're up to hanky-panky," she chuckled.

"You sound like Gunther. American slang will ruin the language. But you're right, I'm beat."

"Come along!"

He followed her into the bath and tried to convince himself that where there's a will, there's a way, when she slithered out of the gown and bent over the tub to turn on the taps.

He thought he might just make it when she let her hands roam while removing his clothes.

"You are tired," she said.

"Close," he sighed, "but no cigar."

She joined him in the tub and soaped him as best she could under water. He couldn't move.

Out of the tub, she dried him with a huge, soft towel and led him into the bedroom. Her hands were strong yet sensual and therapeutic as she massaged him. In seconds, he was slipping away.

He managed, just before going over the edge, to mumble, "Five."

"What?"

"Wake me at five. I have a six-thirty flight."

"Where?"

"Geneva."

She thought and rubbed and then thought some more. "Can I go along?"

But there was no answer. He was already fast asleep.

8

Carstairs Limited was indeed a well-financed company. The Geneva bankers processed the letter of credit and the transfer of funds quickly and efficiently. They also assured him that his "letter of demand" would be honored with no question by their Amsterdam representative upon his return.

That meant that the raw diamonds would practically be waiting for him.

Before heading back to the airport he paid a call on another old acquaintance: his European attorney, Hermann Heinzmuller.

"You're a genius, Hermann."

"That's what you pay me for," replied the gruff, white-haired man. "You're practically a rich man from these investments. Why don't you quit?"

"Maybe I will...some day. In the meantime, you just keep making me richer."

"Do you still want the same beneficiaries...in case?"

Barrabas nodded. "And here are powers of attorney and the other papers on the nine I mentioned. Their account numbers are already in there. I made the down payment deposits this morning."

The old man sighed deeply and leafed through the papers. "Well, I suppose it's a business, like any other business."

"That's right, Hermann, it's just a business."

Sipping his drink on the return flight, Barrabas felt like a man who had just completed the first one-third of a job well done. If anything did happen, Erika Dykstra was going to be one very wealthy woman.

He called Brookler as soon as he landed.

"Tangier is set. The goods will be ready for inspection here by noon tomorrow."

"We'll do it all at once, when we load. Eight tomorrow night?"

"Fine. 'Til then."

He cabbed into Amsterdam and spent the rest of the day with Gunther and the silent Pepe. By seven o'clock that night everything was set, including the diamonds for Brookler and the guilders for Zelzig.

He called Erika.

"I've rented a car. How would you like to spend the night in Alkmaar eating cheese?"

"Among other things?"

"Whatever strikes your fancy."

"SHE DIDN'T LEARN all that at medical school." Vince Biondi was massaging a well-bruised shoulder and watching Dr. Hatton toss Alex Nanos around like a sack of raw rice. She had just done the same thing to him.

"I know," Liam agreed. "I think, laddie, we've got us a ringer."

"Lady, I'm gonna stop worrying about where I grab you!" Nanos panted.

"Please do," she replied, feinting under the big Greek's pawing arm and jolting his ribs with her shoulder and his groin with her elbow. He barely got out a loud grunt before he was sailing over her back. He landed with a bone-jarring thud and she was on him, her palms and thumbs digging into the pressure points at the side of his head and neck.

O'Toole called a halt just before Nanos passed out.

Her performance was no more than a continuation of the whole day. She'd lasted well on the morning's fifteen miles. And then she had astounded them all by breaking down and reassembling both an M-16 and a Mauser in near record time. During practice, she had proved that she could fire them as well as she could handle them.

She outshot all of them, with the exception of the two real experts, Billy Two and O'Toole himself.

Though she had lagged slightly during the afternoon fifteen miles, she seemed to regain strength and energy when it came to the hand-to-hand.

The only person who bested her completely was Al Chen.

"Would you say, Chen," O'Toole asked, drawing him away from the group, "that she was trained?"

"Trained ain't the word for it, Liam," Chen replied. "If this was competition, she'd be close to a red belt. That's expert."

"Yeah, yeah," O'Toole mused. "That's what I figured. Okay, that's it. Short straw boils the chicken!"

Much later that night, Liam broke his own order and crossed the compound to the main house.

"Why, Liam, this is an occasion. Come in!"

He followed her into the sitting room. There was a cozy fire and that, coupled with the figure-fitting white dress she wore, made him slightly uncomfortable.

"Drink? It's Irish whiskey."

"I don't mind if I do." He waited until she was at the sideboard, bottle in hand. "You're more than a doctor."

The bottle paused only momentarily above the glasses before she poured and turned to face him. "We're all of us more than we seem," she said calmly, extending one of the glasses.

He took it and eased himself into one of the high-backed leather chairs. "But you, lass, are more than that."

Leona gripped her glass with both hands as she moved to one of the chairs herself. "I've been trained by my father, my brother and my husband since college. I wanted to be a doctor. I became a doctor. But falling into my father's business seemed a natural thing. The medical profession only allowed me access to countries and situations where I could do the real work I was trained for. I've worked as an undercover agent for most of the agencies in Washington, Liam."

"I figured it was something like that." The tone in his voice was almost one of relief. "You're going in with us, aren't you?"

"All the way." She nodded. "I can hold up my end."

O'Toole tipped his glass, emptying half the contents in one swallow. "Yes, I believe you can."

"And there's another reason. How much do you know about the mission?"

"Just about all of it, I think."

"Then I'll tell you something you don't know." Now it was her turn to drink, neat, as Liam had done. "Joseph Noboctu is a diabetic with a heart condition."

O'Toole digested this slowly and she let it sink in before she spoke again.

"What are you thinking, Liam?"

"I'm thinking," he said, holding his glass out for a refill, "that the colonel is gonna shit in his pants when he finds out."

THE SIDES OF THE CRATES had been carefully sanded and then restamped with the word DELFT in large black letters, and, under it, AMSTERDAM. What the original words had been was impossible to guess. Everything in the crates, from ammunition to clothing to medical supplies, had been originally produced in separate countries. The material had probably then been sold ten times in as many different countries before coming to rest in Brookler's warehouse.

Barrabas hefted one of the lightweight, deadly Armalites and checked the action. Satisfied, he replaced it in the crate and signaled for Gunther's men to nail it up.

"All right?" Brookler asked, lightly tapping his fingers together in front of his thin chest.

"Good. How did you do on the heavy stuff?"

"I got you the .60s with a few thousand rounds each."

Barrabas nodded and moved away from the loading area. He didn't have to inquire about the Tangier half of the shipment. He'd already clarified that it matched, item for item, and had been released to Hadege there from one of Brookler's agents.

He extracted a chamois bag from his briefcase and passed it over. The tall man's skeletal face immediately became infused with life. All small, illicit arms dealers like Brookler bared their greed like a flag at the consummation of a deal. Only one thing could elate them more: the ruination or complete demise of a competitor.

Barrabas had seen it many times.

Brookler took a collapsible scale from his pocket and set it up on an empty crate. Lovingly he rolled the stones from the bag into his hand and weighed them in groups of five.

The whole operation took three minutes, and then everything disappeared back into his cavernous pockets. He extended his hands, the face frozen with his humorless smile.

"Success in your war."

Barrabas reached to shake the hand and, at the last second, grabbed the extended thumb instead. Brookler grunted and tried to pull away but the pain quickly brought him back.

"There was an ad in the *International Herald Tribune* yesterday, Brookler. Did you get an answer yet?"

"I don't know what you're talking about."

A twist and another growl of pain. "How's it going to happen? Customs? Police? Or were you just supposed to blow me away at the last minute?"

Now the pain seemed to be a catharsis for him and the grin returned. "It's part of the business, Nile, you know that."

He wrenched hard. Barrabas hung on and heard the bone crack, but he was loose. Brookler sprang back with a curse, snatching a gun from his pocket. The Walther looked small but deadly in his bony hand.

"I won't kill you here, Barrabas, it's bad for business. Now get out. Our deal's over."

"How much is Heiss putting out for my skin on the open market, Simon?"

"Move. . . while you can!"

That was all the answer Barrabas would get and he knew it. He nodded into the shadows behind Brookler. There was a slight, barely perceptible movement from the darkness and the Walther clattered to the concrete floor.

It had happened so fast Brookler didn't even have time to feel the pain. But he could see it. Pepe's hand held the hilt of the stiletto steady. The blade was clear through Brookler's hand, extending six inches from the palm.

Barrabas nodded a second time to Pepe and walked out of the warehouse. Brookler's three men were nowhere in sight. Both of the crates were bound securely and loaded on the truck bed. Gunther's men were just crawling in behind them and rolling down the tarp as Barrabas climbed into the cab and lit a cigar.

"Well?" Erika said from the center part of the seat.

"It was his ad, I'm sure of it. Heiss knows we're coming but he doesn't know when, and he thinks we'll be forty in strength."

They waited ten minutes before Pepe emerged from the warehouse and crawled into the cab. They were rolling away from the loading dock and heading toward the wharf when he spoke.

"In the number six and nine Delft crates. Plastique, with a twenty-four-hour fuse."

Those were the first words Barrabas had heard the little Latin say in the three days he had known him. In the dim light from the dash Barrabas could see the top of the chamois bag protruding from Pepe's jacket pocket.

Barrabas wondered if Jessup always guessed right. Simon Brookler, the merchant of Death, had used and sold his last gun.

THE CAVERNOUS SIDE of the *Dora Zee* out of Libya yawned open with ramps from the dock into the hold. With only a pause to shift into a lower gear, Pepe drove up the ramps and they were engulfed in the bowels of the ship. Behind them the massive hatches ground shut and minutes later they were moving into the North Sea canal.

It took three hours to clear the canal and another hour plowing through the North Sea to reach international waters. They knew they were there when the fighter's big diesels throttled down, and the hatches slid open again.

The doors had barely parted before the powerful Packard engines of the ex-RAF rescue launch bobbing in the sea outside took over from the diesels.

Gunther's huge bulk and smiling face loomed behind the wheel. "Any problems?"

"Pepe took care of it," Barrabas replied, jumping into the launch and giving Erika a hand.

"I told you he was a shady character."

The two pallets were transferred quickly and quietly with the help of a minicrane, and the launch was easing away, heading south, before the huge doors had completely closed.

Gunther idled along, keeping just enough knots to maintain course, as Pepe and the other three men went to work on the crates.

It didn't take long to find six and nine. When they had the lids off, Pepe motioned Barrabas aft.

He estimated over a hundred pounds of plastic explosive in each crate; more than enough to blow Zelzig's surplus B-25 into a few million pieces and out of the air.

Working by the flashlight held in Pepe's hand, Barrabas readjusted the timers and then renailed the lids. When both were overboard and sinking, Barrabas gave Gunther a wave and the powerful Packard engines lifted the bow of the launch from the sea.

In seconds they were streaking toward Ostend at the pace of fifty knots, enough to leave any customs launch behind.

"ANY PROBLEMS?"

"None that couldn't be overcome," Liam replied. "Lopez and Nanos took off one night and terrorized half the women in the village."

"That's normal." Barrabas smiled, rubbing the sleep from his eyes. He hadn't had much since leaving Gunther and Erika at the airport in Belgium. He'd caught a direct flight into Madrid and a Cessna charter over to Majorca. "Any repercussions?"

"None that a few pesetas couldn't handle. Actually, I think the four ladies they ended up with enjoyed it."

"Four?"

"They're healthy boys." Liam grinned, without the slightest trace of shame.

"And in the field?"

"Solid, every one of them. They're training each other well. Actually, I think they're ready to go right now."

"We'll see after tonight. What about the woman? Did you break her?"

There it was. Liam turned the half-empty glass of stout in his hands, weighing his answer. His loyalties were with the Colonel, but he had grown to like and admire the spunky woman.

Should he break it, or let her?

"She *is* a ringer, Colonel, a pro. She'd done most of it before."

Barrabas nodded. "I sensed it."

"I figured you did." O'Toole took a deep breath and went on to tell him the rest of it.

"Son-of-a-bitch!" Barrabas hissed, and cursed Jessup under his breath. He toyed with the idea of telling the whole story to O'Toole. He felt he needed someone to confide in, someone blindly on his side.

But grudging admiration for Jessup won out, even if he hated the deviousness of the man's style in parceling out information and controlling them all like puppets.

"I'll get it over with later with her," Barrabas went on, weighing the importance of one thing at a time. "Did you locate a boat?"

"It's perfect," Liam replied, relieved to pass the female problem off to his superior. "A sixty-footer, and the old fisherman who owns it was practically willing to sell it to us for the price I quoted, rather than just rent."

"What excuse did you give him?"

"Sunken treasure, very hush-hush. He thinks we're crazy."

"Good, I'll take Nanos and Boone with me." He was fully awake now, his mind clicking off the necessities of the moment like a computer. "Send Nate, Vincent and Lopez in here!"

Liam left and Barrabas moved to the window. He watched the big Irishman move across the compound toward the morning cookfire and the men...and the woman.

Damn, he thought, even if she is capable—a woman? He found it hard to place a woman, any woman, in a firefight in the bush. Worst of all, a beautiful woman. In his mind he placed Erika in the middle of a column being overrun by fifty screaming Simbas.

It made his stomach churn.

"You wanted us, Colonel?"

"Yeah, sit down. Nate, I'll give the rest of the men the whole story this afternoon, but right now I want to know if you can plug into a computer for me."

EACH OF THEM carried identification, excellently forged by Lopez, when they walked into the Madrid offices of Commex Systems International. Commex Madrid was one of the five huge computer processing systems storing data for corporate conglomerates and banks around the world. The other four were in London, New York, Paris and Brussels.

Barrabas hoped that in one of these computers lay the intelligence they needed: what was the strength of military hardware on Kaluba, and how deep was foreign involvement, financially, in the Kaluban government?

The former would tell them what heavy equipment was available for theft by the Eagle Squad to use in their own mission, and the latter would give Joseph Noboctu the ammunition he needed to discredit the country's current leaders once he was landed on the island. They were equally important.

Lopez talked in rapid-fire Castilian, introducing them to a pretty young secretary and waving his credentials past her nose.

"We're here to feed some test flowcharts and programs through the local computer, ma'am. The on-line terminals seem to have developed some bugs, so preventative maintenance and the running of some diagnostics will be necessary."

The girl smiled and shook her head, obviously not understanding one word of the jargon Lopez was throwing at her.

But it worked. She disappeared into the inner offices to find someone of authority, and Lopez leaned his head toward Nate Beck.

"How'd I do?"

"Fine, fine, you sounded like you knew what you were talking about. But save some of it for the big man."

The big man proved easier than Nate had expected. He was of the new breed, a business-oriented manager recently converted into data systems. His only concern was the security of the "big brain," the network computer connecting them to other cities and holding very classified information.

When he was sure that they would be working on only the "local" computer, used for in-country transactions, he saw no reason to check their credentials further with the home office in London. He escorted them to the computer room himself.

The moment they stepped into the huge, well-lit, sterile room, Nate smiled. Computer architects, ninety-nine out of one hundred times, will store all computers in one room, all storage disks in one area, and so forth. The computer room of Commex Madrid, was no different. The room was separated by a long, wide aisle. On the right was the local computer, and on the left was the network brain that he was after.

He nodded to Lopez and Biondi and moved to the right bank of computers. Their guide exchanged a few words with a young, bored operator and left. The young man returned to his desk at the far end of the room and the manual he had been reading.

"What do I do?" Biondi whispered.

"Take this plate off and just make like you're disgusted at what you find." Vince went to work and Nate turned to Emilio. "You do the same with this one, but intercept the kid if he starts wandering about."

Nate grabbed his own briefcase, checked the desk, and scatted across the aisle into the narrower passageways of the larger computer banks.

In no time he found the main twenty-five conduit cable and traced it to the storage modem he needed. Right beside the black box, on the computer processor side, he found a plastic-enclosed encriptor, or scrambler. It was the security system he expected.

"Eureka," he hissed, and pulled the black box he had built himself from his briefcase.

Lopez was suddenly crouching by his side. "What's wrong?"

"Not a damn thing. Why?"

"I thought you called me."

"No, no, I was being elated. It's going to be easier than I thought."

Lopez watched Nate's flying fingers. "Easy! It looks like the underside of a 747 control panel to me!"

Nate was in his element. He couldn't resist explanations. "You see this black box?"

"Yeah."

"It's called a modem. It stores information in what we call characters." He held up the black box from his briefcase. "There are eight silicon chips in here. They form eight bytes, which in turn form a character. That's how the computer talks. This plastic bubble is a scrambler, or security encriptor. If you don't have the right codes when you contact it, you get back gibberish. By taking this cable apart and soldering it to my modem, I can turn the scrambler off and on at will and divert the first sixty-four thousand characters of information so they'll play back to me."

"What was the eureka for?"

"Some lazy installer didn't use modular connections on the cable. Like a wall plug? That's a break. It allows me to cut and resolder each wire, one by one, and the whole connection won't be broken."

"How many wires are in there?"

"Here, plug in this iron. Just twenty-five."

"Twenty-five?" Lopez exploded. "We'll be here all damn day!"

"Just a couple of hours."

"Then how long to get the dope we need?"

"Four, maybe five days."

"Four...you mean we gotta get back in here every day?"

Nate chuckled. "Oh, no, we do that over the telephone."

Lopez just shook his head. They heard voices from the center aisle. "Gotta go. The kid's up and around."

Nate started peeling and resoldering the wires. Ten minutes later he was back.

"Okay?" Nate asked.

"Yeah, he's back at his desk. I gave him my dirty pictures to look at." Emilio was no computer whiz, but he had a logical mind. He had begun to see the implications of what Nate was doing. "When you get that done, you gonna be able to tap into computers all over the world?"

Nate nodded. "All the computers in the Commex system."

"Lots of banks transfer funds through these computers, don't they?"

"That's right," Nate replied, halfway through the wires now.

"Damn, I wish I had you back in the Bronx with me fifteen years ago. We could'a stole a million!"

Nate chuckled. "I already did."

"What?"

"Stole a million dollars."

"What the hell happened?"

"My wife turned me in."

"No shit. It's like I always say, wives ain't really women! 'Least, not ones you can trust."

THE SKY WAS PATCHY, clear in spots and dark in others, with a heavy overcast. Liam had been right about the boat; it was the perfect size and passed for nondescript among many others plying the waters between the Balearic Islands.

They had been circling with the engine at idle for about an hour. Alex Nanos and Wiley Drew Boone sat in the wheelhouse, smoking and poring over their charts. Barrabas was aft, with his ears turned to the sky, while Claude Hayes squatted in the bow working over his gauges and tanks. Barrabas had decided, at the last minute, to bring Hayes along because they might need his diving ability.

The radio had started storm warnings just after they had pulled out of Palma Bay. The thickening of the cloud cover attested to its approach.

Nanos broke the silence. "He's a half-hour over."

"I know," Barrabas sighed. Far off the port bow he could faintly see lights from the tiny island of Ibiza. He could see nothing of the giant Majorca behind them. "Are you sure we're on the coordinates?"

Boone answered his question with another. "How's your Zelzig with a chart?"

"He and Gunther both are excellent."

"So are we, Colonel," Nanos said. "If his drops are right, I can sail this tub another two hundred yards two points to starboard and catch the load on the deck."

Barrabas nodded without answering. They were right. Boats were their business. That's why they'd been hired.

He was about to light his third cigar since leaving port, when the radio started to crackle.

"I'm a bird, I'm a bird...talk to me, Eagle! Here's a bird lookin' for Eagle!"

Barrabas was five long strides into the wheelhouse grabbing the mike from Nanos. "Eagle back to bird! What's your situation?"

Gunther's voice was fading and floating, but there was no mistaking Gunther. "It's soup up here, my friend, pure pea soup. We're about a hundred twenty-five south of the checkpoint as the crow goes. Comin' right down the chute...I think!"

Barrabas did some quick deciphering in his head. They were 125 miles south of Barcelona and dead on target in the center between the big island and the mainland.

"Gimme an ETA!" Barrabas barked.

"I'd say about ten minutes if the wings keep flappin' on

1. How do you rate _____ ?
   (Please print book TITLE)

   1.6 ☐ excellent   .4 ☐ good   .2 ☐ not so good
   .5 ☐ very good   .3 ☐ fair   .1 ☐ poor

2. How likely are you to purchase another book in this series?

   2.1 ☐ definitely would purchase   .3 ☐ probably would not purchase
   .2 ☐ probably would purchase   .4 ☐ definitely would not purchase

3. How do you compare this book with similar books you usually read?

   3.1 ☐ far better than others   .4 ☐ not as good
   .2 ☐ better than others   .5 ☐ definitely not as good
   .3 ☐ about the same

4. Have you any additional comments about this book?

   _____ (4)
   _____ (6)

5. How did you *first* become aware of this book?

   8. ☐ read other books in series   11. ☐ friend's recommendation
   9. ☐ in-store display   12. ☐ ad inside other books
   10. ☐ TV, radio or magazine ad   13. ☐ other _____
   (please specify)

6. What *most* prompted you to buy this book?

   14. ☐ read other books in series   17. ☐ title   20. ☐ story outline on back
   15. ☐ friend's recommendation   18. ☐ author   21. ☐ read a few pages
   16. ☐ picture on cover   19. ☐ advertising   22. ☐ other _____
   (please specify)

   N123

7. What type(s) of paperback fiction have you purchased in the past
   3 months? Approximately how many?

	No. purchased		No. purchased
☐ contemporary romance	(23) ____	☐ espionage	(37) ____
☐ historical romance	(25) ____	☐ western	(39) ____
☐ gothic romance	(27) ____	☐ contemporary novels	(41) ____
☐ romantic suspense	(29) ____	☐ historical novels	(43) ____
☐ mystery	(31) ____	☐ science fiction/fantasy	(45) ____
☐ private eye	(33) ____	☐ occult	(47) ____
☐ action/adventure	(35) ____	☐ other	(49) ____

8. Have you purchased any books from any of these series in the past
   3 months? Approximately how many?

	No. purchased		No. purchased
☐ Mack Bolan (The Executioner)	(51) ____	☐ Phoenix Force	(55) ____
☐ Able Team	(53) ____	☐ Other Adventure series	(57) ____

9. On which date was this book purchased? (59) _____

10. Please indicate your age group and sex.

    61.1 ☐ Male   62.1 ☐ under 15   .3 ☐ 25-34   .5 ☐ 50-64
    .2 ☐ Female   .2 ☐ 15-24   .4 ☐ 35-49   .6 ☐ 65 or older

Thank you for completing and returning this questionnaire.

PRINTED IN CANADA

NAME _____
(Please Print)

ADDRESS _____

CITY _____

ZIP CODE _____

BUSINESS REPLY MAIL

FIRST CLASS   PERMIT NO. 70   TEMPE, AZ.

POSTAGE WILL BE PAID BY ADDRESSEE

NATIONAL READER SURVEYS

1440 SOUTH PRIEST DRIVE
TEMPE, AZ   85266

this thing and my friend's feet don't get tired pumpin' these damn pedals!''

"The guy's a comedian," Nanos chuckled. "Who is he?"

"An old drinking buddy," Barrabas replied. "Shhh."

"I can hear 'em, but I can't see 'em," Boone hissed, straining his eyes up at the darkening sky.

"We've got your sound," Barrabas said into the mike. "We're lighting up."

He turned to give the order and saw that Hayes had already lit the fore and aft beacon lights.

"Can't see you," came Gunther's voice. "Fact is, can't see nothin' past the bird poop on the Plexiglas."

The sound rose to a peak above them and then began to diminish.

"You're fading. I think you've passed us."

"Figures," Gunther replied. "We'll make another pass under the cloud cover. Liable to mangle the merchandise down there a little on the drop. You got a swimmer?"

"Affirmative."

"Good show. Here we go!"

They followed the drone of the prop-driven engines as the plane made a sweeping arc, and then they saw it fall out of the clouds. One wing dipped and they were in a direct line.

Gunther's voice practically screamed over the radio. "Got you, Eagle—now! Bombs away!"

A half-minute later, eight pairs of drop chutes blossomed under the retreating plane and they could make out the outlines of the crates.

Hayes was in the water and his body already resembled a dark, twisting torpedo. He was practically under the first crate when it hit, and by the time the fourth one was down, he had bobbing yellow pontoons attached and inflated on the first three.

Zelzig and Gunther had made a second round, and Barrabas waved at their dipping wings even though he knew they couldn't see him.

"How'd we do, Eagle?"

"Right on, big bird," Barrabas replied. "Thumbs up all the way south and beyond!"

He was about to click off the radio when Gunther's voice came back on. "Got a bit of news."

"Come back?"

"A friend of Pepe's got to Brookler's African contact."

The short hair on the back of Barrabas's neck became electric. He could hear the strain in his own voice when he said, "And was he successful?"

"Just like Pepe," Gunther replied. "The bush people won't know about your arrival. Gonna cost you though."

"Worth every penny," Barrabas said, as he felt the first raindrops on his face and saw the first crate being rolled aboard.

"One more thing, crazy man. Why, I don't know, but little sis says she still loves your body. Fly high, Eagle!"

"Fly safe, big bird."

At the rail, Nanos and Boone exchanged glances as Hayes pushed the second crate into position. They had heard the reference to "little sis," and were both thinking the same thing; maybe the Colonel was human, after all.

But Barrabas already had his mind back on the mission. Gunther's news that their attack was still going to be a surprise was more than welcome. Everything else was falling neatly into place.

Now if Nate was successful, Kaluba itself would supply the heavy hardware they needed.

Barrabas held off a head-to-head confrontation with Hatton for the next few days of training. He preferred to study and evaluate Liam's assessment of her through his own eyes. For the most part, she did measure up, and slowly the men were beginning to accept her as one of their own.

He did, however, try to shock her whenever possible to detect any weaknesses.

On their makeshift range he mounted a couple of large cans filled with gasoline and a stuffed dummy resembling a man.

"Have you ever fired anything as powerful as an Armalite, Doctor?"

"No, Colonel, but I can learn."

"Learning and then doing can be vastly different."

He raised the rifle, shifted to semiautomatic, and sprayed the cans. The explosion was deafening as they disappeared, sending twin sheets of flame forty feet in the air.

She didn't seem impressed.

He handed her the weapon. "Got any idea what a .223 shell can do to flesh and blood, Doctor? Imagine that dummy is a Simba with a panga knife bearing down on you."

She curled her lip in a slight smile as she brought the rifle up. "Easy. I just imagine he's got rape instead of murder on his mind."

She squeezed off two bursts, cutting the dummy completely in two and scattering the remains over a twenty-yard area. Then she calmly handed the rifle back to Barrabas.

"I just shot his balls off."

NATE BECK WAS EXCUSED from any field work whenever he deemed it necessary. During these times he sequestered himself in the main house with the only telephone and the H-11 portable computer he had constructed from a kit purchased before flying back from Madrid.

The modem he had installed was working like a charm. By the third day, he had collected the full 64,000 characters and processed the first 40,000 through his own homemade computer.

It was here that his early Air Force training and creative programming came into play. He discovered that the Kaluban government accounts were being fed and coded on a daily time factor with the word CHARLEMAGNE. The sequence was: the full word at noon, HARLEMAGNE at one o'clock, ARLEMAGNE at two, and so on.

The following day he placed the calls himself, and by that evening he had the key to tap all of the Kaluban government's bank accounts.

Like any good computer man, Nate was thorough and did everything in sequential steps. Before recommanding his modem to feed him back cross-references of the bank accounts, he went ahead and processed the remaining twenty-thousand-plus characters.

It was a wise move.

Before he was half through, he spotted a pattern and quickly realized its significance. Someone, probably a high bank official wanting to find out for personal reasons where to invest some of his own money, had been punching up programs on the London, Amsterdam and Brussels accounts of several arms dealers.

Without wasting valuable time and tediously running through code after code searching, Nate was able to scan the deposits of the arms dealers on a given set of dates, in comparison to funds transfers on those dates from Kaluban accounts.

In less than an hour he was able to match Kaluba's codes to the files status and access codes of a huge Czech arms dealer, Olarum. From the ongoing research file on Olarum, he was able to determine an itemized arms sale to Kaluba.

Nate was like a ten-year-old turned loose in a malt shop as he hopped from the computer to the typewriter. When he finished, he had twenty-six pages in one file folder containing every dime of legal and illegal aid given to Kaluba in the last five years, what countries had made the contributions, and what moneys had been skimmed off by leaders in the current ruling party and illegally invested in foreign corporations. All the information Noboctu would need.

In another folder he had a complete list of the country's military hardware and its current status.

He drove like a wild man across the ranch to where the rest of the team worked burying the arms and other equipment that had been used during the group's training period.

It would no longer be needed, since they were jumping off the next day.

"Colonel, I think I've got it all!" Nate yelled, jumping from the jeep and passing his treasure to Barrabas.

A skim reading of the folder containing the financial report brought a whistle to the big man's lips. A careful scrutiny of the second folder brought a wide grin, especially when his eyes fell on the helicopters and motor launches.

"Fantastic, Nate. I think we're in business. Biondi!"

"Yes, sir?" Vince crawled from the hole and trotted toward them.

"Vince, think you can still handle an old H-24 Marine copter?"

"A banana boat? Hell, yes, Colonel, I can make one of those babies roll upside down, fly backward and spit red peppers!"

LA ESCABORAL was the finest restaurant in the tiny village of Consell, an hour's drive from the ranch. It was also the only restaurant open serving the evening meal. A heavy scent of fresh pastry and the heady aroma of cooking Sollarian sausages greeted them as they walked through the Moorish, tunnellike entrance and entered the restaurant.

Ancient wooden beams looked down at them through a sea of hanging greenery, and color was everywhere, highlighted by the natural red stone of the walls. The tops of the natural wood tables gleamed with years of polish and the friction from countless hands and elbows.

"A beautiful place," Barrabas said, following Leona into a sunken, open courtyard where they were seated by a bubbling fountain.

"The food is even better than the atmosphere," she replied.

And it was.

They both ate in silence, as if the change from field cooking and rations and respite from the tension and week's training was the only reason he had asked her to dinner, rather than accompany the men to Palma.

"I'm flattered," she had said. "There won't be time for a last fling after we leave tomorrow."

"I'm not such a romantic," he'd replied. "No fling is ever the last."

Over espresso and brandy she looked up to find him studying her intently. "You approve?"

"You're a very beautiful woman, Lee."

"And that's another reason you'll try to talk Jessup out of sending me along?"

Barrabas shrugged, lighting a thin cigar. "I guess the time for talk is over. We discussed it this morning on the scrambler phone. He says you're essential to the group for several reasons. Of course, he didn't mention any of them."

"But besides being a physician, able to treat Noboctu if necessary, you think I'm along as Walker Jessup's personal representative or spy. It that it?"

"Yes," he nodded. "That's part of it."

"Well, you're right. This is a very questionable group. This mission could get sticky, politically. Before it's over, diplomacy could be important. Besides my other attributes, I'm quite an astute diplomat."

Barrabas took a few moments to digest this and then spoke again. "Jessup did say that the only way for you not to go in with us would be if you made the decision yourself."

She stayed silent for the remainder of their dinner and most of the ride back to the ranch. The silence was broken only when an enormous moon burst from behind a cloud cover and bathed the entire valley before them in pale blue light.

"It's an idyllic place. . .serene and beautiful."

"It's a nice place to regroup and rest between wars."

She studied his profile, trying to look at the man past the jutting jaw, the irregular nose, and the wide, deep-set eyes under heavy dark brows that didn't agree with the whiteness of his hair.

"Everything revolves around war for you, doesn't it?"

"Yes."

"You live for the action."

"Yes." He cast a quick glance at her and then returned his concentration to the angling road. "But I won't die for it. I have a job, not a cause. I leave causes for men like Joseph Noboctu."

"And me," she replied. "You see, I really believe Joseph Noboctu should be running his country."

The mood didn't lighten when he handed her from the car and accepted her offer of a nightcap. He was still trying to conceive of some magical, worthwhile argument when she suddenly stood and glared down at him with her hands firmly planted on her hips.

"Colonel, I've been racking my brain. . .and suddenly I think I've got it."

"Got what?"

"The real reason. You've built and built this situation until you've blinded yourself to the real reason you've been objecting to me. As a woman in a, quote, man's domain, mainly fighting and war, I've proved to myself and you that I'm capable of keeping up."

He started to rise. "Look, you're going, and there's. . . ."

"Goddammit, I'm not through yet!" The unexpected fury in her words set him back in his chair. "It's not because I'm a woman, Colonel, that it's bothering you. That's what's been throwing me off. It's sex!"

Barrabas started to interrupt and she stopped him with a raised arm.

"It's sex, because that's how you think of a woman... she means sex. And you don't want those guys to be thinking of sex instead of survival. Did you ever stop to think, Colonel, that maybe it has never entered their minds, only yours?"

From the sudden spread of realization across his face she knew she had hit a nerve, the right nerve.

"Well, Colonel, since that's what's bothering you... only you... not me, not them... I suggest that we get it out of the way right now."

Her hands went behind her back. Her shoulders wriggled and the silky summer dress billowed to her feet. Her underwear quickly followed and she resumed her previous stance, only this time stark naked.

"Since the presence of sex, or the curiosity about it, bothers you so much, I suggest we go upstairs and get it over with and out of the way... now. Then maybe we can both forget about it."

Barrabas slowly rose, crossed the room, and retrieved her clothing. His face, when he handed her the garments, sported a wide, almost boyish grin.

"Be packed by eight. Briefing will be short. We go to war at nine. Good night, Doctor."

"Good night, Colonel."

PART FOUR
THE TARGET

9

They came into Dar es Salaam from several directions, using every airline that stopped in the Tanzanian capital. In ones and twos they filtered into the city and registered at several hotels under the false names of their forged passports.

At the sleek, Israeli-built Kilimanjaro Hotel, O'Toole and Leona registered as an English husband and wife. They immediately went to work obtaining permits for a camera safari into the interior.

Nate, Lopez and Boone separately checked into the spacious New African and went right to work procuring jeeps outfitted for the bush. Under the whirring overhead fans in the walnut-paneled bar, they were loudly over-joyed to learn that they were all in the country for the same reason: to explore the bush.

In less than an hour they had the equipment and several offers of trained guides.

From the New Palace Hotel, Billy Two scoured the city for provisions and other necessities that wouldn't be in this second drop of vital supplies.

Barrabas himself had preceded them into the Dar air-port, but he had never left it. He was working his way through the list of night air controllers supplied to him by Jessup. He needed one who was not above accepting a generous amount of *baksheesh* to okay a change in flight plan that he knew was highly irregular.

Baksheesh is the Arab word for a bribe or payoff, but all over Africa—from Algiers to Cape Town, from Dar to Luanda—it is a term that is universally understood.

When he found the right man and the right amount had been bartered, Barrabas explained his needs.

"At midnight tonight, Mambassa control will pass over a Ghanian plane registered 6G14 to you at Dar. His flight plan is for Tomalave, Kaluba.

"6G14 will have experienced difficulties all the way down from Addis Ababa. Just across the Tanzania-Kenya border, he will have to feather one engine and ask to divert."

The explanation was clear and the procedure quite normal. Both the controller and Barrabas knew that 6G14 would then drop below radar, swing inland, para-drop whatever Barrabas was smuggling, and then fly back to Dar airport. Miraculously the engine would refire and 6G14 would receive clearance to continue on to Kaluba.

Baksheesh is a way of life.

The air controller smiled, thinking how much closer he was to the new Fiat he had been dreaming of.

Barrabas smiled and selected one from many of the marked envelopes in his briefcase.

The transaction was quickly concluded, and Barrabas descended from the airport restaurant to search out a helicopter bush pilot who had pontoons on his craft and some knowledge of the Rufiji River. It took less than an hour to find the pilot, and slightly more than double that before they were setting down approximately forty miles up the wide, navigable stream beside a tiny village.

Barrabas met the village chief or headman at once, because the headman greeted every craft that came upriver in the hopes of hiring his men out as guides or porters or just finding out bits of information about the travelers that could be passed along for money to any interested party.

With the help of another envelope from Barrabas's briefcase, the chief willingly agreed to hide, store and repaint the boat that the crazy foreigner was going to deposit with him in the wee hours of the following morning.

Back at the airport, Barrabas thanked and paid well the German pilot who claimed his family were the earliest colonials in the godforsaken country, and left the building to find a taxi.

He had to inquire through four drivers before he found one who was willing to go outside the city. Then it would be done only for an exorbitant rate. Barrabas didn't care. There was a crossroads restaurant far out of Dar on the Morogoro highway that served just the Ethiopian delicacies that he had come all the way to Tanzania to eat.

The driver thought he was insane. But then all foreigners were insane, especially if they were white and rich.

At the restaurant, Barrabas did in fact sit down to one of his favorite meals, and to wait for nightfall and the camera safari that would pick him up for the rest of the trip into the bush.

SECURITY AT KALUBA'S Tomalave airport was tight. The city itself had already started sprouting bunting, flags and general festive paraphernalia for the coming elections a week away.

From the fifteenth story of the newly erected Pan-Kaluban luxury hotel, Vince Biondi studied the airport layout just across the wide boulevard. The airport had almost equal numbers of military and commercial aircraft.

As Biondi called out the layout, landmarks and areas where aircraft were parked, Al Chen quickly transcribed everything onto paper.

"I count two H-34s and two H-21 copters, plus the three MiGs."

Chen noted the aircraft and their placement in proximity to fences and hangars. "That leaves one copter," he said.

"Probably on patrol. My God...."

"What, what?"

"You should see the tits on the Pan Am stew leaving the terminal."

"Jesus, Biondi, concentrate on the hardware, man, the hardware!"

Two miles away, in the Kaluban Ministry of Defense, Claude Hayes was presenting his credentials to three openly disinterested government officials. Their interest grew, however, as Claude implied that he had a good-sized shipment of Finnish 20mm Lahti cannons that he needed a quick sale on.

A quick sale in any language meant that they could be purchased cheap. It was the bait in their delicate double-cross that would neutralize Kaluba's air power.

Hayes also tendered an allusion here and there in his conversation that he knew of their previous deal with the

Czech firm, Olarum. These hints of their very secret previous arms purchases were more than enough to convince the three gentlemen of Claude's authenticity.

They were sure that he had been connected with Olarum himself and had decided to go off on his own. In so doing, he had probably bitten off more than he could handle with the Lahtis, and now needed to dump them for ready cash.

All of this they supposed on their own, without any prompting from Hayes. Such maneuverings were commonplace in the cutthroat arms trade. And since their government was already in the market for approximately this number of Lahtis or comparable cannon, they began chomping at the bit when Hayes suggested that the deal go through his company, Carstairs of Tangier.

They were eager to believe their own presumptions because if the purchase were made government-to-government, as the original deal was, there was no room for *baksheesh*. With Carstairs being a private company there would be a great deal of *baksheesh*.

The deal was made quickly. Carstairs would bill the Lahtis out at two hundred American dollars each, and then accept payment at twenty American dollars each.

The three men were already assembling cables to the Swiss banks and mentally multiplying the number of Lahtis times one hundred eighty.

The capper was put on the deal when an aide walked into the room and announced that there was indeed a Carstairs, Ltd. located in Tangier and, yes, a flight plan had been filed from Tangier to Dar es Salaam by a Ghanian plane, 6G14.

The gentlemen were only too happy to quietly lend Claude a government helicopter, complete with armed guard and pilot, for the pickup that evening. One of them was already reaching for a phone to call the airport and make arrangements as Claude walked out of the office.

The driver of the ancient taxi was more than happy to take the Swahili-speaking stranger up and down the ocean boulevard as many times as he wanted to go. There was nothing to see except the three government gunboats that never went to sea, and a few old fishing boats.

He mentioned several times that the real sights were

farther down the beach: the foreign women with their tiny bathing suits. But his passenger seemed more interested in the navy. So what did he care. He charged by the time. The only meter in a Kaluban taxi was in the driver's head, and the charges usually agreed with the way a passenger was dressed. This light-skinned black man was dressed very well indeed.

"There, in front of that shop. We'll pick up the white man with the suitcase."

The taxi lurched to a sputtering halt. Nanos slid the heavy case onto the rear floorboards and took the seat beside Claude.

"The hotel now," Hayes told the driver. "The Pan-Kaluban."

Oh-ho, the driver thought, gunning the car up to its maximum of forty kilometers, a good fare indeed. These foreigners stay in the city's most expensive hotel!

Nanos opened the top of the case. "These all right?"

Claude made a quick inspection of the two sets of scuba tanks and nodded. "You gonna remember how I taught you to use 'em?"

"Got it in my head like the alphabet."

Two bellmen caught them in the lobby and insisted on carrying the case upstairs. Claude tipped them heavily and, as soon as they were gone, opened the connecting door into the adjoining suite.

"How'd it go?" Biondi called from the window.

Hayes chuckled. "*Baksheesh* works every time. They're even clearing an overflight with somebody high up in the government over there." He glanced over Chen's shoulder at the drawings, notations, and figures on the table in front of him. "What do you think?"

"I think, my African comrade," Al Chen replied, "that coupled with the lack of spare parts we already know about and the lack of security we can see from this little ol' window, it should take us approximately forty minutes to put the entire Kaluban air force out of business."

BARRABAS HIMSELF drove the first jeep, with Lopez and O'Toole wildly maneuvering the other two to keep up. They were well within their time schedule, but they had already been stopped by two army patrols and had their permits and papers checked. If it happened many more times, or if one of the patrol officers started to do some hard wondering about the party's strange makeup—different passports, different nationalities, lack of professional guides—they might be detained too long. Then it would be curtains for Noboctu. They couldn't fight a war without firepower.

The highway was the only land artery across Tanzania. It ran from Dar clear to Ujiji on Lake Tanganyika, with little more than outpost villages along the way.

They whirled through one of these—less than a minute of slumbering bush civilization—and were once again riding the narrow ribbon of highway between two unbroken columns of tall, dark trees.

"That was Dodoma," Billy Two offered, raising his eyes from the map on his lap. "Watch it now. Should be coming up in about twenty-five or so kilometers."

Barrabas checked the dash and nodded. "How's our time?"

"Right on," Billy replied. "I just hope there's some semblance left of the road."

Barrabas set his jaw and nodded a second time. He hoped so, too. The mud road they were looking for would take them to an old British fort. The fort itself had long been abandoned. That meant the road leading to it would hardly have been used in years. And Barrabas knew how fast the jungle reclaimed its land.

In the second jeep, Lee Hatton's eyes were wide in total awe. "My God, it's amazing."

"What's that, lass?" O'Toole called over the roaring engine.

"How much we take electricity for granted. Now I know what darkest Africa means!"

The big Irishman chuckled. "Out here about the only light comes from a palm-oil lamp or an occasional cookfire. And those you can't see over a few yards away."

In the third jeep, Wiley Drew was laughing his head off at Emilio's cursing at the potholes. "Hell, Lopez, don't go around 'em, just hit 'em!"

"I tried that, dammit," Lopez retorted. "I think I'm gettin' a hernia."

In the back, Nate Beck valiantly tried to stay in the center of the seat while balancing the delicate radio in his lap. "Amazing, just amazing."

"What's so damn amazing?" Lopez hissed.

"I thought all cars nowadays, even jeeps, had power steering."

This forced an eruption of laughter from both Lopez and Boone.

"There it is!" Billy cried. "Off to the left!"

Barrabas braked, geared down and careened off into the jungle. The first hundred yards were fairly clear. Then limbs, vines, creepers and a hundred other forms of jungle vegetation began slapping at the windshield and closing in like a hungry mouth around them.

All three drivers cursed, braked, clutched and shifted as they plowed ahead. They lasted another six miles until the jungle literally became a wall in front of them.

Barrabas rocked his jeep to a halt, alighted and started barking orders. "Okay, everybody out! We walk from here. Nate, get that radio going. Drape the vehicles with those bigger fronds. Everybody, jump to!"

Twenty minutes later they were slicing through the seemingly impenetrable undergrowth in a single column, with Billy Two and O'Toole alternately leading the way with panga knives.

Leona tugged at Emilio's sleeve. "What's that sound...around our feet?"

"Bush rats," he replied.

"Oh...is that all!"

"If you feel a claw, kick fast. They get really pissed off when you step on 'em."

Suddenly they were climbing. The dense jungle grew sparse, and they were wading through tall savanna grass.

"Quick time now!" Barrabas yelled from the rear of the column, and they all broke into a jogging trot.

As they moved steadily forward, the rancid smell of mangos and jungle rot left their nostrils to be replaced by a cooling, sweet breeze. Mist hung like a light blanket just over the waving savanna to their left.

"Mist, Colonel. Should be the tail end of the Ugalla River."

"Right. How much farther?"

"A mile, can't be more than two," Billy replied, swinging the column to the right a few degrees.

Then they were descending again, from a plateau to a wide, jungle-clogged ravine. But just as quickly, they broke through and found themselves in a clearing. They had found the fort. One long mud-brick building dominated the clearing, with a few thatched huts on the perimeter. The huts had long since given up and returned to the jungle.

With just a wave of his hand as an order, Barrabas guided them on a quick reconnaissance. Luck was with them. There wasn't a living soul around and hadn't been for months.

Nate went to work with his radio as oil torches were set up to form a drop zone. When everything was in readiness, each of them snatched a few moments' rest. Only a few of them realized it, but they had just stumbled, lurched and run through fourteen miles of jungle.

They didn't have long to wait. They heard the drone of the engines first and not long after it Gunther's voice crackling over the radio.

"Bird to Eagle...Bird to Eagle."

Barrabas smiled to himself. Gunther was all business now; get in, get out. There wouldn't be any of the lighthearted wit and repartee that there had been for that first ocean drop.

Zelzig was flying less than five hundred feet over the trees and partially blind between mountain peaks. Add that to the danger from detection by the Tanzanian air force, and there wasn't much time to be lighthearted.

"There he is!" Billy cried.

And there he was indeed, outlined against the sky like a dark, noisy specter. Besides the roaring sound, the plane's only sign of life was the eerie flame shooting from its exhaust.

"Eagle to Bird...am I there?"

"Got you, Eagle."

"You're nearly on line. We're lighting up."

Flames licked up the poles to oil-soaked rags and the clearing was turned into daylight. Zelzig dipped his right wing ever so slightly and headed in.

The clearing was small, but from five hundred feet it

wasn't hard to hit. All but one of the crates landed on target. The chutes had barely blossomed when the plane's engines revved back to full, the nose lifted and they were heading west, back toward Dar.

"Got the goods, Bird," Barrabas whispered into the mike.

There wasn't even a reply from Gunther, only the singing sound of his frequency switch. He was already raising the Dar tower and reporting that his engine had ceased its malfunction.

Without waiting for an order, Billy Two had already strapped on a pair of climbing spikes and was halfway up a tree to cut down the one misdropped crate.

O'Toole had cracked the others open and jungle greens were being passed out as everyone started stripping, including Dr. Leona Hatton. Her bra gleamed like a strip of alabaster against her tanned skin.

O'Toole tossed her a jacket, pants and shirt and chuckled. "Damn shame we don't have some for you, Doc."

The men all sported green shorts.

CLAUDE HAYES KNEW how to read his fellow man, particularly an African official. He and Biondi were challenged only once, and then very briefly, as they left the commercial side of the terminal and walked through the two sentries onto the tarmac leading out to the neat row of helicopters and the three MiGs beyond.

There was a conspicuous lack of guards around any of the machines. It was much better for the three gentlemen in the Kaluban Ministry of Defense to have no witnesses of some foreigner riding off in a Kaluban helicopter. They had marked the cards and stacked the deck. But they still had to deal the hand.

The only sign of life at all was a mercenary soldier leaning against one of the H-34s, idly cradling a Soviet AK in the crook of his arm. The pilot, complete with a flowing white scarf, lounged in the hatch opening, smoking.

Al Chen nudged Claude in the side with his elbow. "There's our missing chopper."

Hayes followed the other man's gaze. The H-21 they hadn't seen from the hotel room window was completely dismantled and spread all over the floor of a nearby hangar. "Well, there's one we won't have to work on."

Claude showed his passport to the pilot and they sparred until they found a common language, finally settling on French.

"They told me there would only be two of you."

"There will be," Hayes replied. "This gentleman has to check the other aircraft. We also may have some spare parts the government can use."

"Makes no difference," the pilot shrugged.

"You and I can go over the flight plan in the meantime," Claude offered, climbing into the aircraft.

Biondi turned to the guard. "Czech?"

"Belgian," the man grunted.

"Ah, I knew a girl in Antwerp...." The guard still looked bored. "Cigarette? American?" This interested him more. And as they lit up, Biondi deftly turned him away from the other aircraft where Al Chen was already unhooking the engine canopy on one of the H-34s.

Al Chen hummed quietly to himself as the tiny pair of snips in his hand severed the "brain" wires of the copter's electrical system. That done, he replaced the canopy and whistled his way around the machine to its open loading door.

Once there, he bent to tie his shoe, and when he stood again, a six-inch Kewi knife lay in his palm. The blade was honed razor sharp on both sides and would cut through anything short of rock and steel.

Still whistling, he reached through the opening and ran his hand along the interior aluminum skin of the aircraft until he found the main hydraulic pressure line leading up to the single-rotor actuators.

The Kewi went through the tubing like butter, and Chen kept slicing until the thickly sweet odor of hydraulic fluid filled his nostrils.

He whistled his way through the rest of the copters, averaging not more than four minutes apiece to dismantle their electrical systems and ruin their hydraulics.

The MiGs posed a different problem, not the least of which was the trio of mechanics in a nearby hangar who had begun to eye him.

He smiled and waved as he edged nearer the planes.

None of them returned the greeting, and just as he ducked under a wing, one of the men started walking toward him.

"Was machen Sie?"

"Nein Deutsch," Al replied, hiding the Kewi behind his thigh but keeping it ready.

A second mechanic joined them and, out of the corner of his eye, Al saw Biondi start to move. Chen stopped him with a look and addressed the newcomer.

"You speak English?"

"Ja, some little."

Chen pulled out his wallet and flipped it open to his old "Royal Eastern Airways" security card. "I was just hired. Thought I'd look over what I have to fly."

The mechanic chuckled and slapped the MiG's skin for emphasis. "Goot, damn goot machine."

"Yeah, yeah, that's what I hear. They say these babies are glued together with borscht and they'll run on vodka."

"Ja, ja, no gas, goot. Vodka, goot!"

Both mechanics roared their approval and moved away. Al sighed his relief and replaced the Kewi with a screwdriver.

Quickly he moved back to the area between the scoop and the turbine and knelt under the plane's belly. In seconds he had the plate off and was chuckling to himself as he placed an innocent piece of clear cellophane tape between the contacts of the relay.

When the pilot kicked in the cockpit starter switch to activate the relay and the electric starter to roll the turbine, nothing would happen.

Al could visualize their chief engineer and all their mechanics going crazy trying to figure out why, when they were looking right at a functioning relay, it wouldn't function.

As an added twist, from his own warped sense of humor, Chen took the wire from the cockpit switch and attached it to the seat ejection activator.

After performing the same simple feat on MiG number two, he strolled, humming to himself, back to the helicopter.

"Everything okay?" Vince asked.

"Just the way Barrabas planned it," Chen replied. "Of course, I added a twist of my own. The two dudes who try to start those MiGs are gonna get one hell of a rise out of it!"

"Let's hope Nanos has as much fun knocking out the Kaluban 'navy.'"

Al Chen was still chuckling as he left the airport terminal and headed back toward their rented car.

Bill Metzger, his old electronics prof at Cal Tech, would be proud of him.

It WAS PITCH DARK when Nanos picked his way out through the rocks, until he felt sand under his flippers. When the water was nearly chest high he wet the inside of his mask and slipped it on. Reaching behind him he adjusted the air mixture and popped in his mouthpiece.

With one last bearing check off of the bare bulbs of the marina two hundred yards down the beach to his left, he slid under the water. He concentrated on what he had learned from Claude Hayes during the training period; legs straight, even kick to conserve energy, use the hands off your hips as rudders.

At what he guessed to be fifty yards, he bobbed to the surface. Very close, and only a little too far out into the bay.

Back under, swimming again, rolling his body from side to side to get the most from his momentum. Then he saw the reflection of light knifing into the water and rolled to his back.

Wooden hulls. Fishing boats. He went on another twenty yards and practically ran into the bow of the first gunboat. Silently he pulled himself aft until he found the power shaft down to the prop.

It was pitch black that far under the boat's hull, but that didn't make any difference. By feel, he found the three cotter-keys holding the prop to the drive shaft. The needle-nose pliers from a kit on his belt had soon extracted two of the keys.

Now came the dangerous part. The salvage acetylene was a small torch and it threw an equally small light, but if someone were standing on the deck directly above where he was working, they might be able to see the light directly through the water.

But it was a chance that had to be taken.

Nanos felt up and down the rudder shaft until he found both guidance rods. Then he fused the torch and went to work on the lower rod. It was barnacled and rusty, but the powerful little torch was engineered to cut through layers of anything as well as steel.

He felt a light pop and then some give. Off went the torch and back into his belt. Then Nanos braced his feet against the bottom of the rudder and grasped the prop shaft for leverage. It took more of his strength than he had expected, but finally the rudder began to give.

By the time Alex slid under the hull of the second gun-boat, the rudder on the first one was extended out from its base a good ten inches; more than enough, when under way, to give a helmsman an ulcer.

A half hour later he had performed the same operation on boat number two. Before dousing the torch this time, he checked his chronometer. He was fifteen minutes ahead of schedule.

Then he slithered the distance to the third boat, patted its rusty hull lovingly, and hooked an arm through the prop shaft to float and wait.

Alex Nanos had done his part to equalize the odds before they started their war.

AL CHEN PARKED across the wide boulevard from the guarded gate leading down to the boat docks. As he walked toward the guard, he noticed the rifle casually slung over the man's shoulder; a World War I vintage Lee Enfield. The guard was one of the few Kaluban army regulars. The government obviously didn't arm them as well as they did their mercenaries.

Chen was about ten feet from him when the guard came to attention and unslung the rifle. The language was a cross between the Swahili Al had heard Claude use and pure gibberish. But the meaning was clear: Hold it right there!

"Good evening, pal, sprechin' a little Englaise... English?"

"Notto fu gabbe-do."

"Oh? How about parley vous some Francais?"

"Notto. . .notto, gabbe-do."

"No French either, huh?" Al smiled broadly, warmly, as friendly as he could. "That's good, you big, ugly bastard. That means neither one of us knows what the hell the other one's talking about." He then nodded vigorously and stretched his grin even wider.

The guard frowned, shook his head and looked very ill at ease.

"What do ya do around here on Saturday nights?"

"Notto. . .notto."

"No shit."

Al didn't smoke, but now he pulled out a pack of American cigarettes he carried for such occasions and lit up. American cigarettes seemed to have some magic for the locals and this guard was no different. When Al offered him first one and then the pack, the guard quickly checked the street both ways and the docks behind him.

"Sago mi tuton." The pack disappeared into his tunic.

"Oh, you don't know, stud, but if that meant later, you're outta luck."

Al checked his watch: straight up to zero hour.

He'd already done his recon on the situation. It was twenty yards, down some steep wooden steps, to a small shack where a second guard dozed over a newspaper. The boats themselves were all equally equipped with .30-caliber, tripod mounted machine guns on the cabin roof and 20mm recoilless cannon on the bow.

From the look of it, there were only six or seven sailors on board, scattered between the craft, and one guy with some braid.

Then Al saw Nanos break the surface by the aft ladder of the far left boat. When he started up the ladder Al began jumping up and down and pointing.

"Look, look, you big ape, a creature from the black lagoon!"

The guard whirled, already working the bolt on the old Enfield. When he spotted Alex, there was a lot of screaming, *"Notto, nottos!"*

The butt of the rifle had barely touched his shoulder when Al's knee crashed into his kidneys. There was a grunt and he tottered as the callused side of Chen's hand smashed the bridge of his nose.

He went down and out while Al grabbed the Enfield from his lifeless hands. Alex Nanos was performing a similar operation on a sailor in the boat's aft deck.

The second guard was out of the shack and yelling. Chen dropped him with a slug in the spine. Two sailors were scrambling up the cabin ladder of the middle boat, trying to get to the machine gun.

Al worked the bolt action twice and they were both in the water floating facedown.

Then he was leaping, five steps at a time, down the stairs, pumping a round at anything that moved.

Two more sailors and an officer came boiling out of the bowels of the boat toward Nanos as Chen leaped the rail to his side. The Greek dropped one with a chop to his windpipe while Al made hamburger out of the other's face with the butt of the Enfield.

The officer was clawing a .45 from his hip holster, but he stopped and threw his hands in the air when Chen flipped the rifle around and shoved the muzzle against his chest.

"Jump," Alex told him, "overboard!"

He didn't understand.

Nanos made himself clearer by picking him up by the back of his neck and his belt and tossing him into the water. Then he ducked into the wheelhouse.

"All clear. Get on the gun!"

Chen discarded the rifle and took the ladder in three steps. He jammed the slide to full fire and in seconds the circular 500-round magazine on top of the gun began to rotate. Quickly he sprayed the decks of the other two boats to discourage any heroes. Then a barrage of fire pelted the roof around him.

"Shit," Chen hissed, and wheeled the muzzle around to stitch an even line back at the fiery spurts. "Get hot, Alex. Man, the cavalry's arrived!"

Below, Nanos was feverishly switching the port and starboard generators to start, and checking his oil pressure and cooling flow as the starter engine built up enough revs to kick over the diesels.

"Here goes...do it, baby!"

The twin diesel sputtered, coughed and kicked into life. Glass shattered behind him and he ducked, but not before he felt most of his shirt and a lot of the skin on his back shred from the flying splinters.

Al Chen did a neat gainer through the now-shattered window and lit flat out on the wheelhouse deck. "Too damn hot up there for me, pal. Let's get the hell out of here!"

"I need more revs."

"Screw the revs! Here they come!"

Alex could hear them, then he chanced a quick look and saw them; nearly a whole platoon spilling over the embankment, firing as they ran.

He shoved the throttles to cruise power and sighed in relief as the big boat surged away from the dock. They both stayed low as bullets thudded into the walls around them and the bow cut a crisp vee at the sheer.

"What will this baby top?"

"About thirty-five knots at full," Alex yelled above the humming engines.

"You better try for forty," Chen yelled back. "They got the other two cranked up and they're comin' fast!"

Nanos threw a quick look over his shoulder and roared with laughter. "Wait 'til they hit the channel slot in the breakwater," he grinned.

Then, at full throttle, they hit the tricky channel, slithered through the turn and made for open sea.

"One of 'em stopped!" Chen cried.

"He didn't stop," Nanos replied. "His prop fell off."

The other boat wasn't even that lucky. He made it to the channel, but when he tried the turn, the rudder gave way. The boat did a crazy twist and the bow splintered as it tried to climb the rock seawall. Halfway over, the tanks exploded, lighting up the night sky.

"Cool," Chen laughed, "very cool. Take a letter! Dear Barrabas, your laughing Greek and cunning Chinee have just scuttled the Kaluban air force *and* the Kaluban navy!"

THE ROTOR CHURNED above them as the lights of the airport fell away behind. Claude had slid into the second seat when they lifted off. Now, as the faint string of lights along the coastline gave way to the darkness of the Mozambique channel, Biondi stood behind both seats, carefully studying the various dials on the control panel.

When he was satisfied that the copter was functioning well and the tanks were full, he returned to his newfound friend.

"That's Soviet, isn't it? An AK?"

"*Ja, ja,* goot."

"Mind if I take a look at it?"

The pilot was monitoring both the Dar es Salaam channel and Tomalave. He requested and got permission for an overflight, as per Claude's charts, with no definite destination. He killed the volume from Dar just as Tomalave control started calling his number.

He answered and his face turned white, even in the bluish lights from the dash.

"*Merde.*"

"What is it?"

"I'm to return to base. Invasion or something."

"Stay on course," Hayes said in a low, even tone.

"Impossible, it's an emergency! I'm to return and mount guns. All other aircraft are grounded!"

"I know," Claude said. "We grounded them."

Then the pilot saw Vince Biondi's reflection in the bubble, holding the guard's assault rifle. Behind Vince, on the floor, he saw the guard's body stretched out peacefully.

"Is he dead?"

"No," Claude replied. "We don't really want to kill you. After all, we're all in the same business. All we want is the machine."

"What do you want me to do?" the pilot said, shrugging, knowing that he had just lost his job but also knowing that he would find another in less than a month.

"Crawl back there and put on a chute. Put one on him, too." Hayes relieved him of a fancy-handled Mauser pistol and guided him aft with it.

Vince slid into the vacated seat and tested the reaction of the controls.

"Okay?"

"So-so, but it's okay. Let's face it, this old crate is twenty-five years old."

They said goodbye to the two mercenaries just inland from Dar, watched the chutes flutter open, then Vince banked south toward the Rufiji.

The SOBs now had an airborne contingent.

On the makeshift pier, Claude and the village chieftain yelled at each other over the roar of the chopper's engine and its pumping rotor.

Under the pier, totally hidden from them and the river by carefully arranged jungle foliage, was the recently liberated Kaluban gunboat.

"What did you tell him?" Alex asked, as he and Al Chen handed Claude back aboard.

"I told him we were dropping you two farther upriver, and that you would be watching if anybody shows to inspect the boat before we're ready for it."

"You think he bought it?"

"It's just insurance," Claude chuckled. "The Colonel only gave him half down. He'll wait until he gets the other half before he sends a runner out to sell his information. Let's go, Vince!"

Chen crawled forward and slid into the bucket across from Vince. "Hey, guy, let me take this mother up?"

"It ain't no turbo, Al."

"I don't give a damn," the smaller man laughed. "It's got an engine, ain't it?"

Vince lifted his hands from the rotor control levers under the seat and his feet from the rudder blade pedals.

"It's all yours."

Chen chuckled merrily as he sweetened the mix and away they went, skimming over the water. Claude and Nanos hung on for dear life as the copter's sleds plowed the water under them and the machine itself wobbled like a constipated goony bird.

A hundred yards later they were still spraying water like a huge water skier. Biondi leaned over and yelled in Chen's ear. "You plannin' on sailin' this thing or flyin' it?"

"A little of both!" Chen laughed.

At last they were airborne, just missing a line of trees, before banking north.

"Christ, Chen," Nanos declared, "remind me not to loan you my Porsche when I get it."

"Hell, that wasn't bad," Chen yelled back, "for the first time."

"The what?"

"First time. I never flew a chopper before."

THEY HAD SLEPT and worked in shifts, but it was finished. Barrabas and O'Toole sat quietly smoking on top of one wide wall of the fort's main building. Stretched across half of the rectangle across from them was a newly constructed thatched roof. It rested on rollers so it could easily be moved.

"Almost dawn."

Barrabas nodded. "They'll be here."

O'Toole chuckled. "If Nanos and Biondi didn't stop for a piece of tail."

"You like 'em, don't you?"

"Hell, yes," O'Toole said, a wide smile illuminating his rugged face as he clung to the cigar. "They're gutsy lads. Hell, they've all got what it takes. . . even the woman."

"Especially Lee," Barrabas murmured in agreement, remembering the last night at the ranch and recapping, in his mind, how she had pitched in since they had hit the bush.

The sound of a chopper flying low doesn't carry far. It was almost on them before they heard it.

"Everybody up! Let's go, jump, jump!" Barrabas yelled.

All hands scrambled up the makeshift vine ladders. By the time they were all assembled around the tops of the three walls and the thatched roof, the popping, explosive sound of the helicopter's engine was less than fifty yards away, skimming over the treetops in the moonlight.

"All right, everybody sit down! Spread your legs and hang on to the wall with your knees. And hang on tight! The wash from that rotor could suck you away!"

Lee's self-mocking voice came out of the darkness. "Oh, dear, it's just going to ruin my hair!"

It was the tension-breaker they all needed, and the laughter as they switched on their pocket flashes was genuine. The copter had been overdue for the past hour, and during that time there had been some speculation and even more silent prayer.

Now there was elation as Biondi hovered the big gray

machine overhead and then skillfully lowered it, like some prehistoric bird, into the building's innards.

The twin sleds had barely touched the dirt floor when Vince cut the engine. The side doors opened and all four men spilled out. Everybody on the wall was already tugging the thatched roof over the copter.

"Welcome to the bush, lads!" O'Toole called down.

"Nice country you got," Al Chen replied.

"Anybody got a drink?" Vince asked.

10

They spent the better part of the day checking out the newly acquired weapons, then transferring them, with the ammunition and the rest of the gear, into the copter.

Vince, with Emilio's help, checked out the chopper from stem to stern. Liam and Claude mounted the two .60s, one in each hatch opening.

All of them sweltered in the 100-plus humid heat that seemed to bake them even in the shade of the thatched roof.

Lee Hatton spent a great deal of her time just drawing buckets of water for them. She would barely douse their half-naked bodies, allow them another ten minutes on the guns, and they would be begging for more.

Late in the afternoon, the skies opened. The rain was a solid sheet coming straight down. It broke a portion of the heat, relieving the stress and allowing them to work in longer spurts.

But it created another tension; the late-afternoon rain signaled the swift approach of dusk and departure.

"Whatta ya think?"

"I don't know, Colonel. The H-34 was designed as a troop carrier, and it was designed for twelve and the fliers, but—"

"But what, Vince?" Barrabas said, sucking on his cigar.

Vince did some mental calculations as he wiped his sweat- and grease-covered hands on a rag.

"It's an old bird, been around one hell of a long time."

"I know that."

"Yeah, well, everything on the surface is okay, but I can't tell what might be frayed in the guts. It's a hundred twenty-five miles in, with a full load, then a good fight, then a hundred twenty-five back out again."

"Will it do it, Vince? That's all I give a damn about."

Biondi looked up at the falling rain, his forehead furrowed. "We might have to chuck some weight before pulling out...with the extra passenger, I mean." Then he smiled. "Other than that, Colonel, I'll make the son-of-a-bitch fly if I have to put a rubber band on the rotor."

Liam put the finishing touches on the two sled extensions, then he and Claude hoisted the rocket packs into place.

"Man, I don't know about this," Claude grunted, ratcheting the bolts on one side of the tubing while Liam held the screws on the other. "These babies pack a lotta kick when they go boom."

"That's why we built up the sleds."

"Yeah," Claude nodded. "But this tubing wasn't designed for this kind of stress."

"That flooring wasn't designed to handle anything stronger than .30s, either. Those .60s are gonna shake this bird like a popcorn popper."

"That ain't what I'm scared of," Claude said.

"What is?"

Hayes's teeth gleamed evilly in his dark face. "Dat it's you and me what's doin' the poppin', and we done jettisoned all de chutes to lighten de load. Dat's what got me worried, white man!"

"Well, now, if that's what's worryin' ye, lad," Liam laughed, "just be thankful we got this old bird. You're the one that told me what it would be like if we had to walk back!"

"Liam?"

"Aye, Colonel?"

"How much longer?"

"I'd say about a half hour, sir."

"Good. Final briefing in forty-five minutes."

"You sound as if you really don't care about Noboctu...the man, his background, or why we're putting him back on Kaluba."

Leona Hatton couldn't believe all of this. She had thought that, during the final briefing, the colonel would explain the political core and reason for the mission to the men, as well as the tactics involved in rescuing Noboctu.

Instead, he had cautioned Biondi about which of the three buildings none of the rockets should be fired into. He had laid out careful details to Liam and Claude about where the .60 machine guns should be directed, and he had detailed the procedure for the actual rescue to the rest of them, the ground troops.

Quickly, he went over the plan again, covering just the major points: "Okay, the chopper flies us in over the border. Then we split into two teams. I'll lead one; Lopez, the other. We march in the rest of the way, dispose of the guards, and get in position. If anybody gets dropped, we'll leave them. Then Biondi and the others fly in as our air support. Got it?" Everyone nodded. Barrabas seemed satisfied. "We hit 'em with everything we've got—designated targets only. The object is to get Noboctu back alive."

Still he made no mention of the broader ramifications of the raid; so it was that when Leona found herself alone with Barrabas, sipping camp coffee and waiting for dusk, she felt she had to say something herself.

"Granted, Kaluba is just one very small African nation," she continued, "but its people have known nothing but ignorance, widespread poverty and political instability. Don't you care that by putting this man back on Kaluba you can end coups, mutiny and assassinations and create a whole new world for these people?"

"Doctor, it's not a question of caring or not caring. It's a question of the job. This squad's *job* is to topple the existing power, neutralize the mercenary rebellion and place Noboctu back in front of his people. If I, or any of us, starts worrying or caring what he does after he gets there, then we become politicians, not soldiers."

She just shook her head and pulled back into herself, trying to fathom the enigma of this man and the men he led.

In the time they had spent together, Lee Hatton had grown to respect each of them, even to love them. They were like no men she had ever known. She sensed in them an overpowering, total sensuality, and also a curious gentleness. All of which they seemed totally unaware of.

It seemed inherent in the way they walked, in the way they moved within their lithe, athletic bodies. And when they talked, revealing little bits and pieces of their lives, they grew in her eyes far beyond the mere killing machines she had at first thought them to be.

They seemed incapable of calculated violence for its own

sake. And that was why she had begun to trust them, implicitly and instinctively.

And when she had realized that, she knew that a large part of the psychological gap between herself and them had been spanned. Perhaps that's why she felt she had to retain her own conscience and pass it on to them, because she needed to do what she was doing as a cause, not just a result.

Barrabas watched her face mirror these thoughts as her mind raced over all that had happened. It was as if he could read those thoughts.

How could he tell her that what she believed was a theory, out of some book. He knew reality because he knew Africa and, yes, he knew African politics.

Its basic ingredient was tribal division. Africa was, in reality, a conglomeration of tribes, most with their own language, customs, rituals and beliefs. These tribes all centered in given geographical areas. When the colonial powers sought to divide up Africa, they totally ignored these tribal groupings, and as a result there wasn't a country in Africa that wasn't a forced mixing of opposing cultures.

Consequently, Africa was a hotbed of separatist movements and vindictive governments. Whenever one tribe gained control of the government, it usually set out to eliminate its rival tribes, and usually this elimination was cruel and bloody.

Barrabas had been a part of some of these bloody eliminations. It went with the territory. Sometimes the leader he had helped to put in power had been a good leader. Sometimes he wasn't.

She was talking again, telling him about Joseph Noboctu.

He was born in southern Africa, on the island now called Kaluba, and raised in Johannesburg. His father managed to rise to a token position of some authority in Johannesburg government. This enabled Joseph to gain more education than the average black.

As a youth, Noboctu became involved in the black cause. He felt his own opportunities in life were the result of accident of birth, and he wanted to see all blacks have the chances that he had been given.

He studied political science and sociology at the University of Johannesburg, going on to do his doctoral work at Oxford, England. He then returned to Africa to take up his cause.

He became respected for having mixed his studies in school with summers spent among the varying rural tribes. He actually lived with them, studied them, in an effort to search out common denominators and points of similarity between them that would enable them to band more closely together, to unite.

Noboctu was unflagging in his attempts to find the points of unity from one tribe to another, but no effective unity ever seemed to emerge. It was, however, this background, and Noboctu's ability to bridge many of the gaps that separated the blacks, that made him the central figure for South African blacks.

Because of his unceasing efforts to achieve black rule, Noboctu was one of the most revered and loved black leaders in all of South Africa. Even among the guerrilla movements, his influence could be felt, the only difference between them and Noboctu being that they wanted black rule under a Marxist government.

"So you can see, can't you, that he is the perfect leader to end all this political and military strife? If it's done in Kaluba, maybe other countries will follow suit."

"Maybe," Barrabas replied, gently squeezing her shoulder and smiling. "And maybe not. By the time we know, we'll have another cause somewhere."

Stalemate.

Leona smiled and nodded.

"But, nevertheless, I'll keep my conscience."

Barrabas was about to reply when Claude's voice came out of the darkness. "Ready to roll, Colonel."

Barrabas was up and away. Lee followed and fell in step with Claude as they moved toward the helicopter. It was uncharacteristic of Claude Hayes, but he was smiling broadly.

Then she realized. "You heard?"

"Most of it."

"And. . . ?"

"And right on, lady, right on!"

BIONDI HAD LIFTED empty out of the shell of the building and set down at the farthest end of the clearing to load.

Now, inside the big, banana-shaped H-34 dull blue cabin lights glowed, eerily mixing with the red glow from the instrument panel. The lights reflected off the Plexiglas and made strange masks out of Vince's and Al Chen's faces.

"Pulling pitch!" Biondi yelled.

Black smoke belched from the tail of the big machine, followed by a spurt of blue flame into the jungle night. O'Toole and Hayes were already feeding belts of ammunition into the .60s as the engine caught with a shattering roar.

Everyone squatted along the aluminum floor, using webbed belting attached to the sides to stay in place. Here and there a cigarette glowed between taut lips.

"Ready, Colonel," Biondi yelled back, coarsening the pitch of his rotor to get the feel and make sure the engine was putting out enough power to lift such a load.

"Ready back here, Vince. Let's go."

And then they were rolling across the clearing, much like a conventional plane taking off. The lift was slow, gradual, and perfectly executed; just enough so the sleds would clear the trees.

Biondi checked his gyro and headed northeast at eighty miles an hour.

"How is it?"

"She's lumbering a little," Biondi said, answering the colonel's question without turning his head. "But she's a brave old bird."

"Sounds like she's airsick to me," Nate offered. He disliked flying in anything, let alone a twenty-five-year-old shell-shocked helicopter. Especially when he judged the pilot to have a death wish.

"Don't worry about a thing, Nate," Alex Nanos chuckled mirthlessly. "Hell, Vince damn near won the Monte Carlo Grand Prix in a Volkswagen."

"Who told you that?"

"He did."

The moon had come from behind the clouds now and sparkled brilliantly, as if greeting them. Its light shone through the oval portholes on tense, grim faces. The banter continued, but there was little or no laughter.

Clips were released and nervously slammed back into

weapons. Shells were jacked into chambers of Mauser pistols. Leather tops were popped open from knife sheaths and folded back.

"Talk to me, Al," Vince yelled. Al Chen consulted a map, scanning it with his pocket flash, and rattled back their current coordinates. "Banking," Vince warned, and rolled the machine a little to the right to adjust their flight pattern.

They flew low, just above treetop level where it would be hard to spot them from the ground. Peering out into the darkness, several of them wondered how Biondi could see where they were heading, how they could avoid crashing into a tree or a suddenly rising hill.

But the craft droned on, as confident as a migratory bird, the only sound the monotonous drone of the whirring blade.

"Going over the line, here. Open 'em up, Liam!"

The twin side doors of the copter rolled open and a rush of cool air engulfed them along with the engine's deafening roar.

"Okay, close enough," Al Chen declared. "Look for a clearing."

"Got it," Vince cried.

The nose tilted up. The big chopper slowed and settled to the ground like an ungainly bird. Everyone was standing, bunched near the hatches, peering out.

The tall elephant grass lashed in wild waves across the clearing as the beating rotor caused a hurricane below. Biondi slowed and stopped the descent about seven feet above the ground.

"How's it look, Colonel?"

"Safe as far as I can see," Barrabas replied.

"What's he mean?" Leona asked Claude Hayes who stood beside her, his finger hovering nervously over the .60 trigger.

"Could be anything down in that grass... big rock, tree stump... tear the belly right out of this thing."

She didn't reply, but she swallowed heavily.

Then they were down and everyone was leaping out, each getting a friendly whack on the butt from Hayes or O'Toole.

They quickly formed up in two groups, one led by

Emilio Lopez and the other led by Barrabas. With rifles above their heads, they trotted in columns through the chest-high grass.

Behind them, Biondi had stilled the copter's engine. He would start it up again and come, rockets firing and machine guns blazing, at a prearranged time. And by that time the rest of them would have disposed of the perimeter sentries and be in place just below the camp.

If nothing happened.

They moved out of the high grass into the close-growing jungle bush.

"Paths, Colonel."

"Yeah, I see 'em. Nate!"

Nate Beck jogged to the head of the column. Barrabas removed the portable heat-sensory screen from Beck's pack and plugged it in. Then he passed it to Nate who fiddled with the battery-powered, transistorized controls until the screen came to life. It glowed red with an occasional dark shadow. Beck turned to the others and blurred white images formed on the screen. The sensor had picked up their body heat.

"Nothing yet, Colonel, except us."

"Keep a close eye. Move out!"

They crossed open fields linking one clump of heavy forest to another, tripping over roots and hillocks, their faces, shoulders and chests taking a beating from disguised tree branches and swinging vines. Thorn bushes raked their arms and ankles, ripped through their fatigues and clawed at their bare skin.

There were bridges to cross, no more than decaying tree trunks felled over wide, water-filled ditches. They inched over them, lurching and teetering on bark slippery with mud.

"Colonel!" Nate whispered.

Everyone stopped in their tracks.

"Where?"

"About forty yards straight ahead. One. A pair about forty yards to his right."

"Lopez will get those two from his side. Billy!"

The tall red man nodded and passed his gun to Barrabas. He moved off down the path without a sound, seemingly not even touching the ground.

They waited ten minutes and Nate whispered again. "Emilio's taken one of his."

Five more minutes and Billy Two appeared on the path before them.

When they passed the body, Lee forced herself to look at it. The throat had been cut, nearly severing the head from the body.

But it was Nate who threw up.

In the next half hour, they disposed of three more sentries in the same way and linked back up with Emilio's group.

Slowly the path widened until it became an old, wide elephant walk. The trees opened above them, letting in the bright moonlight. It illuminated the winding road like daylight.

"At least we can see where we're going."

"And they can see where we're coming from. Keep a sharp eye on that thing, Nate!"

A hundred yards farther on, Billy stopped abruptly and threw his arms wide. "Colonel!"

"What is it?" Barrabas edged up to his side and sighted down Billy's pointing finger. "Hell. Mines. Everybody stay put!"

Alongside the road was a metal slab with rows of small, dark objects. Each was topped with a plastic button. Just underneath, attached to the button, was the detonator.

"Antipersonnel?"

Barrabas nodded. "We'll have to defuse a couple of them to get across."

Both of them knew what an antipersonnel mine could do if stepped on. The explosion could tear the legs off or rip open the crotch and the gut, depending on the victim's angle.

Barrabas lay spread-eagled on his belly and crawled toward the tiny pillows of soft sand. He circled the first one, looking for a second mine that could have been planted to booby-trap anyone moving in to pick up the casualty from the first one. He saw nothing and crawled to within inches of the deadly little mound.

Gently, as if his very breath could set if off, Barrabas blew away the top layer of fine dust. The plastic button grew in size until it was protruding from the earth. Then, ever so gently, using his knife, he dug a shallow trench around the metal slab. With all his weight on his elbows, he then lifted the mine out and twisted onto his back.

Billy was there, ready to take it from his hands.

Barrabas repeated the operation twice more, opening a hole for them to pass through. When the last mine was exposed and placed out of the way by Billy Two, there was one long exhalation by the whole group.

"Okay, let's go. Walk only where the ground is hard and step exactly in my footsteps."

Carefully they inched along until no more of the little pillows of earth could be spotted. Then they broke into a trot for nearly two miles until Billy pulled them up short again.

"Everybody into the bush," Barrabas hissed. "We're there!"

"Where?" Lee whispered. "I don't see a damn thing."

"'Bout fifty yards," Nate replied, putting the screen up to her eyes. Half of it glowed a hazy white.

They moved separately, side by side now, instead of in a column. Suddenly the clearing, and its buildings, loomed up without warning.

Hidden away on the hillside, the rebel center was like all African villages had been through their ages of wartime strife. It was so well camouflaged that it would be impossible to find without a guide. Or Nate's electronic eye.

Crouching at the edge of the clearing, just under cover of the bush, Barrabas mentally gave credit to Walker Jessup's intelligence. The camp was laid out just as they had been told.

Three mud-brick buildings, about forty by twenty, were nestled into the hillside on a plateau about halfway to the top. The buildings were thankfully spaced wide apart. Biondi shouldn't have any trouble blowing the two end ones to hell without hitting the center one where they hoped Noboctu was kept.

Around the hill leading up to the buildings were huts. Their sides of woven raffia were supported by poles, and the sloping roofs were made from bundles of dried savanna grass.

A few well-placed incendiaries and they would go up like fire traps.

Between them and the first set of huts were two rows of barbed wire and sandbags piled in front of trenches. About every ten yards, Barrabas would see the snout of a .30-caliber machine gun poking through.

"They ain't fartin' around, are they?" Wiley Drew whispered.

There was no need for an answer. The camp was well entrenched and heavily gunned. And all through it, there was a hushed sense of military efficiency. Mogabe could thank Karl Heiss for that.

"Billy, you know what and when."

"Got it, Colonel."

"Wiley, Emilio, let's go."

The three of them crawled around the perimeter of the camp until they reached the base of the hill. There they used snips on the double strand of wire and wriggled through on their backs.

"They might have mined a few feet inside," Lopez whispered.

"If they did," Barrabas replied, "we'll never know it."

Through the wire, they cautiously and quietly climbed the hill until they found a path leading above the three main buildings. Crouched down they moved along it until they were directly above the thatched roof of the center building.

They were barely in place when they heard the coughing drone of the H-34 in the distance.

Below them, Billy, Alex and Leona heard it too, and fitted cartridges into flare pistols.

"Wait for my signal!"

Men were appearing in the doorways of the huts, their eyes toward the sky. The snouts of the machine guns drifted in the same direction as slides were clicked, setting the weapons to "fire."

Five miles, four miles, three miles, two miles. . . .

"Let 'em rip!" Billy shouted.

11

"There's the flares! Get set, Chen...right one first!"

"Got it," Al replied, mentally sighting the building off the two sleds under the copter as his thumb poised over the red button of the launcher by his side.

"Fire!" Vince yelled.

The pair of 2.75 rockets made a horrifying roar as they streaked through the night sky. Half the building erupted into flying brick and bodies. The roof became an instant torch lighting up the rest of the camp.

Answering fire was already coming from the trenched machine guns and the huts. In the copter, both .60s had begun to chatter. Orange tracers spewed from the hot muzzles and drifted toward the ground as hundreds of spent cartridges and machine-gun belt links poured from the guns.

Biondi lifted the chopper and rolled right for another pass. Two thuds, like steel landing on a hollow oil drum, hit them in the side.

O'Toole and Hayes both screamed in agony and their backs were immediately coated with blood.

"How bad?" Vince cried out.

"Just fragments, the bastards," came the reply.

Two heavy-caliber slugs had left a jagged hole in the side of the machine and torn hundreds of fragments from an aluminum structural beam.

"There!" Chen cried. "On the hill above the colonel... two machine guns dug in!"

"Have they spotted the Colonel yet?"

"Don't think so," Chen said. "But they will when they make their move."

"Dammit," Liam hissed. "We'll get 'em on the next pass. Get this duck movin'!"

"COLONEL, THERE'S TWO BIG ONES on the hill above us," Emilio said.

"I know. Wiley, can you get 'em with an M-79?"

"Pretty tricky, sir. Besides, we'll draw their fire like some goddamn magnet."

"Can we wait for another pass from Vince?" Emilio asked. "Liam and Claude should be able to get 'em with the .60s."

Barrabas looked down at the center hut. Half of its roof was on fire and spreading. It had caught from the explosion next door. "One pass," he said, "but, Jesus, that's all. Start playing out the rope!"

Billy and Alex were lobbing grenades toward the sandbags and the trenches behind them. Lee's and Nate's guns were already barrel-hot from firing in the same direction, trying to draw the fire from the machine guns away from the H-34.

They were successful. Three of the white-hot barrels dropped in their direction. A solid sheet of bullets covered the air inches above their heads. No one person had to tell another to get down. All four of them tried to dig holes in the jungle floor with their knees, their hips and pelvises, and their chins.

Billy howled and craned his eyes down the flattened length of his body.

"You hit?"

"Yeah," he hissed. "Some son-of-a-bitch just shot off my little toe. Slide that goddamn grenade launcher over here!"

AL CHEN'S THUMB pressed the rocket-firing mechanism and the second building went the way of the first.

"I'm gonna hover," Biondi yelled. "Get those bastards on the hill!"

Tracers flew toward the heavy foliage, answering their kind coming like fireflies toward the copter. The interior of the cabin was full of black smoke now from both the guns. They were broadside to the hill, so only Liam could fire.

"Claude, feed me...!"

He didn't have to finish. Claude had already scrambled across the blood-slick floor, falling twice on the spent cartridges, and was feeding a new belt into O'Toole's gun.

"Good God," Hayes cried.

Liam looked, his finger still on the trigger. Claude's prediction had come true. The sheets of aluminum under the tripod had ripped away. The big, powerful gun was starting to dance along the floor.

"Get on it!" O'Toole screamed.

"Huh?"

"Stand on the son-of-a-bitch!"

Claude grabbed two of the support struts overhead and stepped up onto the gun. It wasn't as maneuverable and it still bucked and shuddered under his weight, but it could still be fired in the general direction of the hill.

Claude's face was controlled with pain and the smell of burning rubber joined the stench of spent powder. The barrel was burning the shoes off his feet.

ON THE HILL, Barrabas shook his head and spat a wad of phlegm from his throat. Wide gouges were more than evident in the side of the copter and the erratic fire from Liam's gun was coming dangerously close to where they were crouched.

It was either take their own chances now or lose the copter.

He pulled a handkerchief from his pocket and frantically waved it at Biondi's white face through the Plexiglas. The face nodded and the helicopter lumbered away in a tight arc, only to swerve back at the last minute.

"What's he gonna do?" Lopez said.

"Try for 'em with his last two rockets," Barrabas replied.

"FIRE!" YELLED VINCE, lifting the nose slightly as they groaned toward the ridge.

Al Chen fired and there was a scream of rending metal as the H-34 shuddered and came to a full stop in midair. The rockets flew off, useless in the night sky.

"Jesus, what the hell was that?" Chen cried.

O'Toole was already leaning out one of the hatches. He pulled himself back in and yelled forward.

"The rocket fins came out too soon. They ripped all hell out of the pod!"

"What about the sled?" Vince asked, banking the machine away from the deadly fire from the ridge.

"What sled?" Liam replied.

"YOU RECKON WE BETTER GO anyway, Colonel?" Wiley drawled.

"Yeah. The hell with the ropes. We'll jump. I just hope there's enough roof left to cushion our fall."

"Take off!" Lopez hissed, stepping out from beneath the overhang that had been shielding them from the two machine gunners.

He crouched on one knee, brought up the Armalite and began pumping away in the direction of one of the tracer lines.

His fire was quickly answered by two screams, and a headless body rolled down the hill toward them.

He swiveled around to look for the second gun as Barrabas crouched beside him and leaped out into space, closely followed by Wiley Drew. They both hit the very inner edge of the roof, rolled over, and fell on down to the dirt floor below.

Behind and above them they heard the pop, pop, pop of the Armalite and the answering chatter of the machine gun. Neither of them had time to worry about Emilio, however. They had jumped into their own hornet's nest.

Four black mercenaries and a white man were at the room's two front windows and opened door. Two of the blacks turned when they heard the thud behind them. Wiley cut them both in two with his Armalite while Barrabas got a third in the face.

Before he could get another shot off, the fourth black was on him with a panga knife. He blocked the blow with his rifle and spotted the white man sprinting for the doorway.

"Wiley, that's Heiss. Get him!" At the same moment he spoke, Barrabas brought the butt of the Armalite up against the black's elbow. The panga flew from his hand but he was far from stopped. He continued his forward momentum. They hit belly to belly and sprawled. Somehow Barrabas got turned around and they came up with the man on his back, his arm closed and locked in a viselike grip on Barrabas's throat.

Nile reached over his shoulder and grabbed a handful of wiry hair. At the same time, he twisted hard backward and sideways.

Having loosened the man's hold on his neck, Barrabas

fell to his knees and twisted the head with all his strength. As the black went over his shoulder, Barrabas clawed at his belt.

The man grunted from loss of air when his spine hit the hardpacked floor. But he never got the chance to get his air back. Barrabas's trench knife was clear through his throat.

Barrabas whirled, replacing the still bloody knife in its sheath. "Heiss?"

"Got away, over the hill," Wiley replied. "I missed him."

Barrabas just nodded. "Check in there!" He motioned with the Mauser pistol now filling his hand toward the door to their left. "And be careful!"

Wiley padded to the door as Barrabas bolted to the one on the right. He kicked it open, fell to his knees and rolled through, coming back upright with the Mauser ready.

A heavyset black man was just turning to face him, a mike still in his hand. Behind him a radio was crackling.

"I am Haile Mogabe. I have reinforcements nineteen miles south of here. Lyinga is already on the way. You'll never get him out alive. Surrender now and you'll be treated with leniency."

Barrabas raised the Mauser. "Call them off!"

"I won't do that."

"Then you're my hostage."

Mogabe dropped the mike and reached for the top of the console. Barrabas let his hand grab the Colt and actually start to swing it around before he shot him in the middle of the forehead.

Back in the center room, he found Wiley with a tall, gaunt black man.

"Have you come to kill me too?"

"No, Doctor Noboctu, we've come to take you back to Kaluba."

The politician shrugged. He couldn't see how they would manage that. Mogabe had more troops close by. And the firing outside had not abated.

12

The grenades from the M-79 launchers, coupled with the small-arms fire, were only partially effective. It became a stalemate, with no way for Billy Two to get an opening in the line of fire for the Colonel once they got Noboctu.

"Nate, get Vince up!" Nate went to work with the radio, and seconds later Billy was barking into the mike.

"Is that thing still flying, Vince?"

"By the cheeks of my ass."

"I saw you lose one of the sixties. Is the other one still operable?"

"Yeah."

"Pass a couple of strafing runs across those trenches... oh, my God."

"Yeah, I see!" Vince yelled.

The Colonel and Wiley had taken their dive into the building and Emilio was pinned to his ledge under murderous fire from the machine gun.

"Make that run to cover me, Vince," Billy said. "I'm goin' up after him."

"You're on, Chief...give 'em hell!" Vince replied, and Billy saw the H-34 bank.

"The second he finishes his run, the three of you pour everything you can at 'em until he can come back for a second run."

The chopper came roaring down, with Claude firing the heavy .60 while Liam fed the gun. The guns in the trenches started opening up again but a little more sporadically, telling Billy that their grenades had done some good.

Then he was up and running in the crouching zigzag that was natural to a fighting man. He saw puffs of dirt spurting across his path as one of the machine gunners spotted him. He dropped, lobbing a grenade at the same time.

The exploding fragments got all but one in that end of the trench, and that one was up and after him. Billy brought the Armalite up and squeezed off three shots in quick succession. There was a startled cry, and Billy was running again before the body hit the ground.

He went under the wire where it was already cut and made the hill. As he climbed, he reconned the trenches. They were pretty clear and got clearer with more height. He fully expected to see another machine gun turning his way, but instead he saw the results of Vince's second strafing run.

Bodies were splayed across guns on both sides of the trench. Some of them were moaning, with a kneecap blown away, their stomachs hanging open or a shredded sleeve where an arm had been.

Jesus, he thought, I'd almost forgotten what it was like.

He reached the first path and ran along it until he found one cutting off farther up the ridge. Ahead of him, the machine gun was still hammering away but he couldn't hear any return fire from Emilio.

He chanced another look down. The big .60 had done its work well. There were about fifteen left alive in the trench and they were taking off, led by a white man, and running like hell for the safety of the jungle before Vince could completely finish the job.

Right then Billy couldn't think about anything but his own job. He broke free of the undergrowth and there they were; one standing directing the fire and two lying flat out, delivering it.

He emptied the clip in his Armalite back and forth into the two on the ground and dropped the gun, replacing it with his knife, without breaking step.

The one standing was clawing for a pistol when Billy sank his knife, hilt deep, in his chest. He gagged and, a little blood dribbling from the side of his lips, dropped dead.

Billy retrieved his piece and slithered down the hill, breaking his fall on vines and small trees until he hit Emilio's ledge.

"Don't fire, Lopez, it's me, your red-man savior!" But he needn't have worried about drawing any fire from Emilio. "Oh, Jesus!"

Billy looked down in the ruined shell of the building. The Colonel was staring up at him. "Billy...what is it?"

"Better get the Doc up here, Colonel. Emilio's been hit bad. Looks like he's had it."

VINCE MADE ONE of the more creative landings in the history of helicopter flight. Over the radio he instructed them exactly how to improvise a right sled from the sandbags on the level part of the clearing.

Then he brought it down, left sled first, and, at the last second, tilted the big machine over so it rested, nearly level, on one sled and the bags.

"Well, I'll be damned," Chen cried. "This here heathen Chinee has to salute you: One hell of a landing!"

"It's the next one I'm worried about," Biondi replied, unstrapping and climbing out of his bucket. "C'mon, let's see how much of this crate we've got left."

Not much. Besides a third of the Plexiglas in the front being blown away, the skin on both sides of the copter had more gashes and gouges in it than they could count.

Several slugs had partially splintered a few of the steel-wound control cables, but they could be repaired with clamps. But the big problem was still the rents in the craft's skin.

"That's gonna be hell for handling," Vince mused, surveying the huge rents. "Air flow will be a bitch. We'll never have the maneuverability for top speed."

"Vince, look!" Chen said, holding his hand up after running it down the side of the main pressure hose.

"Oh, Christ."

When they brought Emilio aboard on a makeshift litter, they had a difficult time finding enough floor to stretch him out on. He was a mess. From his crotch to his neck and clear across his chest was blood, dark maroon now, almost black, from soaking into his fatigues and exposure to the air.

Lee Hatton went to work on him right away. Nate remained in the chopper to help.

Carefully but with speedy fingers she cut away the bloody fatigue shirt and washed away the mess from the wound. The slug had entered under his left collarbone and angled toward his left armpit. It had emerged there and made a good-sized hole. Some of Emilio's arm had been taken with it on the way.

Luckily, the slug must have been a WW I or II steel jacket without a fragmenting nose. The wound was clean, but painful and still bleeding like hell.

Lopez screamed when she probed for splinters and checked the bone, but he didn't pass out.

"Jesus, Doc, I can't take it. More morphine."

"You've had three ampules, Emilio," she said, working quickly. "We're limited and you'll need it later." She didn't tell him that he'd need it when she started sewing him up.

"No!" he screamed. "I can't take it!"

His face was twisted in pain and tears were streaming from the corners of his eyes. He'd bitten through his lower lip until it, too, was bleeding badly. The blood ran into his mouth only to be coughed up again to roll across his cheek and chin.

Nate mopped it away.

Leona looked for something in her pack to shove between his teeth and settled on the sheath to his trench knife.

"Just think, it can't hurt worse than when you were hit," she smiled down at him encouragingly.

"That was different," he mumbled around the leather. "I had my mind on something else then."

Her grin broadened. "Then get your mind on something else now." She took his good right hand and flattened his palm over her breast. "Just don't squeeze it off," she said, and spread the wound for packing.

"Damn, any other time..." he managed to get out before one more ear-wrenching scream.

That one did it. He passed out, and his right arm fell to the deck as lifeless as his left.

With Nate's help, Lee started applying pressure dressing to both ends of the wound. They soaked through as fast as she could put them on, and she thought of Claude's words in training: "If you get a wound in the bush...you die."

The hell he will, she thought. I won't let him.

"My God," Nate gasped, and nearly choked.

She looked up. Nate's face was ashen but he was standing his ground, his hands working as gently as her own.

"You all right?"

"Yeah," he nodded.

"You threw up before." She needed his help, but she didn't want him being sick all over her patient.

"That was different. The guy was dead. It's not blood that makes me sick, it's death."

Everyone who wasn't in the planning procedure around the copter was on the alert, their eyes constantly scanning the jungle. Heiss might be crazy enough to regroup what was left of his ragtag group and try to hit them one more time.

Barrabas was barking questions, answers and orders while Billy and Al Chen pored over charts.

"Claude, how's the ammo?"

"Real low, Colonel. I mean we poured some amount of junk on 'em."

"All right. Check around. If you can find extra ammunition for their AKs, we'll dump the Armalites and trade."

"Check, Colonel." He moved off.

"Vince?"

"Sir."

"Can we get this crate up?"

"I hope so, sir. How long I can keep it up is the question. We caught a slug in the right main pressure line on that last pass. A copter can take a hundred hits and still fly, but one hit in the right place and...pssssssst!" He made a thumbs-down motion and went, "Boom!"

"Can you repair it?"

"I did, with a hunk of wood and some tree bark rigged like a bandage. But if the seam starts to split we lose our hydraulics."

Barrabas knew, without being an engineer, what that meant. Hydraulic fluid to an aluminum bird is like blood to the human heart.

"Pack it as best you can!" Barrabas growled, and turned to join Billy Two and Chen at the maps. "Well?"

"Sixteen miles would put them right about there, Colonel and getting closer all the time," Billy said, poking a finger at one of the maps. "That is, if Mogabe wasn't speaking with forked tongue."

"I doubt if he was."

Al Chen made a lot of wrinkles in his face and spoke as if to himself. "If we head southwest, back to the jeeps, and make it...we're cool. But if we go down before we make the lake, we'll have Mogabe's other goons and probably your man Heiss on our ass, and government troops in front of us."

"So, gimme an alternate," Barrabas said.

"I think what Chen's saying, Colonel, is that we've got a better gamble heading due south and trying to get over them."

"You see, Colonel, there's an elephant walk here wide enough for a road," Chen continued. "My guess is that they're hightailing it up toward us right now. If we get over them and we can make the cross into Zambia. . . well, if we went down then, we'd only have one force to worry about."

"Also," Billy chimed in, "that way it's a shorter march to the rivers that form the headwaters to the Rufiji."

"So we forget about the jeeps and get through by boat?"

"That's my vote," Billy said.

"Mine, too," Al agreed.

"Claude!"

"Yes, sir. Found a big stash of Rusky ammo. Everything's shifted over."

"Good. Take a look at this." Barrabas explained the situation to him as Claude nodded his understanding. "How long will it take them to reach us?"

"If what Al says about that road is right, I'd say. . . another twenty-five minutes. And, Colonel—"

"Yeah?"

Claude frowned. "That's probably the real weapons company. They'll have mortars and light cannon. We could never take them on."

"But you think this is the best gamble?"

Claude nodded and looked at the copter. "If what's left of that bird can get us over top of them." He turned back to Barrabas with an even heavier frown on his face. "And if it doesn't, that group's probably commanded by Joshua Lyinga."

"It is," Barrabas said. "So Mogabe said."

"One bad dude. If he gets us, it's worse than the Simbas."

"I know. All right, let's load up. Ten minutes." Barrabas spotted Noboctu standing by the copter's hatch watching Lee work on Emilio. He moved to him. "She'll check you over, sir, as soon as she's through there. We have insulin and anything we need for an emergency."

The gaunt man shook his head. "I'm fine. Tend to your own wounded. That man looks like he's dying. I wish I were a doctor of medicine, instead of philosophy. I feel helpless."

Barrabas disregarded his words and motioned to the papers in his hand. "Did you look those over, sir?"

"Yes. How in the world. . .?"

"That man, there. He's a computer expert. I don't know how he did it, technically, but it doesn't matter. All that information is fact."

"If that's so, there needn't be more bloodshed if you can get me back into my country."

"We'll get you there."

The old man looked up, first at the tall, white-haired man in the cocked beret, and then at the carnage. "This is an awful price to pay for freedom and self-rule."

"Depends on how you rule, Doctor." Barrabas moved back to Al Chen and the charts. "Forget the case for those. Just use the oilskin and carry it in your shirt. We can't afford to lose them."

Chen nodded and moved away. Barrabas chewed the end from a cigar and started discarding what Armalite ammunition he had left and replacing it with the AK clips that Hayes and the others had stockpiled.

Lee appeared at his side, wiping her bloody hands on her fatigue pants.

"How is he?" Barrabas asked.

"Bad. Damn bad. He needs a transfusion and I need to sew him up. He's lost a lot of blood."

"No time now. How long can he last?"

"A few hours. . .but damn few. He might lose that arm."

"How about the rest?"

"Liam and Claude caught hell across their backs. They'll have some nasty scars, but the bleeding has stopped. Billy's toe is a lot more serious than it looks. If I don't get to him soon he'll have complications and one hell of a lot of pain."

She was about to say more, but Vince lumbered up to them. "Colonel?"

"Yeah?"

"I got an idea. . .crazy, but it might help."

"Talk!"

"If I can get up about fifteen feet, so I can get some tilt, the weight won't matter."

"I'm way ahead of you," Barrabas said. "Al, rig some rope slings for yourself, Nate and Nanos. And one for me." He turned back to Vince. "That do it?"

"That'll do it," Biondi said, and moved off.

Lee was still there, staring across the clearing. He followed her gaze. Bodies were strewn grotesquely all the way up the hill. "Wondering what your own body count is?"

"Yes. How did you know?"

"Common," Barrabas said. "You did good. The best. Does it bother you...them?" He nodded toward the corpses.

"No." She faced him. "Oddly enough, it doesn't seem to bother me as much as it should."

The lift-off was rough, with every movable part on the H-34 straining like the muscles of a weightlifter trying for that last ten pounds that will win him a medal.

Its rotor flapping wildly, the big machine finally heaved itself into the air. Ludicrously, the four men below pushed, as if pushing a mired auto from the mud.

But it worked.

Vince got his fifteen or so feet and the H-34 tilted. He gave them thumbs up through the Plexiglas and the four of them backed off until the lifelines, looped like chairs around their thighs, were taut.

Biondi gave the engines more revs. The rotor sped up, swirling the hair on the heads of the four men below and pulling the skin of their faces into stretched, grotesque grins.

Then they were airborne themselves, swinging and dangling from the copter's hatches. All were climbing as the H-34 topped the treeline and turned due south. Chen's agile body was the first one in and the three others quickly followed, aided by the pull of topside hands.

Barrabas charged forward. "How's she taking it, Vince?"

"We're up and moving, Colonel. That's about all I can say."

"Can you get any more airspeed than this?"

"Don't dare. I got the rotor dancing all over hell now to keep it in a straight line."

Barrabas noticed Al Chen making the sign of the cross constantly back and forth across his chest. "I didn't know you were Catholic."

"I'm not. But I already went through Buddha, Shinto and Moses. I'm just touching all bases."

In the back, Billy Two was screaming war whoops as Lee Hatton sutured his toe. "My God, woman, you're killing me!"

"Do you want to lose the foot?"

"I'm debating." Another war whoop.

Alex Nanos wiped something sticky from the side of his face and began sniffing the air.

They climbed painfully to a thousand feet and Vince idled back. "There's your road, Chen!"

"Yeah, and that's not all," Al replied, handing over his binoculars. "About six miles off, Colonel!"

Barrabas adjusted the glasses and sighted along the road. His jaw set in a grim hard line and the artery in his neck swelled.

Three jeeps jammed with men and an armored heavy weapons carrier. The dust they were making had already formed a cloud in the sky behind them.

Alex Nanos felt a steady stream of hot liquid on the side of his face and whirled. "Good God...*Vince*!"

Biondi swiveled his head and saw at once what had happened. The lift-off pressure had been too much for the ruptured line. The rent was three feet down now and hydraulic fluid was pouring out in a steady stream.

13

"Look!" Chen cried. "There's another dust cloud about eight miles farther up. Their column must have been split up."

"Colonel," Vince said, already feeling the fatal sluggishness creep into the controls. "I got to take it down now. If I lose any more altitude we're dead."

"Do it!" Barrabas replied, a plan already forming in his mind.

"I ain't gonna be able to get over both sets of 'em. Shall I try for a clearing in the bush?"

"No. Set it down between them on the road!" Barrabas moved back into the copter. "All right, everybody down on the deck. Make a cushion for Emilio. Doctor Noboctu, you get in the center. I don't want to lose you now."

"How are you feeling, Doctor?" Leona asked. It was the first time she had spoken to him.

"Physically, fine," the black man replied, settling himself full length beside Emilio and cushioning the wounded man's body with his own.

Emilio was awake. "You the guy we came after?"

"That's right, son."

"Got any dancing girls in Kaluba?"

They all scrambled, and when they were set Barrabas joined them.

"Billy, Liam, here's what I want you to do...."

They were weaving and rolling from side to side now like a kite in a high wind. Vince reacted swiftly from years of experience and a thorough understanding of machines, particularly the bitch he was currently trying to fly.

All helicopters are equipped with clutches. The clutch can be disengaged. Vince did this, throwing the rotor into autorotation, hoping that they had enough forward momentum to allow the rotor to freewheel and create more, rather than less, power.

He let out the air he'd been holding in his lungs for a full minute when he felt the machine steady into a glide pattern.

Beside him, Al Chen let out a whoop. "Hot damn, man, you are a genius! Even I could guide this baby in now!"

Vince stayed grim. "Yeah? Well, we've still got to set down on one leg."

"Got it, Colonel," Billy said, unwrapping a pack from where he lay.

"Damn, we must be right over 'em," Alex said. "We're drawing fire."

They could all hear the ping of bullets against the chopper's hull. "Carbines," Barrabas said. "Can't hurt us too bad from this distance."

Alex was peering over the side, out the hatch. "That first mob is already turning around, sir."

Then they all had their hands to their ears from the sudden change in air pressure as Vince nosed over and plummeted toward the ground. Less than twenty feet from the ground, he brought the nose up and they settled into a forward glide.

Then, before he lost the momentum from the rotor, he descended and rolled slightly to the left. The single sled hit and began to grind into the packed earth, sending up a veer of dust like it was water. More and more weight was applied until the sled started to give and finally curled under the belly before it, too, ground into the road.

They made one complete revolution and finally skidded to a halt, facing back the way they had come.

The silence was sudden, like the eye after the rampaging wind of a hurricane.

Barrabas's voice sounded loud even though he barely whispered. "Anybody busted up?" When he got no answer, he got them moving. "All right, everybody out! Rig a litter for Lopez. Billy, Liam, get on those Claymores. When you're set, we run!"

The Claymore mine is curved like a horseshoe. It has an optical sighting device and hurls a blast of shrapnel directionally at the point toward which it has been preaimed.

Liam mounted two of them directly under the copter's fuel tanks while Billy spaced the remaining six on down the road, fusing them as he moved.

In case the exploding copter didn't ruin the narrow road enough, he set two more regular charges that would be set off by the chain stretching from the copter.

"Ready?" Billy panted.

"Yeah, let's go!"

They picked a place fifty-odd yards down the road in the bush to wait.

The rest of them were running, fifty, a hundred, a hundred fifty yards, their legs pumping as fast as they could. The soft-soled shoes made a slap, slap sound on the hard-packed earth that vied with their panting gasps as the only sound.

Dawn, like its brother dusk, broke fast in the jungle. When they had taken off, first light had just been peeking over the trees. Now the sun was up and the locusts were already chirruping, welcoming the dawn of another hot, humid, African day.

A day of intense running and intense heat, for they were all sure they could never take another step and, at the same time, they were all positive that they were going to have to run forever.

"Faster," Barrabas rasped, "faster!"

Two hundred yards.

Impossible. ESP among them all. Can't go any faster. Just broke the record for the hundred-yard dash...twice.

Barrabas led the column. He was ten yards ahead and pulling away. He's an old man, all of forty or more. How can he do that?

Vince, Claude, Wiley and Nate were coming in second, each carrying a corner of Emilio's litter. How can they run that fast and hold that litter straight?

Joseph Noboctu managed to run the first fifty yards himself, beside the litter, holding Emilio's hand in a comforting grip as the wounded man groaned with each step.

Then he began fading. The valves were old, tired, damaged. There was no way he could keep up the pace. His grip on Emilio's hand loosened as he faltered.

Wiley Drew saw the old man grasp his chest as he moved up beside him. "Hop aboard, pal!" he drawled.

"What?"

"Mount up! On my back!"

"No, I—"

"Bullshit! You're the reason he's bleeding like an Arkansas razorback. Now jump!"

Noboctu managed to crawl up Wiley's back, and the big southerner let out a cackle as he wound his arms around the black man's legs and tugged him in close.

"What's the matter?"

"Nothin'. I was just wonderin' what my daddy would say if he saw me now."

Al Chen and Nanos brought up the rear with Lee Hatton. She was taking great gulps of air and her eyes, the irises, were doing funny things. They were disappearing up into her head.

She stumbled and felt herself hurled forward. How did a sheet of sandpaper get in the jungle? On the road? It was scraping all the skin off the left side of her face.

Hands under her armpits and she was back on her feet. Was she running? Yes, she could feel her feet hitting the ground. Each hit sent a jolt up her spine that exploded somewhere in the back of her neck. Her brain? The subcutaneous fascia muscles? Remember it from anatomy class.

You're being a doctor. Be a soldier. Run. Run. *Run!*

Her chest was expanding, she could feel it. She was dropping back. She could see Chen and Nanos. Chen looked like he was jogging through Central Park.

No, it wasn't her chest expanding; it was her heart; probably going to blow up. Will it expand my left breast? Don't need expanding. Always had more than I needed. Don't want to be a sex object, want to be a doctor. Besides; look funny...double D on the left side, a B on the right.

Stop that. Think like a doctor. No, think like a *soldier!*

Only I'm a woman. Got shorter legs. Falling again. Got the sandpaper on the right side this time.

Again she was yanked to her feet, only this time her feet didn't touch the ground, just her toes.

Chen had her under the armpits. They were carrying her, with only her toes now and then touching, and they were catching up with the rest.

Nanos was close to six-four. Chen was five-seven. She was running at a ridiculous angle.

She looked at Chen, eye level. "You have a very strong right arm, Al."

He smiled. When he spoke it was in a very calm voice; he was hardly breathing heavily. "I played with myself a lot when I was a kid."

Barrabas halted them. "Scatter into the bush! Al, Alex, Vince, get up those trees! Claude, get on the .60! Doctor, take care of Lopez!"

They were hidden, waiting, when they heard the first explosion behind them.

LIAM AND BILLY lay in a gully, with the assault rifles resting on a decaying log. The Russian sights, particularly from a distance, were awkward, but they knew the quality of the weapon from past experience. It was the perfect sniper's rifle, so it would take more than one shot, but not more than three, to set off the Claymores and create chaos on the road.

"Here they come, lad."

"I got 'em," Billy chuckled. "Man, just like Custer."

The three jeeps came on full bore, with the weapons carrier bringing up the rear. The first one slid to a stop not more than ten feet from the ruined nose of the copter. Men from all three jeeps were piling out and running before they came to a full stop.

There wasn't a white man among them. Obviously, Heiss and what was left of the home force hadn't caught up yet.

Half the men milled around the copter. Then one of them spotted the endless trail of barely distinguishable footprints leading on down the road. He started jabbering like a wild man. At the same time, two soldiers, crawling around the side of the machine looking for a way to clear it off the road, spotted the Claymores.

Their squawking was even louder.

"NOW!"

Liam and Billy both fired in unison, on semiautomatic. It seemed to take an eternity, but at last the Claymores went off, their steel fragments ripping at flesh and fuel tanks alike.

"Keep firing, lads! Aim for the fuel!"

They did, but there was really no need. The secondary charges went off with an even more ear-shattering explosion. What was left of the machine split in two. The forward section went high in the air, turned over once gracefully, and came down...a direct hit on the first jeep.

Both tanks on the aft section were spreading flaming fuel down the road like twin flamethrowers. Several men, human torches now, ran forward screaming and twisting blindly in no direction. They fell like burning timber into the six-foot crater created by the blast.

Liam and Billy turned their fire on the men as a few of them bunched for a charge around the sides of the copter wreckage.

It was a slaughter. The few that the AK-47 bullets didn't mutilate were ripped apart by the exploding Claymores.

Even with the gentle morning breeze, the air hung heavy with the scent of burnt powder, mostly from Liam's and Billy's guns. There was little return fire. The enemy couldn't find them in the chaos.

They clicked empty, jammed in new clips, continued firing until the entire force fell back behind the armored weapons carrier. It had already tried moving around the one jeep left intact and now teetered at a precarious angle between road and ditch.

"They might make it," O'Toole chuckled, "if they don't get mired in the mud."

"Yeah, but even if they do, it'll take an hour to push all that iron off the road. Let's go."

They faded farther into the bush until they found the semblance of a trail and started dog-trotting. It was doubtful they had been spotted, but they stopped every few yards to detect the sound of pursuers.

Then there wasn't any need for that. Ahead of them they heard the group open up on the second half of the column.

FIRE FROM THE TREES shattered the windshield of the first jeep, killing its occupants instantly. It veered to the right, slid off the road and began to settle in the mud.

The second jeep fared the same, but the driver instinctively jammed on his brakes and spun the wheel. The little vehicle slid sideways a few feet, then gently rolled to its side.

The one-and-a-half ton, its canvas-covered bed loaded with troops, slid several feet like a sidewinder and gently nudged the underside of the upturned jeep as it came to a stop.

Al, Vince and Alex leaped from the trees and took cover in front of the big truck. Claude was in the bush twenty yards behind it on the .60.

As the tarp came up and the men poured off the bed, they were caught in a withering cross fire that annihilated half of them in seconds.

Suddenly from his place by the gun, Barrabas saw Noboctu run from cover and cross the road to the first jeep.

"Jesus, that damn fool!" Claude hissed, releasing the trigger on the .60 for fear of hitting him.

"What the hell?" Barrabas echoed.

Fire from the front of the truck also stopped. The remaining men on the truck bed reacted instinctively to the respite and brought their own rifles up.

Then Noboctu was screaming at them from the jeep.

"What's he saying?" Barrabas barked at Claude. "He's speaking too fast."

"He's telling them that Lyinga is dead, Mogabe is dead, their war is over."

"Not these boys," Barrabas growled.

But he was wrong. Weapons made a clatter on the wooden bed and, one by one, they stood.

Barrabas retrieved his AK and the group sifted out of the bush. Down the road he saw Liam and Billy loping toward them.

"Okay, line them up against the side of the truck!"

It was all too evident what the Colonel had in mind. Vince and Alex were already moving into place beside the road.

Noboctu ran up to him, panting. "No, Colonel, please."

"They're crack troops, Doctor. That's what they get paid for. And Heiss is still back there somewhere."

"They've surrendered!"

"We don't have time for prisoners. If I turn them loose, they'll rejoin Heiss. Do you want to take that gamble?"

Noboctu drew himself up to his full height and nodded. "Yes. Yes, I do. Returning to my country behind your guns is one thing, but this? No. Not over their bodies."

Barrabas looked over his shoulder as Lee Hatton came into view. "You heard?"

"I heard," she replied.

But if Barrabas thought she would take a side, she didn't. Her face remained totally impassive.

"All right, strip 'em and get 'em moving down the road. The rest of you, load up!"

THE TRUCK WAS SLOW but reliable, allowing them to pass south into Zambia by the late afternoon. By dusk they were at the southern tip of the lake, just above Kalambo Falls.

They roared off the main road and crashed through the brush as far as possible before burying the .60 and abandoning the truck.

"Think they're still behind us, Colonel?" Vince asked, as they started through the bush.

"I doubt it. They know where we're headed. They'll probably try to cut us off cross-country."

"Colonel?"

It was Lee. She padded along beside him. "I know. He's worse."

"Worse than worse. He's dying. Claude said there's an aid station at Kalambo Falls. They probably have something there I can convert into an operating room."

"No way. If we stop there we'll be interned and it's all over. There's a village, very small, about twenty kilometers into the bush on the other side of the lake. We'll stop there."

"He might die, Colonel."

"Doctor, you go back there and tell him I've ordered him not to."

Lee slackened her pace to drop back in the column and Barrabas sped up to meet Claude and Billy Two who were crouching just ahead of them. They stood and fell in step when he reached them.

"What about it?"

"The ferry captain was very unwilling when he got a hard look at my fatigues," Claude chuckled.

"But he agreed when you showed him your shillings," Barrabas said.

"Oh, yes. He makes his last official trip across at seven. He'll come back for us after that."

"And land us where we want?"

"Colonel, for enough shillings I think he'd take us over the falls."

It took them another half hour to reach the ferry landing. Three boatmen were lounging around the tiny shack that served as a ticket office and a shelter during the rains.

They took one hard look at the column, the fatigues, the shouldered hardware, and turned away. Barrabas was right. They had seen many mercenary units before, during and after the revolution.

But Claude had already passed among them with *baksheesh*. They would forget they saw this group.

The ferry returned just after nine. The captain and two crewmen paid no attention. The only time the captain seemed to admit that any of them were even on board was when Claude paid him the remainder of the promised shillings and pointed out, on one of his charts, where they wanted to land.

He even managed to totally disregard the mad ravings of Emilio, whose pain had sent him into some other world beyond their reach, beyond Lee Hatton's help.

The village was old and poor. But, despite its state of decay, there was an air of permanence about its straw huts that carried over to their inhabitants.

They treated the group, with watchful eyes, as intruders until they were sure that the gun-wielding men weren't thieves or marauders. When Claude finally convinced them that the unit meant no harm, but would pay for any food or quarters they used, they began to smile.

Then they learned of the wounded man. It was a situation they knew only too well. They quickly made one of the huts ready for him.

The dirt floor was swept clean. Because of being practically a part of the surrounding vegetation, the interior was nearly as dark as the night outside.

Leona immediately took over, barking orders very much as Barrabas had done during battle. "I'll need light, lots of it, and the biggest mosquito netting in the village. Someone take these instruments, gloves, everything here, and sterilize them. The inside of this bag is steel. Boil it, too. Then put the instruments in it with tongs when you come back. And bring plenty of boiling water!"

They stood for a second, a little awe on their faces along with faint smiles. They knew how tired she was. A half hour ago she'd looked as though she couldn't walk another step, as if the next vine would strangle her before she could plow her way through it.

They jumped, and a half hour later everything was ready. The headman, wise in the ways of war and the owner of good eyes, volunteered his own people to hold the many palm-oil lamps. The members of the group that weren't needed filed gratefully outside to slump wearily by the campfire until they might be needed.

Only Nate was retained to help Lee, and Joseph Noboctu insisted on volunteering.

She consulted the tiny notebook of the records she had kept during the training period and stepped to the door.

"Nanos!" she barked.

His eyes flew open and he jumped to his feet. "Yes, sir, ma'am... whatever."

"Take your shirt off. Get in there and lie on the upper cot across from Lopez." He was through the low door like a shot. "Chen, you, Alex and I are the only others besides Claude who can give him blood. Be ready, Claude. You've lost too much already, but it might be necessary."

"Don't you worry, Doc," Hayes smiled at her. "I got plenty, and that boy needs some soul anyway."

She patted his shoulder, ducked back through the door and went to work.

She laid out the six sets of sutures already threaded in their needles, and looked from them to the wound. They didn't look like nearly enough.

She shook that thought off quickly and readied the tubing. From the bag that was now a tray she selected two 16-gauge needles, ripped off the protective covering, and attached them, one to one end of the tube.

"Let me see your antecubital fossa, Alex."

His smile was broad, all teeth. "Does that mean what I hope it means?"

"It means make a fist so I can find a vein in the bend of your arm." He did and she found it.

"Ow!"

"Start pumping, squeezing your fist when I tell you to." He nodded and she handed her last saline bag to a giant native wearing an ankle-length coat, a huge, ostrich feather headdress, and a pair of sunglasses. "Hold this!" He stared at her dumbly. "Doctor."

Noboctu interpreted and the giant's face lit up. He ripped off a string of Swahili at Noboctu, who interpreted again to Leona. "He tells you that he is most honored to assist and if your magic doesn't work he is willing to help you with his."

"Magic?"

"He's the village magic or medicine man."

Leona nodded. "Tell him to stand by." She cleared the needle in the saline tube and started for Emilio's battered arm, thought better of it, and used the great saphenous vein in his inner thigh. "Doctor Noboctu, I'll show you how to take his blood pressure."

"No need, Doctor," Noboctu replied. "I've had to do it for myself hundreds of times."

She opened the valve on the saline bag, made sure the I.V. fluids were flowing well, and turned to Nanos. "All right, Alex? Nate, let's go to work!"

Internal stitches first. They took half the sutures. Nate did a good job pulling, stretching, holding. And, now and then, mopping the sweat from Lee's face.

"Okay, Alex, that's all for you."

"Hey, Doc, Greeks got a lot of blood. I'm good for another gallon, at least."

"Get outta here! Send Chen in!"

Chen entered, his shirt already off. "How's it going?"

"Good, so far." Lee found his vein and gave him the same instructions she had Alex.

"I had the clap when I was a kid, Doc. I won't give it to Emilio, will I?"

It was no time for jokes. But when she looked at the frown on Chen's face, she realized that he wasn't joking. "Don't worry, Al."

She had to stretch the last twelve stitches for the exterior wound. It wasn't good, but it was the best she could do. "That's enough, Al."

He climbed off the cot and she climbed on. "Hey, Doc, what the hell are you doing?"

"Saving Claude for last." She put the needle in her own arm and started pumping, mentally building toward a pint and wondering if she dare go beyond that.

"Doctor?"

"Yes?"

"There's something funny," Noboctu said. "The needle is jumping in his arm."

Lee leaned from the cot. She was still squeezing her fist, but the flow of blood into Emilio's arm had nearly stopped. Then she saw them.

"Get some light down here!"

Three of the palm-oil lamps were lowered close to the life-giving tube.

Clots. The blood was clotting.

Her mind raced. *Emboli. Blood through the heart to the*

lungs. Emboli. . .a shower of emboli to the lungs. Got to stop it. A filter. Need a filter. Saline bag.

She slid from the cot, pulled the needle from Emilio's thigh and began ripping the bag apart until she found the tiny filter. She emptied the tube, fitted the filter, and started to replace it in her own arm, when she slumped against the cot.

"Doc, you all right?"

"Yes, I just—" Her eyes were rolling. *"Claude!"*

Hayes saw the situation at once. He grabbed the needles and tube from her hand, inserted them expertly in his own arm, and crawled up on the cot.

"Where. . . where did you learn to do that?"

"Long time ago," he smiled, "before I started blowing things up. . .on a bloody road outside Selma."

The blood flowed smoothly. She watched Emilio carefully. Color was finally returning to his face, and his blood pressure was distinctly stronger. A few more pumps from Claude's arm, then she carefully removed the life-giving tube, scoured the area with more alcohol and clamped a wad of cotton over the tiny hole. She looked into Claude's dark eyes. "Thanks."

"Any time," came the reply.

She watched Emilio for another ten minutes, then, satisfied that he was sleeping comfortably, emerged from the hut.

Barrabas caught her by the shoulders as she staggered.

"You look worse than your patient."

"Frankly, Colonel," she said, "I feel like hell."

"C'mon."

She couldn't believe it, and yet there it was: a bath. They had shifted the huge cook pot to a dark part of the clearing and filled it with warm water. Liam, Wiley, Vince and Billy Two stood around it, holding tall, wide raffia curtains.

Lee couldn't hold it back. It started as a sniff, and then the dam broke and the tears ran like twin rivers down her cheeks.

"Hey, you're acting like a woman!"

"I know," she mumbled. "I can't help it."

Barrabas pushed her toward the pot and the curtains

closed around her. Gratefully she removed her clothes and sank into the water. In no time she was gleefully splashing like a child.

Then she was giggling. "I wonder," she said, "if anybody was ever cooked in this pot."

"Got it from the headman himself," Wiley drawled. "They ain't ate anybody around here in years."

The four men grinned at each other as the splashing continued. Then it stopped. Silence. Five minutes. Ten minutes.

"Doc...uh, Doc, you okay?"

"Doc, it's awful quiet in there...."

They waited a few more minutes, then Liam took the risk. He lowered his side of the raffia curtain and peeked over.

"Colonel?"

"Yeah?"

"She's out like a light."

THE OVERLAND TRIP to the river was slow but not hazardous. Emilio's fever had broken and he was slowly climbing out of his delirium.

They used pirogues purchased from the river people, and traveled only at night, rowing ceaselessly and silently for hours. There was still a chance that Heiss and what was left of the Mogabe force might guess their route and try to intercept them.

But it didn't happen. On the morning of the second day they didn't stop but used the swift seaward current of the Rufiji to take them all the way down to the village where the stolen gunboat awaited them.

There they all gratefully slept the day and most of the night away.

At three in the morning, they boarded. Nanos nosed out into the river and headed downstream.

One thought was on all their minds; at noon that day, they would be watching the tall, gaunt black man now sitting in the bow mount the speaker's platform at Kaluba's Festival of Elections.

Once they hit open sea, they headed far south before turning seaward. This would allow them to skirt the farthest southern tip of Kaluba: the least populated and hopefully the least patrolled section of the country.

During the trip, Barrabas pumped every scrap of information he could from Noboctu about the few Kalubans still loyal to him. Chief among them were two men who could be very helpful, perhaps absolutely necessary, to the Colonel's plan to get Joseph Noboctu into the city just at the height of the festivities.

Mustala Alisisti, headman of Noboctu's native village, was one who could be counted on. The other was Jacques Mouton, an aging planter who loved the country as much as Noboctu himself.

Nanos maneuvered the big craft as skillfully as a small power launch into a well-hidden cove on the ocean side of Kaluba, opposite the capital of Tomalave. They hastily camouflaged the boat as best as they could in the time allowed, and set off for the village of Noboctu's birth, ten kilometers inland.

The trip should have taken less than an hour. But, because of constant government patrols, it took much longer than that.

Noboctu voiced his amazement. "This is strange, indeed. Patrols are rare outside the capital and almost non-existent on this side of the island. It's as if they were expecting an invasion."

"My guess is," Barrabas whispered, as the uniformed men passed within yards of their place of concealment, "that's just what they are looking for."

The black man's face twisted in puzzlement, but the Colonel didn't explain. The area was clear and it was time to move again.

The rebel force on the mainland was shattered now and the team had retrieved Noboctu. The first two-thirds of the mission had been achieved. Now an unforeseen problem in the culmination of the last third had come up. Kaluba's current demagogues knew that the Doctor was alive and headed for the island. As soon as they found the boat they would know that he had landed.

Barrabas swore to himself. Now he knew why Karl Heiss hadn't tried to cut them off in the bush. His paymaster, Mogabe, was dead. Ergo, change sides and find a new employer. Barrabas was sure that Heiss was somewhere on Kaluba and had already spilled his guts to the men still in power.

The village was more modern than those they had encountered in the deep bush of the mainland. But it was
poor and lacked any modern conveniences, such as plumb-
ing and electrical power. Shabbily built wooden shacks
lined both sides of a quagmirelike street.

The column was halted deep in the trees, far short of the
open space. Barrabas waved Billy Two and Noboctu up to
join him.

"It doesn't look right."

"No," Noboctu agreed. "It's a half hour after dawn
and not one bit of smoke from a cookfire."

"They're in there somewhere, waiting for us," Barrabas
said. "Where would your man be?"

"There!" Noboctu pointed. "The larger house on the
end, the gray one."

"Billy."

"Yeah, Colonel, no sweat. I can circle around there and
come up damn near under it."

"There will be a trapdoor, on the far side, somewhere
between those three support stilts." Billy nodded, and the
Doctor continued. "He will come with you if you tell him,
'Luinda's mistake was not crossing the bridge when Joseph
won the match.'"

Billy melded into the trees.

Barrabas and Noboctu moved silently back to the group.

"Who's Luinda?"

"My loyal friend Mustala's wife," he replied, with a
grin. "She should have married me."

MUSTALA ALISISTI was a wiry little man with a fierce sense
of determination and an even fiercer loyalty to his boy-
hood friend, Joseph Noboctu.

The two men exchanged greetings, and the new arrival
immediately turned his attention to Barrabas's interrogation.

"Yes, we knew at once that Joseph had arrived," Mustala answered, "when they took over our village."

"How many are there?"

"Twelve, well armed."

"And how many of you?"

"Thirty," the man replied, grinning, "and just as well
armed...all buried under my house."

"Can you take them?"

"Colonel, without even the weapons."

"Good. If we can enlist the aid of Jacques Mouton, that should be all the help we need."

"The planter has long been our friend, Joseph," Mustala said. "He will do all he can."

Barrabas spread out a map of the island nation and spoke in low tones.

"All right, everybody gather in close. There are three vehicle roads into the city; here, from the presidential palace, here, from the mercenary encampment, and here, from Mouton's plantation. That will be the only road that's guarded from the ground, here, at these four checkpoints. Mustala, I'll need five of your men...four of them for the checkpoints and one to deliver a prerecorded tape."

"I know just the men."

"The radio station is here, just up from the bay. Take half your force, infiltrate the city, here, and take that radio station. The other half will, with their weapons concealed, gravitate toward Government Square."

"Ah...do we just sit and watch, Colonel?"

"No such luck, Liam. The president, in his limo, will leave the palace at eleven sharp. Since he has two helicopters in the air, the roads have been scanned and the mercenaries that prop up his government are only twenty-five minutes away, his guard should be small. We'll intercept him on the road, here."

"And Mustala starts playing the tape," Noboctu said.

"That's right, sir," Barrabas replied. "That should cause chaos at the square among the hundred regular Kaluban troops."

"A hundred? Against fifteen?" O'Toole frowned.

"We hope not, Liam. The Kaluban army has long been vacillating. Without their mercenary advisors or the president to whip them up, Doctor Noboctu's voice from the tape, and what he will be saying, should confuse them for a while. That's where the time element—and you—come in, Vince."

"I'm listening."

"When we have the president, and the tape starts, the mercenaries will be instantly alerted. From their barracks to the square by jeep is twenty-five minutes. You've got to have Doctor Noboctu, in person, on that square, preferably on the platform, in less than twenty. Can you do it?''

Vince studied the map and looked up glumly. ''In a pickup?''

''That's what the help drives on a plantation, Vince,'' said Barrabas, then continued with a grin, ''but the boss drives a five-twelve Boxer.''

Vince's face glowed.

Nate looked puzzled. ''What's a five-twelve Boxer?''

''What you would have bought if you'd gotten away with that million, Nate. It's a Ferrari that'll do a hundred and ninety flat out, all day long. And there isn't a curve in that road that I can't take topping a hundred.''

JACQUES MOUTON CARRIED his morning coffee out to the veranda and hand-rolled the mosquito netting up before easing into his favorite chair. He looked out at his once proud and profitable part of the world, and sighed at its present state of decay.

He sipped his coffee and thought of the thirty years of his life that lay in near ruination before him.

How many mornings would he be able to sit like this?

''Monsieur Mouton?''

Slowly, not really caring who the intruders were—there had been several of them lately—the old man swiveled his head and shoulders. *''Oui.''*

''My name is Nile Barrabas. I'm heading a mercenary unit to put Joseph Noboctu back on Kaluba.''

Mouton's face didn't change expression. ''Joseph is dead. It was on the wireless...*mon Dieu.''*

''Jacques...my friend.''

''My God...you are alive!''

''Monsieur Mouton, we need three things: a place to hide a wounded man, the use of your tape recorder...and your automobile.''

THE GUARD LOLLED half-in and half-out of the tiny two-by-two windowless shack. He was thinking about the parade and the festivities that would soon begin in the city below.

Only the chosen got to guard the square and be ogled in their dress uniforms by the girls. He wasn't one of the chosen. All this day of days, he would stand in the hot sun, guarding a road where no one passed anyway.

The army was a lousy life.

But someone was passing, walking directly down the side of the road toward him. How did this worker get by the other three guard posts?

"Halt! You will have to go back!"

"But I must go into the city to vote," came the reply.

The guard threw his head up, stretching his neck, and roared with laughter.

Vote, this fool thinks he will get a vote. How can he be a Kaluban and not know that his vote has already been cast and counted, in absentia. This fool believes the elections are for real.

He saw the glint of sunlight on steel just over his left shoulder, but he felt nothing as the knife passed across his throat.

Quickly his body was dragged into the trees.

"Look at that," Billy hissed at Claude Hayes. "You got blood on his collar! I'll take the next one."

The guard was stripped, and by the time a helicopter passed overhead checking the road, he was replaced in the shack and the group was moving through the trees toward the next one.

"WHAT HAPPENS, COLONEL," O'Toole asked, "if those Kaluban troops don't decide to swing our way when they see Noboctu alive?"

"Then they won't turn on the mercenaries when they arrive."

Liam hunkered down farther behind the fallen trees where they had hidden themselves, and thought about this.

Barrabas chuckled. "They will, Liam, as long as Vince gets him there ahead of the mercenaries. First leader on the scene is the new leader. That's how coups are made around here."

"Colonel!" It was Wiley, high in a tree above them. "He just came out. There's four men to a jeep, two jeeps...one in front of the limo and one behind."

"Everything ready up there?"

Wiley nodded and patted the swaying butt of the tree they had topped earlier. He was holding it by a line he had already snaked through the crotch of another tree. Barrabas glanced across the road, high up in another tree.

Nate Beck gave him a thumbs-up sign. Barrabas smiled to himself. If the electronics wizard was out of his element high in a Kaluban tree, he didn't show it, as he tightly gripped the rope holding the other end of the tree. The jeep roared down the drive, scattering rocks until it hit the road with its tires screaming. On the bucket seat opposite the driver lay a tape recording recently made by Joseph Noboctu, relating to his people how they had been swindled time and again during the past three years and urging them to lay down their arms. He had never sounded more persuasive.

Behind the big house, in a small shed that served as a garage, Vince Biondi turned the key on the Boxer and felt the low rumble of power sift through his legs to his groin.

The car was the fantasy of every young boy who had ever dreamed of owning or driving the ultimate in high-performance machinery.

Beside Vince, Joseph Noboctu fastened his seat belt and accepted the stop watch from Biondi.

"It's twenty-four miles."

"Sixteen minutes, Doc, I guarantee it. We got a five-litre, twelve-cylinder flathead back there that will fly. In fact, if this baby had wings I wouldn't even need the road."

Vince let his foot toy with the accelerator, and the resultant roar gave even the gray-haired black man a thrill that brought a smile to his face.

Martial music blared from the two studio speakers. An engineer adjusted his levels and yawned, wishing the day was over rather than just beginning.

He checked the clock. The first newscast of the day, the one predicting the government's popular return to power, was five minutes away. And, as usual, the government man who was to read it was late. He was probably hung over from last night's celebration. A celebration of "counting" the votes that supposedly wouldn't be cast until this afternoon.

The door behind him opened and he turned to urge the man to hurry. He found himself staring into the muzzle of a pistol.

"We have taken over the radio station. Your five comrades are below in our custody." The man handed him a slip of paper and a reel of tape. "When I tell you, you will read this, several times, over the air. Then you will play this tape!"

"But—but, I'm an engineer. I'm not an announcer."

"You will read it anyway, or I will shoot you."

He looked down at the slip of paper. ATTENTION! JOSEPH NOBOCTU IS ALIVE. JOSEPH NOBOCTU IS ALIVE AND ON KALUBA.

"Do you understand?"

"Quite clearly," the engineer smiled in reply, reaching for the prepared government tape and tossing it in a wastebasket.

IT WAS THE FIRST TIME Al Chen had ever felt uncomfortable in civilian clothes. It was because both men in the car they had stopped were nearly the size of Nanos, who now stood beside him at the customs gate, looking natty in a European, three-piece pinstripe.

"Ghanian 6G14 is hangar three," the official said, pointing it out.

His English was very broken but Al understood enough as they were waved through. In his hands he carried 6G14's release papers, a paid voucher for storage and fuel, and a customs release for the aging B-25.

They entered hangar three and spotted the plane. It looked ready to fly.

They were just passing the hangar office when a solo man in blue coveralls came loping toward them.

"Sie! Es ist Sie! Ich weiss es!"

"Alex, what's he saying?"

Alex quickly interpreted as the man went on sputtering in German and waving his arms. "He thinks you look just like the guy who fucked up the copters and the two MiGs. He wants to know what you did to the MiGs. They still can't get them started."

"Alex," Chen said calmly, "this is a very dangerous man."

Alex stepped in close to the mechanic. In one smooth movement he pulled the silenced Mauser from beneath his coat, jammed it into his gut, and tilted the barrel upward under his rib cage. There was a muffled sound like the popping of a champagne cork, and the mechanic slumped into Nanos's arms.

"In here," Chen said. "It looks like a john."

While Alex propped him up in the lone booth, Chen rummaged in a storage room beside the door. "Hey, Alex, what's this sign say?" It was lettered in three languages.

"Out of order."

"Perfect."

With the door locked and the sign hanging from the knob they headed for the plane.

THE HUGE LIMB fell directly across the hood of the lead jeep. When its occupants offered resistance, Wiley and Nate cut them down from their perches.

Seeing the fate of their comrades, and the readiness of O'Toole and Barrabas to deal them the same fate, the men in the second jeep threw down their weapons.

"Mr. President, I know this limousine is too heavily armored for small arms. But if you don't have these doors open in ten seconds I'll instruct my men to put five pounds of plastic explosive under the gas tank. And we will blow you to hell.''

The doors, all four of them, opened immediately.

"No, not you, Mr. President. You stay inside. All right, get these men to clear the road!"

"Colonel." Liam was looking at the sky.

Barrabas looked up. A helicopter was hovering above them at five hundred feet. He was sure the pilot was already radioing the mercenary barracks.

A CROSS between John Phillip Sousa and a steel band blared from the car radio as Vince eased out the clutch and rolled around the corner of the big house.

Then the music stopped and a faltering voice was shouting, "Attention, attention! Joseph Noboctu. . . .''

"Hang on, Doctor, and pop that watch! Here we go!"

Both men sank deep in the soft leather as Biondi tromped the accelerator. The big five-litre engine roared with power, and they lurched forward like a jet being catapulted from the deck of a carrier.

The tires screamed, but the car rocked hardly at all as they hit the asphalt of the road and Vince stiff-armed into the first curve. He geared up all the way through it and they sailed out of it at over a hundred miles an hour.

Three more curves, with Vince's foot never leaving the floor, they sailed under the raised railing of the first guard station.

The guard was smiling and waving them on.

"Time?" Vince barked.

"My God," Noboctu gasped. "Three minutes. We've come five miles!"

"Too damn slow," Vince growled.

MAJOR ORBIN WEISAL had been in Africa his whole life. It was only natural that when the English, Dutch, Germans, and his own native Belgians had given up their colonies, Weisal would stay on as a mercenary. He had fought the colonial wars so long he knew nothing else.

"Major, you will forgive me, but you are a fool!"

Weisal's hands made fists under the desk in his lap as he

ground his teeth and stared at Karl Heiss. He didn't like the man but his orders were to shelter him.

"Herr Heiss, I have my orders. The President does not want a show of white faces—particularly in uniform—around the reviewing stand."

Heiss spat on the floor, further enraging the other man. "Then mark my words, Weisal, you'll be out of a job by noon and lucky to be alive tonight."

A young Frenchman rushed into the office, saluted smartly and gasped out his message. "Begging the Major's pardon, the helicopter reports that the President's car has been stopped. The pilot thinks he's been taken."

"My God. And Noboctu?"

"No sign of him, sir. But—"

"Yes? Dammit, speak up, man!"

"Helicopter Two reports that the planter Mouton's red car is heading toward the square with a white driver and a black passenger, and—"

"That's him," Heiss hissed. "It has to be!"

"And the checkpoint guards aren't stopping the car."

Weisal leapt from behind the desk. "Everyone on alert! We move at once!"

"I told you," Heiss hissed as Weisal passed by him, buckling an automatic around his middle.

Major Weisal had one thought besides reaching the square as he stepped into the lead jeep. He thought of turning at the last minute and killing Karl Heiss, who stood ten yards away, smiling smugly.

But the jeep lurched away and instead he turned to his radio operator. "Get Helicopter Two up and tell him to destroy Mouton's car!"

Heiss watched until they were out of sight, then climbed into the remaining jeep. He followed their dust for ten miles toward the city and then turned abruptly off, heading for the airport.

Lousy luck, he thought, *should have gotten payment in advance. But Brookler will be holding my share of the Mogabe sale in Amsterdam.*

THE .30-CALIBER BULLETS coming from Chopper Two stitched a line in the road within a foot of the car. Then the pilot stalled and rolled around for another pass.

"Jesus, here he comes again!" Vince yelled. He had the Ferrari flat out now and was quickly climbing toward the 190 mph peak.

At that speed it was hard to swerve and veer, but he tried. Bullets from the second pass thudded across the trunk, and Vince geared down for the last curve that would take them to the long, downhill straightaway into the city.

He came out of it two gears down and quickly found high again.

There was an audible gasp from the man beside him when they screamed out of the curve.

"Are you all right, Doctor?"

"Yes," came the weak reply. "But I'm scared to death."

"You mean the copter? Don't worry, he missed the only chance he had. I can literally outrun him now."

"No, not the copter," Noboctu replied. "It's you! You!"

IN THE LIMOUSINE, Barrabas was giving the president two choices of action. The first was to sign the powers of attorney and the release forms that would send the vast amount of money he had milked from the Kaluban economy back to the country. If he did, then they would get him out of the country.

If he didn't, they would continue on to the square and throw him to the mob.

The president was unruffled. "I'll withhold my decision until I see whether your gamble succeeds, Colonel."

The car rocked to a halt on a rise overlooking Government Square. Barrabas jumped out and brought binoculars to his eyes.

VINCE KEPT THE CAR in low, idling through the cheering crowd with watchful eyes. The fifteen or so men that Mustala had sent were closely packed around them, parting the crowd as they moved.

The uniformed men around the reviewing stand were of two minds; half of them looked confused, and the other half had already given up and were cheering Noboctu with the rest of the crowd.

Vince braked by the stairs leading up to the platform. "How's my time?"

Noboctu smiled as he stepped from the car. "Sixteen minutes," he said. "Thank you!"

Biondi watched the sagging shoulders straighten, the back stiffen, and the head raise as Noboctu reached the microphone.

THEY WERE A MILE AWAY but the deafening roar of the crowd that greeted Joseph Noboctu's words could be heard clearly from five times that distance.

"Well, Mr. President?" Barrabas said.

"We shall see!"

"I DON'T SEE the President's limousine, sir!"

"Use the bullhorn. Order the crowd dispersed," Weisal shouted, standing up in the front of the jeep.

His mind was racing, trying to sort out the immediate problems and find solutions to them. The first thing that had to be done was to arrest this Noboctu and then find the president.

The bullhorn wasn't being heard above the crowd. Then Major Weisal saw the Kalubans breaking through the crowd toward them. Their intent was all too obvious.

Treacherous, traitorous bastards, Weisal thought. He turned to the man on the bullhorn. "Order the men to fire at will!"

But the first shots came from the advancing black troops. And the greater part of the volley blew apart the standing target of Major Orbin Weisal.

"THERE ARE YOUR SIGNED PAPERS, Colonel. You do guarantee me safe passage out of the country?"

"That was Joseph Noboctu's wish, Mr. President."

"Very well. Shall we be going?"

BILLY TWO AND CLAUDE finished laying the grenade line along the fence separating the end of the runway from the road and returned to Leona and Emilio in the panel truck.

"Will it work?" she asked.

"Doc, of course it will work. Just a gentle tug, out come all the pins, and boom goes the fence."

A roaring engine outside the truck brought Billy to the back windows. "It's Vince in his hotrod and here comes the limo!"

THE CONTROL TOWER OPERATOR WAS speaking in German. "6G14, you are not cleared for takeoff. I repeat, 6G14, all planes are temporarily grounded. You are not cleared for takeoff."

Alex interpreted for Chen.

"Gimme that thing." Chen grabbed the mike from Alex as he continued to taxi toward the end of the runway.

"There they are!" Alex yelled, pointing beyond the fence.

"6G14 to tower. You speak English, buddy? Over."

"*Ja, ja,* 6G14. You will return to the hangar."

"6G14 to tower. Since you speak such good English, buddy, I'm sure you'll understand my final transmission. Fuck you! 6G14 out."

Chen shut the radio off and worked the rudders with his feet to swing the tail around. He was half through his checklist and adjusting the prop pitch and fuel mix when the fence behind them disintegrated, and the rest of the SOBs plus one started pouring through.

KARL HEISS WASN'T PANICKED, but he wasn't exactly calm either. First he'd been informed that all commercial flights were cancelled, and now the guard on the military side of the airport wouldn't let him through.

"You fool, I'm with Major Weisal's mercenary command!"

"I can't help it, sir. My orders."

Then Heiss saw the B-25 at the end of the runway and the crowd pour through the hole in the fence. Among them, he saw Nile Barrabas. He would know that white hair anywhere.

Ten feet away was a jeep.

Why not? Barrabas always had more heart than brains.

His fist caught the guard on the point of the jaw and he was sprinting for the jeep.

"EVERYBODY'S ON BOARD, let's move it, Al!"

The plane started rolling.

"Colonel, some guy just jumped out of a jeep. He's running toward us!"

Barrabas moved to the open hatch. It was Heiss, twenty feet away and running like hell.

"Barrabas, give me a ride!"

"What for, Karl?"

"What the hell," Heiss panted. "The war's over. Give me a lift. I don't want to end up in some jail down here. You know what that's like."

Barrabas did know what that was like. He did not reach out his hand. Heiss ran harder.

"Al, get us the hell out of here!" roared Barrabas.

Chen jammed the throttles forward, temporarily blinding the gunner with the prop wash, and they were rolling down the runway, Heiss still running after them, gesticulating hopelessly.

"BEST THING OL' BILLY ever did, thinkin' of bringin' along a case of this stuff," Al Chen said, lifting the champagne bottle from between his legs.

"Hey, take it easy on that stuff," Vince said from the second seat.

"Don't worry, old son, this Chinee can drive drunk or sober. And besides, only thing gets me drunk is Japanese sake."

In the rear of the plane the rest of them were all sprawled out, each with their own thoughts, wondering what they would do until the next call from the Colonel.

Wiley, Alex and Nate were already planning nights on the town in gay Paree.

Liam had a mother in Cork that he hadn't seen for years. He might buy her a new house.

Emilio was thinking about investments, maybe a bar or a hotel in southern Spain. The tourist business was getting big down there. It was sort of nice to think about putting something away for his old age now that the Doc said he would probably live to have one.

Billy Two would head back to the States for a while. Maybe Washington and a little lobbying against his family who wanted to strip-mine the tribe's lands.

"What are you gonna do, Doc?" Claude asked.

"Renovate the ranch," she smiled. "Make it the kind of place my father dreamed it would be."

"That'll take a lot of work."

"I know."

"Couldn't use one hell of a carpenter for a while, could you?"

"You're damn right I could," she laughed.

Barrabas listened to them all and smiled. What would he do? Erika, for a while. Maybe Paris. She loved buying clothes in Paris. They would spend a few days, maybe weeks together.

Maybe longer.

Then the next ad would be in the *Herald Tribune*, and it would all start again. Jessup was right—there would always be a need for men like them.

He just hoped it wouldn't be too long.

UNITED STATES ARMY
IN RE: COURT-MARTIAL OF
COLONEL NILE BARRABAS

INVESTIGATIVE REPORT

Defense Investigative Service
Forrestal Building, Washington DC 20314

PP 201 15 May 1975

SUBJECT: Colonel Nile Barrabas
Military Attaché Liaison Office, Saigon

TO: General Staff US Army

Attached are promotion nominations and a newspaper profile, together with the investigation reports of the DIS agents regarding outstanding charges of insubordination, failure to obey orders, and conduct discrediting to the United States Army, which have been preferred against Colonel Nile Barrabas US Army.

The evidence adduced in the DIS investigation supports the charges against Colonel Barrabas. However, further investigation as to the role of Karl Heiss CORD operative is required. Colonel Barrabas is presently in custody awaiting the decision of the Court-martial Board. Karl Heiss unfortunately evaded custody at Tan Son Nhut Airport and has not been located.

Charles Ross
Director DIS

UNITED STATES ARMY
SAIGON

Report of
Awards and Decorations Investigations Committee

CITATION: Captain Nile Barrabas US Army,
Company C, 5th Special Forces Group Airborne: Silver Star

Place and date: southern Quang Nam Province, Republic of Vietnam, 17-18 May 1967. For gallantry in action at the risk of his life on a reconnaissance-in-force mission in Quang Nam Province. Company C was inserted into enemy territory to locate and destroy the enemy. Captain Barrabas courageously led his men against several enemy patrols and basecamps, successfully destroying opposition which impeded company advances. On the evening of the 17th of May, lead elements of Company C came under heavy automatic weapon and machine-gun fire. Captain Barrabas immediately moved into the threatened area to direct the defense of his company. While waiting for reinforcements, Captain Barrabas saw that his men were pinned down by enemy fire from a concealed bunker some 30 meters distant. Captain Barrabas crawled across unprotected ground for this distance and singlehandedly destroyed the bunker with grenades. During this action he received a bullet wound in his left arm and shrapnel wounds in his legs. Captain Barrabas ordered his men to secure their position against enemy fire and wait for airborne reinforcements. During the night, oblivious to the pain from his own wounds, Captain Barrabas distributed ammunition and encouragement to his men and ensured the security of the company's position. Through his gallantry and exemplary conduct in the face of enemy fire, Captain Barrabas was able to protect his company and hold off an enemy force superior in numbers until reinforcements arrived the next morning. He has brought great credit to himself, his unit and the United States Army.

To the best of my knowledge and belief the facts presented in this citation are true and as far as can be determined all pertinent facts have been presented.

16 June 1967

_____   _____
date   Major John Harden
                   Awards and Decorations Board
                   1st Cavalry Division (Airmobile)

UNITED STATES ARMY
SAIGON

Report of
Awards and Decorations Investigations Committee

CITATION: Captain Nile Barrabas US Army,
Company C, 5th Special Forces Group Airborne: Silver Star.

Place and date: Ap Dong, Republic of Vietnam, 19 December 1967. For gallantry in action during an airmobile assault as he led his company across a rice paddy, Company C's rear flank was ambushed by hidden enemy soldiers armed with mortars, Claymores, grenades and machine guns. With heavy fire coming from three sides, Captain Barrabas led his company to a small island in the center of the paddy to establish a defensive perimeter. Seeing that several soldiers had fallen in the initial ambush, Captain Barrabas, with no thought for his own safety, ran across the rice paddy to hoist one of the wounded soldiers and carry him back to safety. Captain Barrabas made three such trips, coming under intense hostile enemy fire, until the fallen soldiers had been brought to safety. On the last trip Captain Barrabas was wounded in his right shoulder and forearm. Through his gallantry and intrepid bravery Captain Barrabas saved the lives of three of his soldiers, bringing great credit upon himself and upholding the traditions of the United States Army.

To the best of my knowledge and belief the facts presented in this citation are true and as far as can be determined all pertinent facts have been presented.

11 January 1968
date

Major John Harden
Awards and Decorations Board
1st Cavalry Division (Airmobile)

*Report of
Awards and Decorations Investigations Committee*

CITATION: Captain Nile Barrabas US Army,
            Company C, 5th Special Forces Group Air-
            borne: Distinguished Service Cross

Place and date: near Quang Ngai, Republic of Vietnam, 14 January 1969. For extraordinary heroism in connection with military operations against an armed enemy of the United States. Responding to a monitored emergency call while aboard a helicopter gunship in the Quang Ngai area, Captain Barrabas and the pilot encountered a platoon of men from Company C trapped on a beach under intense hostile fire and in imminent danger of being overwhelmed by a large Viet Cong force. A number of enemy were in the open, bayonetting and beating the trapped soldiers. Captain Barrabas ordered the helicopter pilot to hold the helicopter steady while he directed automatic weapons fire against the enemy, driving them back into the jungle and killing many. The Viet Cong forces returned fire, killing the helicopter pilot. Without hesitation Captain Barrabas seized the controls of the aircraft, then launched a rocket and machine-gun retaliation against the enemy. He brought the helicopter down into a position where it acted as a shield, allowing his crew to retrieve the wounded soldiers on the ground. Enemy forces continued to rush the aircraft during this rescue operation, but were repeatedly driven back by automatic weapons fire directed against them by Captain Barrabas. When the rescue operation was completed, Captain Barrabas flew the dangerously over-loaded helicopter out over the sea. On two occasions the aircraft almost slipped into the water before Captain Barrabas got it aloft, demonstrating exemplary flight skills. Captain Barrabas's determined heroism and excellent piloting ability saved the lives of American soldiers and brings the highest credit to his unit to the United States Army.

To the best of my knowledge and belief the facts presented in this citation are true and as far as can be determined all pertinent facts have been presented.

8 February 1969 _____
date   Major John Harden
                        Awards and Decorations Board
                        1st Cavalry Division (Airmobile)

clipping

US ARMY NEWS (Vietnam edition) April 1st, 1969
page 9

MILITARY PROFILE: MAJOR NILE BARRABAS
MAC
by Corporal Edward Bloom

A few years ago the word filtered down from Quang Nam
Province that Company C of the 5th Special Forces Group
Airborne had a new CO and were calling themselves the
SOBs. It stands for "Sons of Barrabas"—among other
things—and their new captain was none other than Nile
Barrabas, a soldier and an officer who has a reputation as
one of the toughest, roughest, meanest SOBs anywhere,
and his soldiers say they'll follow him to hell or back.

But it looks as if Captain Barrabas's combat days are
over at least for a while. Four Purple Hearts, two Silver
Stars, and a Distinguished Service Cross later, he's been
promoted to Major and transferred to Military Assistance
Command for intelligence work in Saigon.

"I'll miss the combat, the patrols, and my men," Major
Barrabas told *Army News*. "But if the Army feels they
need me at MAC, then I guess that's where I go."

Major Barrabas is one of those rare officers who began
as an enlisted man, and later attended West Point Military
Academy, graduating near the top of his class. He's had
specialized training in jungle warfare and intelligence. We
asked Major Barrabas why the "SOBs" were able to con-
sistently clean up VC and NVA activity in areas that had
resisted prior attempts at pacification. Says Major Barrabas, "High body counts aren't good enough. In order to
be successful you have to set up your theater of operations
the right way. It's most important to establish healthy
liaison with the local people. My company worked a lot
with the Rhade tribe of the Montagnards. I learned to
speak their language and I learned their warrior customs
and they learned to repect ours."

On one occasion, Major Barrabas and a few men from
Company C were invited to a Rhade feast to celebrate a
victory against a VC unit which had been harassing the

villagers. One dish was chicken eggs which had been in-
cubated to the point of hatching; just as the little chicks
begin to poke their way out, the eggs are plunked into boiling water. These are a real delicacy among the Rhade
people, but C Company soldiers watched with horror as
their hosts ate them. It was Major Barrabas who, for the
sake of respecting indigenous customs, took the plunge
and popped one of those baby chick eggs into his mouth.
His officers then followed suit.

"A few minutes with an unpleasant taste in your mouth
is a small price to pay for taking Rhade warriors on
patrol," says Major Barrabas. "They have about sixteen
jungle senses we can't even imagine. They can smell an
NVA patrol a mile off through dense jungle and they have
an uncanny ability to ferret out punji stick booby traps.
They've saved a lot of American lives, which means the
lives of a lot of my men."

And saving lives is what Major Barrabas is famous for.
C Company has lost 12 men in two years. When *Army
News* asked Major Barrabas about this, his face looked
pained. "It's low," he says, "compared to the amount of
combat action we've seen. It's my job to kill the enemy and
get my boys through their term of duty alive. I work hard
at it. I think they hate me for it sometimes because I'm
hard on them. But as long as they follow my orders, they'll
stay alive. When they don't, that's when they get killed.

"I use a different formation from what we were taught
in school because it works better in the jungle. Some of
those hot lazy days out there, everyone starts to feel that
nothing's going to happen. Then there's a shot. The guy on
left flank got it. Now one of the rules out there is that if
you get shot, or wounded, don't yell. Just sit and wait and
we'll come and get you. Suddenly I hear the guy yell,
there's another shot and he stops. When we got there he
was dead. If he hadn't yelled, he'd be alive today.

"That's when I tell the men, it's too bad what happened,
but this guy broke the rules so he died."

The word from Quang Nam Province was that if you
wanted to fight a real war you got into Company C. It's
because it's full of the finest fighting men in the US Army,
put there by Major Barrabas. He was known as a man who
on more than one occasion risked his life to save the lives

of his men. His decorations prove it. "None of Company C's success was possible without the men," says Major Barrabas. "I led it. I got decorated. But they did the fighting."

Major Barrabas has another reputation—as the Captain who goes for "church music," and he's been known to turn it up full volume on his tape deck and let it waft through the air of Ban Me Thuot Special Forces Camp all Sunday long. Major Barrabas laughs. "On one of those rare Sundays when we're not on patrol I guess that's true. I like classical music, especially when it's accompanied by a lovely woman, candlelight dinner and a good wine. I acquired a taste for that kind of thing at West Point. I have two weeks of leave coming up in Tokyo, and I'm going to indulge!"

There's one other part of the legend of Major Barrabas that *Army News* wanted to ask about. Apparently when he puts through a supply requisition for equipment, he takes about twice as much ammunition as required and a few bottles of good Scotch. "The ammunition," he says, "is so that when another Company we're working with runs out, we can keep on shooting to cover their asses. And we've had to do that on more than one occasion." And the whisky? "Well, first of all it's great to sterilize cuts and scratches that are prone to jungle rot out there. And if we don't need it for that, well, we drink it to kill the worms."

Does Major Barrabas like his reputation as a "fearless" leader? He tells us, "I'm not fearless. There'd be something wrong if I was. Fear keeps you on your toes. Bravery doesn't mean fighting without fear. It means fighting past it."

With that final comment from one of the fine fighting men in Vietnam, *Army News* salutes Major Nile Barrabas. Good luck at MAC!

Defense Investigative Service

INVESTIGATION REPORT: COLONEL NILE
BARRABAS, U.S. ARMY, APRIL 1975

Colonel Nile Barrabas was posted to the Military Attaché
Liaison Office in Saigon, Republic of Vietnam, in June
1973, where he performed his duties in an exemplary man-
ner until April 1975. Colonel Barrabas was responsible for
liaison with the Military representatives attached to the
embassies of allied and non-allied powers. His duties included expediting information between the armed forces of
the United States and the interests of other sovereign
states. As well, an important part of Colonel Barrabas's
duties included collecting and assessing "rumor" and
"gossip" among foreign diplomatic agents and relaying
such information to MAC. By all accounts, Col. Barrabas
was adept at his work.

In late March 1975, when it became apparent that the
defense of the Republic of Vietnam by the Vietnamese
Armed Forces was collapsing under the offensive from the
NVA, Col. Barrabas was approached by a member of the
Hungarian diplomatic corps who had, in the past, provided information of considerable value to the American
government. Colonel Barrabas was informed that 20
American Air Force pilots who had been taken prisoners
of war by the NVA were being held in a temporary camp
near Da Nang and were being marched to prisoner of war
camps in North Vietnam. It was conjectured that the airmen would be used as pawns in international negotiations
between the government of the United States of America
and the government of the People's Democratic Republic
of Vietnam.

Colonel Barrabas passed the information on to MAC. He
also filed an Operations Plan with the Joint Command.
The plan of operation utilized Colonel Barrabas's own extensive knowledge of combat tactics and the particular
region of Vietnam where the airmen were held, proposing
a rescue operation to save the airmen before US military
forces left Vietnam. By this point in time, the RVNA

forces had collapsed and were preparing for the final siege of Saigon.

Colonel Barrabas's Operations Plan involved sending a large Special Forces team (Airborne) by helicopter into the area where the prisoners were held. A back-up of four helicopters was to stand by. The Special Forces team would abandon the first two helicopters, trek overland some distance, attack the NVA base camp, free the prisoners and radio for the back-up helicopters to fly in and take them out. After a great deal of discussion and consultations with the Embassy and the CIA, Joint Command agreed to the rescue plan and assigned it to Colonel Barrabas's old unit, 5th Special Forces Group (Airborne). Colonel Barrabas requested permission to join the operation. Permission was denied because of the danger of the mission and Colonel Barrabas's value to MCA during the impending collapse of Saigon. Col. Barrabas's superiors were also under strict instructions from General Hart of the Joint Chiefs of Staff not to allow Colonel Barrabas any combat position. Colonel Barrabas was engaged to General Hart's daughter at the time.

The rescue operation, codenamed "Argonaut" was to begin at 0230 hours 3 April 1975, with a regrouped 5th Special Forces Airborne unit flying out of Tan Son Nhut airport. At 0100 hours the unit received through regular channels revised orders which altered the landing coordinates. Ten men were dropped from the unit, bringing it down to a level of 10 remaining soldiers. The revised orders also provided for one Karl Heiss, a CIA operative with Civil Operations and Rural Development Support (CORDS) to accompany the rescue unit. It was later ascertained that Karl Heiss arranged for the revised orders through CIA and US Embassy channels. The rescue unit departed at 0130 hours, 2 April, one hour earlier than originally planned.

Shortly after the rescue unit left, Colonel Barrabas arrived at Tan Son Nhut airport to bid the soldiers of his former unit good luck. On arrival at the airport, he discovered the revised orders. A series of telephone calls ascertained the

reasons for the changes, and Colonel Barrabas went directly to Major General English of the 1st Cavalry Division
(Airborne) to report the discrepancy and request permission to assemble immediately a second rescue force to
adhere to the original Operations Plan. Major General
English denied permission and ordered Colonel Barrabas
to return to Military Attaché headquarters in Saigon,
reminding him that he was no longer on combat duty.

In flagrant violation of US Army rules and regulations,
Colonel Barrabas ignored Major General English's orders.
Between the hours of 0230 and 0430 3 April 1975, Colonel
Barrabas went through Special Forces barracks at Tan Son
Nhut rounding up ten regulars of Company C—some of
whom he had commanded some years earlier—and com-
mandeered an assault helicopter. Colonel Barrabas and his
ten soldiers also broke into quartermaster stores at Tan
Son Nhut and illegally removed large amounts of ammunition, arms, Claymores, grenades, automatic weapons,
rocket launchers, radio equipment, clothing and other
gear.

The following interviews with members of the assault
team, and rescued Air Force POWs, detail subsequent
events. All interviews have been transcribed verbatim.

Interview with Sgt. Steven York Company C, US Special Forces

"We flew dark and made good time to the landing zone.
The plan was to land 10 km south of the base camp where
the POWs were held, do a fast march overland and arrive
at the camp just before dawn. If everything went well,
we'd be out and picked up by morning light. But since the
revised orders had changed the plan of operations, the
back-up Hueys had been dropped and we didn't know how
we were going to get out of there. Colonel Barrabas had
given the RTO instructions to send out a code signal when
the POWs were freed.

"Just before we got to the landing zone, we flew over the
landing party that had left an hour before with Karl Heiss

and the revised orders. We knew it was them, because we checked out the coordinates and we could see a couple of flares on the ground but no sign of activity.

"Everything went exactly as the Colonel had planned. We went overland about 8 km through the jungle and came out at the edge of some irrigated rice paddies. For the next 2 km we went waist deep through the irrigation canals, which is a good evasive tactic, and if someone does start shooting, the water will slow down the bullets.

"There were ten hooches in the base camp. Two of them had two guards outside. Another hooch directly across from those about two hundred feet had an RVN flag hanging from it. They didn't expect anyone, so they weren't being real careful. It looked like easy pickings.

"The Colonel had a couple of guys set up grenade launchers, and sent four of the best sharpshooters into positions around the camp to pick off the four guards first, then anyone else they wanted to. The grenade launchers were aimed at the hooch with the flag and at another hooch with a radio antenna. It was just sunrise.

"Everything was set to go off at once and then the Colonel disappeared into the rice paddies. It was uncanny how it worked, as if the Colonel could get right inside our heads to give us the order, tell us to pull the triggers all at the same time. The RVN camp, I don't think they ever really had time to figure out what was going on. The four guards went down and the two hooches went up instantly. There was a pause—probably no more than a couple of seconds but it seemed like a day. I could hear the guys changing the direction of the grenade launcher, the clicks of the machine gun set to go. Next the VC are pouring out of a couple of huts. They never even got to the ground before they bought it. A few Charlies tried to get out of trapdoors under the hooches, but the sharpshooters just picked them off."

The facts presented in this statement are true and to the best of my memory all pertinent facts have been presented.

. . . .
date   Sgt. Steven York

                                      . . . .
                                      witness

INTERVIEW: Captain Cory Patton US Air Force (POW)

"We'd been held at the base camp for a week. All we knew was that they were marching us farther north, and we were due to leave that morning. I woke up with a hand over my mouth and this big guy saying, "Shhhhh...," and he was obviously an American. He motioned with his head for me to wake up the others, which I did. Then he asked me if the other ten airmen were in the other hooch beside us. Then he told us to sit tight and be ready to move, and he left.

"All hell broke loose outside. Two guys burst into the door of the hooch and got us out. There wasn't much left of the other hooches and there were a lot of dead VC lying around. We didn't ask questions or celebrate, but we knew who it was who came after us—Colonel Barrabas and his men. I don't think there's anyone in the U.S. Army who hasn't heard some story about him and his company.

"We were all in standard VC POW clothes, meaning black pajamas and bare feet. Next thing we're being handed boots and fatigues which these guys must've brought with them. Then we got weapons and ammo and headed off overland using standard evasive tactics to cover our trail. We got to the other side of the rice paddies to a strip of land between the jungle and paddies when we heard the helicopters coming, three of them. We knew they weren't Army helicopters before they set down. When they got close enough, I could make out the words 'Netherlands Import-Export' on the sides. I remember the Colonel had a big grin on his face as he watched them land.

"We started going for the helicopters when I saw that Colonel Barrabas was staying behind with four other men. He was speaking to one of the helicopter pilots rather urgently. I was looking at him then and I guess he realized I was wondering what was going on. It was like he knew what I was thinking. It was like he knew what everyone was thinking, all the time—and we all knew what he was thinking too, because I remember everything went so smoothly it was like it had been rehearsed a dozen times. In that whole rescue, no one asked questions or hesitated. We all knew what to do, and Col. Barrabas knew we knew what to do. We all trusted him and I suppose that's what gave us the courage to just go ahead the way we did.

"Anyway, I saw him standing back with four other men and he looked at me with a kind of determined expression on his face and said, 'We'll catch up to you. We've got some work to do first.' As the helicopter lifted into the air, I saw him disappear into the jungle."

The facts presented in this statement are true and to the best of my memory all pertinent facts have been presented.

....
date   Captain Cory Patton

                              ....
                              witness

"Colonel Barrabas asked for four volunteers to stay back with him to check out the first landing party that had left with the CIA operative Karl Heiss. It required an overland trek of some 40 km by day, hard work considering the terrain, the heat and humidity and the fact that we were behind enemy lines. All ten of us volunteered so the Colonel told us to draw lots. I had the job of carrying the radio unit. The Colonel gave me a channel and a code for pick up and told me I'd know when to use it.

"After the airmen and other SOBs were on the helicopters and gone, we started into the jungle and made good time. We were about 2 km from our destination by dusk. The Colonel told us to rest. We hadn't slept in two days. He kept watch. He hadn't had any sleep either. He didn't seem to need it.

"Around midnight we headed for the landing zone. We moved very slowly so as not to alert anyone. There was a moon that night, but the jungle was dark because the jungle is always dark at night. In the clearing where the helicopter had landed, everything was bright as day.

"It was pretty bad. It was obvious the copter wasn't going to fly again, and neither were the seven men we found dead there. We figured none of them got hurt when the chopper came down. It looked like VC took those men alive, but what they did to them after are the kinds of things which shouldn't happen to no one. We couldn't recognize some of them. A couple looked like they'd been burned alive. Like they'd just had flamethrowers turned on them. There were seven bodies, so three men and Karl Heiss were still missing.

"In the chopper and scattered around on the ground were crates stamped 'Military Supply.' Most of them had been left opened and emptied but one looked as if it'd been dropped while it was full. The crate had smashed and all these bags of white powder had fallen out and split open. It probably happened when the copter came down.

"We knew what it was. You didn't serve a month in Vietnam without knowing what heroin was. It ate up the Army inside out. It was one thing to know guys who were doing it—you could understand it a little, what with the kinds of pressure men find in war. But to see this, what was left of those guys and all because of this shipment of heroin. There must have been a ton of it when the crates were full. And we knew that something was seriously wrong here, because of the way those orders had been changed. We knew this one went right to the top.

"Colonel Barrabas didn't say a word as we stood there figuring this stuff out. It was like we all knew that something terrible had gone on. That somehow this guy Heiss was connected to heroin and had used Company C soldiers to get a last shipment out of Nam before Charlie took over. He brought these boys up here, and somehow the helicopter got loaded but didn't get far off the ground.

"The Colonel started walking around the landing area. He looked at the bodies of the soldiers. Then he says, 'VC didn't do this. I'm going to find out who did, and I'm going to kill them.'

"It didn't take him long to find a trail into the jungle and we started on it. It was slow going, but a couple of hours later we'd covered about 2 km when we saw some lights and a few hooches in a clearing. The Colonel told me to circle counterclockwise around the camp to reconnoiter, and he was going clockwise. We'd meet on the far side. The other three he told to stay put and stay alert.

"There were men wandering around among the hooches, and I could recognize Heiss, because I'd seen him bring in the revised orders to Tan Son Nhut. The other men were Americans and they might have been soldiers but they wore the strangest collection of uniforms I'd ever seen. Later we found out what they were: US Army deserters, the scum of the forces and of the earth, the guys who came to Nam to sate their own bloodlust for killing and found the heroin trade more profitable. There were about a half

ozen of them standing around with Heiss, and they ap-
eared to be arguing about something.

I saw three others standing guard duty around the pe-
meter of the camp as I went through the jungle around it. I
vas just about at the other side when I heard the automatic
veapons fire. A few minutes later I saw the other three guys
eing led into the camp. One was pretty badly wounded.
'hen, from the jungle about 50 yards away I see the Colonel
eing led into the camp with a rifle in his back too.

"It's hard to put it all together, what happened. Heiss took
ne look and said something about it being the famous war
ero Nile Barrabas, that it looked as if they'd just found
heir ticket out of there, and that they'd have to find out
vhat the Colonel's back-up arrangements were.

"They took the Colonel into one of the hooches. I climbed
 tree where I had a view of the camp. Every now and then
Heiss and another guy would come out of the hooch where
hey'd taken the Colonel, smoke a cigarette and talk. Then
hey'd go back in, sometimes both of them, sometimes
ust the other guy.

"At daybreak, some of the renegade soldiers went to one
f the hooches and brought out the three Company C sol-
liers who'd gone up there with Heiss, and the three who'd
ome with us. A few of them were in rough shape. The
nen were allowed to relieve themselves and were then
aken back into the hooch.

"Something told me just to hang tight. I knew it would be
uicide for choppers to come in by day and take us out of
here. I decided that by night if nothing happened I'd try to
ake the guards one by one from the perimeter and see how
ar I could get. I fell asleep late in the day and woke up just
s the sun went down. I can't say why, but when I woke up
 knew it was time to use the radio. I didn't even think
bout it, I just did it.

"I used the channel and the code the Colonel had given
ne—Eagle to Flying Dutchman. Flying Dutchman picked

me up right away. I gave the coordinates and said we were in big trouble. Flying Dutchman, whoever he was, didn't even ask questions. He signed out, saying, 'Hang on Eagle.'

"The choppers came in around midnight and they came in fast, a couple of Cobras and a Kiowa. The Kiowa flew right over the camp, dropping flares which lit the place up bright as day. The men in the camp came out of the hooches and the Hueys came in with automatic weapon fire and mowed them right down.

"The Kiowa landed on the side of the camp not far from the jungle where I was hiding. When I got to it, I realized it wasn't an Army chopper. It had Netherlands Import-Export Company painted on the side, like the ones that had come and gotten the airmen the day before. A couple of men were jumping out, and I couldn't believe it because there was a blond woman in the pilot's seat and she seemed to be shouting orders at the guys.

"One of the men getting out of the chopper raised his gun at me, then I think he saw the radio pack and he knew I was Company C too. I knew we were under fire because I could hear the bullets pinging by us. That's the last thing I remember because I guess that's when I took one of those bullets. When I woke up I was in the USAID Hospital in Saigon."

The facts presented in this statement are true and to the best of my memory all pertinent facts have been presented.

. . . .
date   Capt. Alan Bathias

                                    . . . .
                                    witness

STATEMENT FROM ROBERT WOODS PFC, 5th Special Forces:

"We were in, kept in one of the hooches. It was hot, and they weren't giving us any food and just a little water. They let us out once in the morning to relieve ourselves and then tied us up in the hooch again.

"A long while later—it's hard to say because it was hard to keep track of the time—we knew it was night again because the daylight which came through the cracks in the walls of the hooch had faded.

"Suddenly we heard the sound of some whirlybirds coming. One of them came down right over the camp and dropped a flare. Then two others came in with automatic weapon fire and all hell broke loose.

"Next thing I knew a bunch of men came rushing into the hooch, untying us and getting us out of there. The scene outside was incredible, I couldn't tell who was shooting at who. We were hustled toward this big chopper behind the camp. I saw a couple of men come out of one of the hooches, shooting their way out the door, and right behind them was the Colonel. He was shooting too. He was half naked and his skin looked like it had been ground down to the raw meat with steel wool. They'd worked him over pretty good. He wasn't using his right arm, but somehow he was able to hold an M-16 in his left and shoot his way across the camp.

"It wasn't an army helicopter we were on and I knew these guys who come in for us weren't Army regulars. They were fighting men, but not US Army. The Colonel was the last one into the chopper and he had Heiss with him, alive. I don't think anyone else was left alive in that camp. There was a blond woman who started taking care of the guys who were wounded, giving them injections of morphine. The Colonel wouldn't take any. He just stood there during the flight, looking down at Heiss who lay crumpled on the floor of the copter. And the Colonel held an M-16 to Heiss's head the whole way back to Saigon.

"I tell you, feeling that chopper lift off out of the hellhole and head up over the trees toward Saigon was one of the happiest moments of my life."

The facts presented in this statement are true and to the best of my memory all pertinent facts have been presented.

. . . .
date   Robert Woods PFC

                           . . . .
                           witness

HEADQUARTERS
MILITARY ASSISTANCE COMMAND
Saigon

RG 407.33   11 April 1975
SUBJECT: Erika Dykstra

TO: General Command, US Army Vietnam

1. Erika Dykstra is a Dutch national who, in conjunction with her brother Gunther Dykstra, runs a company in Saigon called Netherlands Import Management Company. This company exports native handicraft from warehouses in Phan Rang to Europe. Intelligence indicates that this business is basically a front for large scale smuggling operations involving gold, jewels, antiques and works of art. It has been an extremely profitable business in these troubled times in Vietnam. Most of Miss Dykstra's customers are wealthy Vietnamese, and some wealthy Americans who want to remove valuable properties from Vietnam. There is no indication that Miss Dykstra has ever been involved in drug smuggling of any kind.

2. On a number of occasions CIA operatives have used Miss Dykstra's business to transport arms to operatives in Cambodia and Laos.

3. The nature of Miss Dykstra's relationship with Colonel Nile Barrabas, U.S. Army, is unknown. They have been seen together at social functions and private dinners in Saigon on a number of occasions, and spent at least one weekend in a hotel at Dalat under assumed names.

4. Miss Dykstra left Vietnam for Manila on April 5. Her destination from Manila is unknown.

                    Maj. Gen. J. Green
                    Asst. Chief of Staff, MAC

CLASSIFIED

CENTRAL INTELLIGENCE AGENCY
WASHINGTON DC

MAY 1, 1975

SUBJECT: Karl Heiss, internal investigation

TO: General Staff, US Army

The Central Intelligence Agency is able to confirm the following:

1. Karl Heiss was recruited as a CIA operative in October 1972 after employment with the United States diplomatic corps as 2nd Secretary to the United States Embassy in Saigon.

2. Karl Heiss was given special responsibility for the design and implementation of Civil Operations and Rural Development Support (CORDS), part of a large-scale program to pacify hostile sectors of the Republic of Vietnam by assisting rural villages with redevelopment of community facilities.

3. Subsequent investigation indicates that Karl Heiss had close personal friendship with Vietnamese Army Major General Nguyen Son Ny, a central figure in heroin distribution in Vietnam.

4. The agency has ascertained that Heiss organized an extensive and profitable network for smuggling large quantities of heroin into US Army camps, and into the continental United States. The agency has begun to analyze and dismantle this organization and identify participants.

5. CIA operatives have been notified to locate Karl Heiss. His whereabouts since his disappearance at Tan Son Nhut airbase are unknown, although it is suspected he is in Europe.

Director, CIA

UNITED STATES ARMY
General Staff
Washington DC

Excerpts from minutes of General Staff meeting, 17 May 1975:

. . . Having examined the report of the Committee of Investigation, it was resolved that all court-martial proceedings against Colonel Nile Barrabas, U.S. Army, will be halted immediately.

In view of his dedication to the lives of others without regard to his own life, and in recognition of actions above and beyond the call of duty, it is resolved that Col. Barrabas receive the Medal of Honor, the United States of America's highest award for bravery. . . .